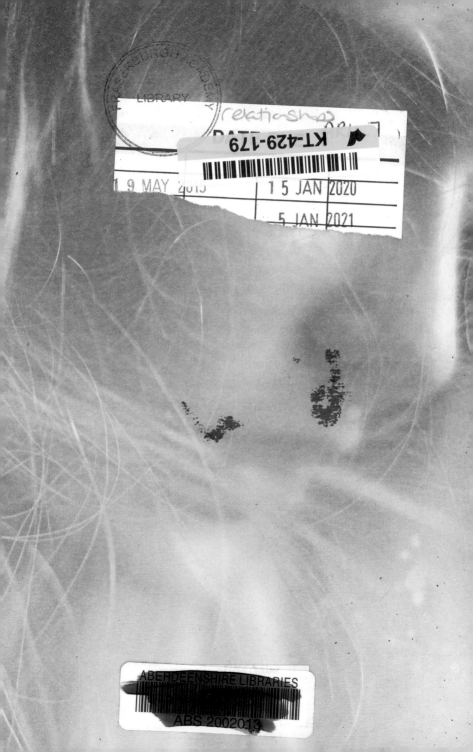

From the Chicken House

Grrrr … don't you want to shake some TV talent show judges? But just when you think these competitions are all about wicked manipulation, real-life moments of humility and magic break through. Sophia Bennett's new novel brilliantly shows both sides of the music game, and the perils of online fame and blame. My own ability to mime to pop songs is apparently not enough to qualify!

Barry Cunningham
Publisher

If you've ever felt alone in a world full of people talking
This book is for you

'In the future, everyone will be famous for fifteen minutes.'
Andy Warhol

fifteen Minutes: Part 1

It's funny how fifteen minutes can change your life.

Sometimes people ask me: would you do it again, knowing what happened? I've thought about it a lot and I suppose the answer is yes, despite everything. Fifteen minutes can be golden. They're all you need to make something beautiful, or save someone from disaster. They can also be black. Either way, fifteen minutes is all it takes to find out who you really are.

We were in Rose's bedroom, at the end of the summer holiday. I was sitting on her window seat, watching a combine harvester in the fields outside and idly scrolling through celebrity news websites on the phone my dad had just given me. School was about to start: GCSE year, where everything really matters and teachers keep asking you what you want to do with your life. These were our last few minutes of peace. Well, relative peace, anyway. As peaceful as you can get when one girl – Rose – was making up a mournful tune on the guitar, another girl – Jodie – was moaning about her ex-boyfriend and a third one – Nell – was trying to calm her down.

'He's evil and I hate him with a passion,' Jodie announced, slumping against the wall next to me with an angry scowl.

'Well, not *evil* exactly,' Nell pointed out. Nell is calm yin to Jodie's ranty yang. Together they make a normal girl. 'I mean, he only changed his status on Interface.'

'In *public!*' Jodie complained. 'Without *consulting* me! Just because I was going to France. He said he wasn't sure he could maintain a long-distance relationship. It was TWO WEEKS. Kyle Stanley is a scumbag and that's all there is to it.'

It was our first time back together after weeks away. I'd been visiting my dad in America, and Nell and Jodie had only recently come back from family trips. Rose had been stuck at home all the time, helping on her grandparents' farm. She was still quiet and gloomy, making up sad songs on her guitar.

I looked across to where she sat on her bed with the guitar, and caught her eye. We shared a private smile about Jodie's ranting. Rose changed her tune from the sombre, folky melody she'd been working on to something Spanish and angsty. It involved lots of fast strumming and dramatic crescendos. You could imagine a Latin singer wailing her distress. Jodie pouted at her.

'Shut up, Rose. I'm not *that* bad.'

Rose merely raised an eyebrow at her and smiled.

'You need something to take your mind off him,' Nell said. She was on the floor, sorting out the pile of junk that had accumulated at the bottom of Rose's wardrobe. 'You can't let a boy like that get to you. Oh look! Wow! Rose, d'you remember these?'

She pulled out a pair of scratched yellow plastic sunglasses with frames in the shape of flowers. Rose has very eclectic dress sense, which means it comes from a variety of sources. 'Eclectic' – a Rose word. She collects them, like I'd started collecting apps for my new phone.

'Oh, I wondered where those had got to,' Rose said, looking up for a moment.

Nell took off her smart red specs and replaced them with the yellow flowers. 'Where did you get them?'

'Can't remember,' Rose said absently, looking back at her guitar. 'I think it was the Bigelow Festival.'

Luckily nobody was watching me at that point, so nobody saw the sudden colour in my cheeks.

Nell went over to the mirror to admire herself. She looked great in the glasses, even though they were probably designed for ten-year-olds. Nell has a small, pretty face and wavy blonde hair that looks good with anything. Peering closely, because she's practically blind without her glasses, she grinned.

'You can't be unhappy in these,' she announced.

Then she started to sing a little tune:

3

*'I put my sunglasses on
My yellow sunglasses on'*

That's how it started. I think I came up with the next lines.

*'And I think of you
And all the things you do
And it doesn't matter any more because . . .'*

Nell laughed and joined in:

'I've got my sunglasses on.'

Rose strummed a new tune on the guitar to go with them. It was quite different this time: fun, silly and catchy. Not angsty at all. And not like that folky, moody number she'd been working on earlier, which had been starting to worry me.

We liked the lines, so we sang them again, and Jodie even added a little harmony. It was something we often did when we were all together. We'd been doing it so long we even had a band name. In fact, several. We called ourselves the Powerpuff Girls. Or the Cheerios (Jodie's favourite breakfast food), or the Manic Pixie Dream Girls (Rose's idea), or the Xtremes, but only if Rose wasn't around – she's a stickler for spelling. Jodie would choose the music. Nell was our lead singer. Rose was makeup and instrumentals. I was wardrobe and catering.

It had been like that since Jodie, Nell and I were in primary school together. Rose joined us later, when she arrived in my class at St Christopher's. We'd get together

4

. . . we'd sing. We didn't normally write our own stuff, though: we were more of a cover band. But that day Rose had her guitar out and Nell looked really funny in those glasses, and the words and music just seemed to flow. They weren't Shakespeare, I admit, but they made Jodie smile and that was enough.

Rose reached over to her bedside table and grabbed a notebook from it. She always has one lying around in case she's inspired to write something, as you do. I used to think of myself as a bit of a poet until Rose arrived, but she is the real thing.

'How does the third line go again?' she asked.

'Are you writing it down?' I was flattered. She'd never written my words down before.

'It's great, Sash! Really catchy. Except I'm not sure if I've got that line right.'

'I can only remember it if I sing it,' I said, suddenly realising this was true. 'I know – why don't we just record it?' I waved my new iPhone at her, thinking this would be the perfect chance to get a new app. That phone was the most beautiful present I'd ever received and I was a little bit obsessed.

Rose agreed, curious, and I found a recording app. We worked out some extra verses, then tried the song out, all clustering round the phone, not sure where the mic was. It sounded OK, but a bit tinny. It was totally working as therapy for Rose's gloomy mood and Jodie's heartbreak, though.

Rose dug out the microphone she uses when she's recording her own songs and, miraculously, also an adapter to fit my phone. We sang it once more, in harmony, then played it back. Surprisingly, we didn't sound too bad.

'That phone's *amazing*, Sash,' Nell said. 'I know – why don't I video us on it, too? Can I?'

Great idea, I said. Go for it. We don't have time now, but why don't we have a band get-together on my birthday? We can dress up, like we used to in the old days, and make loads of videos. It'll be hysterical.

Hahahahahahaha.

So we do.

My birthday is three weekends later, on the last Saturday of September. I invite them all over for a sleepover, and bring home a selection of spare dressing-up clothes from my Saturday job at a vintage shop.

Mum cooks us Thai green curry for lunch, because I'm turning sixteen and it's the most sophisticated thing we can think of. Then we nip upstairs to spend the afternoon dressing up as our favourite pop stars, because we haven't totally mastered maturity *yet*. Not in secret, anyway. Not when it's just us.

Highlights include our Abba interpretation, Jodie as Katy Perry, and Nell as Kylie Minogue, in gold sequin shorts and a white hoodie. She could practically *be* Kylie: it's uncanny. Rose does a long, sad Irish ballad, not entirely entering into the spirit of things, but it's beautiful. I am olden-days Britney Spears, in a mini-kilt and half my school uniform. We are also, if I say so myself, quite brilliant as Girls Aloud.

'Sunglasses' is last. We mime to the audio version we recorded in Jodie's room. By now we're getting tired and I'm half ready for bed.

It's the perfect end to a perfect day. We eat warm

brownies and homemade popcorn. We watch two *Twilights* back to back in our pyjamas and go to sleep at about five a.m., peppered in brownie crumbs, all huddled in a heap under our duvets on the floor.

Precisely four days later, my iPhone disappears.

Secrets

easons why you don't want to lose your brand new iPhone:

- Your mother goes crazy because she can't contact you if you get kidnapped by a deranged serial killer. Or if she suddenly needs you to buy milk on the way home from school. Whatever.
- You can't play your games, or check your apps, or watch TV in bed, or see what everybody is saying about everybody in school. Which is tragic.
- Your mother goes even more crazy because your father gave you that phone in America and even though she thought it was a 'mad, excessive present

for a teenage girl', she is still angry that it's gone.

– You don't know who's got it, or who's looking at all your secrets.

That's the real problem. Secrets.

Secrets like the fact that my dad doesn't work for Apple in California, like I told everyone. He doesn't even own a Mac.

Or that George Drury kissed me behind the speaker stacks at the Bigelow Music Festival last summer and his girlfriend doesn't know.

Or the mean things I've said about people at school that I assumed would remain private, but could be anywhere by now.

Or the videos. Oh my God. All those videos we took on my birthday, of us prancing around to Abba and Girls Aloud. We were so cheesy you could make a fondue out of us. Anyone who saw them would think we were six, not sixteen. If it was someone at St Christopher's who took my phone, just one of them will be enough to keep the whole place laughing for a year.

'I'm sure we'll find it,' says Nell on Friday for the fifty billionth time, taking the cushions off my bed and feeling down the gap between it and the wall with her hand. Despite the fact that my room looks like a clothes shop exploded in a library, Nell still seems hopeful.

'Where did you have it last?' Rose asks, looking up from her place in front of my wardrobe mirror, where she's fiddling with her hair.

I stifle a groan.

'I can't remember. I know I had it in my locker when I

got changed for dance class on Wednesday. And I thought it was in my bag when we were coming home. But I can't be sure now.'

Jodie, wearing an ancient top hat from my vintage collection over her long dark hair, is slouched on a beanbag, checking her own phone. It's a BlackBerry that her dad got a deal on. She was so jealous of my iPhone, and sure it would be stolen. Which is what she's convinced has happened. By someone who is using it, right this minute, to do something terrible.

'Are you sure your wi-fi's switched on?'

'Totally sure.'

'Well, I can't get a signal. I'm trying to check Interface.'

I sigh. If anyone *does* decide to share my secrets, the first place they will appear is Interface. It's the world's fastest-growing website. Ever since it came along, Interface has replaced Facebook, Twitter and YouTube on all our phones and computers, because it lets you share everything, all of the time. It's where we live our lives now: all conversations, invitations, photos and videos happen here. If you're not on Interface, you don't exist. And right now, if someone's looking at all that stuff on my phone, I'm not sure I want to.

'Have you suspended your contract?' Nell asks, glancing up momentarily from her search.

I bite my lip. 'Not exactly. I just keep hoping it'll turn up . . .'

'And have you tried Find My iPhone?'

'Yes. But that says it's still at school, and we've searched *everywhere*, and it just isn't.'

'Looking on the bright side, it might be on eBay.'

'Oh, great. So the good news is, my £400 present from

10

my dad is now being sold to a stranger.'

'Well, at least if it is,' Jodie sighs, 'nobody at school is going to get to see your interpretation of Beyoncé. In the leotard.'

Nell frowns and throws a cushion at her.

'Sasha told you not to remind her about the leotard.'

Rose is busy attempting to see what her hair would look like in Princess Leia-style plaits either side of her head. She has a perfect oval face, with big blue eyes, enhanced by masses of red-gold hair, but the plaits look like Danish pastries hanging over her ears. She catches my eye in the mirror and gives up on them. 'Ah, the Single Ladies leotard,' she sighs. 'It was a seminal moment.'

What is 'seminal'? Apart from being another thing I need to be deeply embarrassed about, obviously. OK, so before the whole Britney thing on my birthday, I did my 'Single Ladies' impression – in a black leotard from ballet and borrowed heels from Mum. I do the dance as a workout occasionally. All I can say is, it seemed like a good idea at the time.

'What does seminal m—' Jodie starts. But then she looks down at her BlackBerry and stares at the screen. She's got a signal now and she's obviously found something. From the expression on her face, it's *so* not good.

'Tell me. What?' I beg, rushing over.

She turns her phone out so I can see the screen. There's a puzzled, worried look in her eyes.

'It's this.'

Zero Mean Comments

'This' is a video. Of us. From that day. And on a website that everyone can see.

As soon as Jodie clicks 'Play', my heart starts to pound. There's my bedroom, with my white wrought-iron bed frame in the background, my ancient fairy lights, my old High School Musical duvet and my poster of a beach in Malibu. My bedroom: on the internet. Oh no oh no oh no.

There's the sound of giggling in the background. And 'Are you doing it, Nell?'

Please let it not be Abba. Let it not be the leotard.

Real-life Nell abandons the phone search and comes over to join us, slipping her arm through mine.

On the screen, Rose enters first, wearing a green crushed-velvet maxi-dress over her purple boots, and her hair in rivers of ringlets around her face. (This was her 'Irish folk singer' look, I remember.) She's carrying her guitar and she sits on my bed and starts to play. But it's not the folk song, it's bright and breezy. In fact, it's the intro to 'Sunglasses'. And, oh my God, it sounds like the proper audio version we did, not the tinny soundtrack that comes with the video.

Somebody worked on this. Somebody went through my phone and *edited stuff together*. This is perverted and bizarre.

While video-Rose plays, video-Nell and video-Jodie arrive to stand near her, moving to the music and beckoning to me to join them. Jodie's still in her Katy Perry outfit of a pink satin top and leopard-print leggings, which is the total opposite of what she normally wears. Nell's in the sequin shorts and hoodie – and no, that's not her typical daywear, either. Funnily enough, Rose does like to hang around in maxi-dresses and purple boots. Only the ringlets were unusual for her. I desperately try to remember what I ended up wearing for this. *Was* it the leotard?

Just before we start to sing, I arrive in shot, looking out of breath and laughing. I'm half-changed for bed, with my pyjama top on over my mini-kilt, and a feather boa quickly flung around my neck for panache. My hair's ultra-backcombed from my Beyoncé moment and I've ended up with the yellow plastic sunglasses. Apart from that, I look *totally* normal.

Oh God.

On-screen, we grin like maniacs and start to sing.

'I put my sunglasses on
My yellow sunglasses on . . .'

Video-me gets carried away, skipping around to the music, making funny faces and doing some of my Beyoncé moves. We look so silly. But I can't help feeling that the song *sounds* OK. We have definitely done a lot worse.

Real-life Rose finishes brushing out her hair with her fingers and comes over.

'Is it horrendous? Is it Abba?'

We shake our heads. Jodie holds her phone out still further so everyone can see.

What's strange is that someone would use 'Sunglasses' of all things to try and humiliate us. Why not, as Rose said, Abba? Or the 'seminal' leotard moment? Costumes aside, this one is relatively normal. In fact, of all the songs we did, it's my favourite, and it actually sounds quite good.

Am I the problem? Is that why they chose it? It's the only thing I can think of. The others have all got beautiful voices. I still love singing more than anything, but in Year 8 I was told in choir that my voice sounded like 'a truckful of gravel being poured down a hole'. Plus the whole skipping thing.

'Is it me?' I ask.

Jodie looks doubtful. 'Could be. Look at that wiggle you did there.'

'Was it terrible? Should I have just stood there?'

14

'I don't think so,' Rose disagrees, peering at the screen curiously.

I still don't get it.

'*What?*' I'm almost wailing by now.

'Look,' Nell says, pointing to the titles above the video. I hadn't even noticed there were any. I was too busy checking out my legs for previously unknown deformities, or my dance style for embarrassing dad-at-a-disco moves I didn't know I had.

But now I see it more clearly. Whoever uploaded this video only did it this morning. And whoever they were, they decided to enter it into a competition. Not just any competition, but Killer Act – the battle of the bands on Interface. It's the biggest online music competition in the country and it feels like half the school has already entered.

Oh help. And there I go, bouncing around my bedroom in a feather boa and half my pyjamas.

I drag my eyes away from myself and look where the others are looking: at the information underneath. So far there have been, surprisingly, zero mean comments about us. And 24 votes.

We have 24 votes.

Call of Duty – who go to Castle College, and are the best band in the area by miles – have been on Killer Act for weeks and they only had about 300 votes the last time I looked. We have nearly a tenth of that in a few hours.

There are two comments but they're both OK.

The blonde in the glitter shorts is awesome.

Loving those dance moves! lol

'I don't get it,' I say, sinking into the beanbag, confused.

Nell, bright pink after that comment about her shorts, stares at the screen hard, as if daring it to change. It does. 25 votes. 26.

'I think it's OK,' she whispers in wonderment. 'I think people like it.'

But then I remind myself: Nell is a cute, fluffy kitten in human form. I look to Jodie for a second opinion. Was that comment about my dance moves ironic, or not?

'It's possible . . .' Jodie announces, sounding as if she can't quite believe what she's saying, '. . . that we don't totally suck on video.'

Moody Blue

On Saturday morning, Mum drives me to Living Vintage, the shop next to her café on the market square in Castle Bigelow. I took the job there last year, partly to help pay my phone bills – an irony that isn't exactly lost on me now.

In the car, Mum can tell I'm quieter than usual. She turns to me and in the bright sunlight streaming through the windscreen, I notice strands of grey in the brown frizz of her hair, which otherwise matches mine.

'Still no luck, then?' she asks, referring to the phone.

The worst of her anger is over by now. I think she even feels a tiny bit sorry for me. She knows how much that phone meant to me.

'No,' I say. 'Not yet.'

I'm certainly not going to tell her about the whole 'I was hacked and now my bedroom is online, plus me in my pyjamas' thing. Mum struggles with the café. It's hard running a business in a little country town these days. Two shops closed last month, and another two the month before. But Mum tries to spare me her worries, and I try to spare her mine. Besides – is it really a worry, having fifty votes on Killer Act, which is what we're up to now? If I only knew *why*, I think I could feel quite happy about it.

We park up behind the market square. Castle Bigelow is an old Somerset town, with a high street leading up the hill to the grand gates of Castle College at the top. Market Square is at the bottom: a collection of old Georgian buildings painted in cheerful colours, housing the café, the vintage shop, a pet shop, a bookshop and two antique shops. It looks quaint and old-fashioned – like something out of an Agatha Christie mystery. All the modern chains are up the other end.

At Living Vintage, Mrs Venning, the owner, greets me with her usual wide-armed hug. She greets everyone this way, including visiting tourists. They usually depart with at least a costume jewellery brooch, if not a hat and a jacket. She narrows her eyes and casts a critical eye over me.

'Jeans, dull; jumper, hideous. I wish you'd let me dress you, darling.'

Mrs Venning is wearing wide black wool trousers, a peacock velvet tunic and a little sequinned cocktail hat over her bright auburn hair.

'One day, Mrs V,' I promise. *When nobody I know is*

18

ever going to see me, I add silently to myself. She looks amazing, but I'd never dare go out like that in public.

'You should copy your friend, you know,' she adds. 'She's got a real eye.'

'I know,' I nod.

She means Rose. Rose has the brave, individual look that Mrs Venning likes to go for.

'Upstairs, today, if you don't mind,' she adds. 'Lots of new bags in. Michael's been trawling the Midlands. There will be some gems but most of it will be absolutely dire. The usual story, darling: charity shop, recycling, pearls and maybes. You are an angel.'

I climb the narrow staircase to the attic. It's one of my favourite places: whitewashed walls and sloping ceilings, plain floorboards and rails and rails of unusual clothes. These are the ones that Mrs Venning has rescued in the past. Her husband travels around vintage markets, charity shops and recycling centres, looking for bargains. My job is to go through the three large cardboard boxes lined up in the middle of the floor and sort out the very worst of the things he's picked up from the very best. Some things are old, filthy, falling apart and frankly disgusting. Others are worth giving to Oxfam, but not selling here. Mrs Venning makes her money by spotting the occasional original Chanel handbag or perfect sixties shift. These are her 'pearls'.

Normally, while I sort through the piles, I play the latest chart tunes on my headphones, but today I can't. I've lost my flippin' iPhone, with all my music on it, and Mrs Venning's little portable radio is out of batteries. I end up singing 'Sunglasses' to myself, to keep myself amused.

After an hour of sorting, I pick out a bead necklace and an old fake-fur shrug I think Rose might love. One of the perks of my job is that I get to take things away that Mrs Venning doesn't think she can sell. Rose gets half her wardrobe this way. I'm checking myself out in the mirror in the necklace and shrug, imagining them on her, when I could swear I see her ghostly face hovering behind me.

'Ahh!' I leap half a metre in the air.

'Are you OK?' Rose asks, coming over, and very much real.

'No. Not exactly. You scared the hell out of me.'

'Well, serves you right for prancing about in front of the mirror like Lady Gaga. Nice shrug, by the way.'

'It's for you. Well, it was. Well, it would be, if Mrs V said it was OK. And if you hadn't scared me witless.'

Rose rolls her eyes. 'I was only trying to be helpful. Gran made me come into town with her. I thought I'd come and find you. I can do some sorting with you, if you like. Found any pearls yet?'

'No. I found these, though.' I point to the things I've chosen for her.

She tries the shrug on and looks fabulous, as I expected. Suddenly, the day is fun. Rose quite often pops in like this, to keep me company. At first, I offered to share my wages with her, but she refused. She gets a generous allowance from her granny. Besides, Rose doesn't actually work very much when she's here. She gets too distracted by the clothes and jewellery, and imagining what the people who wore them thought and did and said.

She wanders around, acting out little playlets for me, while I gradually sort out the piles. '"Oh, Harold! Harold! Will you never come back to me? How could you leave me at the altar, when we swore we'd be true for all eternity? And me in my best lace veil, and fourteen strands of emeralds . . ."'

'Take that veil off!' I instruct her, crossly. 'You'll ruin it. And be careful with those necklaces. They could be pearls.'

'They're glass beads!'

'You know what I mean.'

'Oh all right. Spoilsport . . . Hey, look at these round glasses. "Imagine all the PE-puuuul."'

'Are you trying to be John Lennon?'

'Of course.'

'You look more like Ozzy Osborne. Put them down.'

'You could use them if we sing "Sunglasses" again,' she says, holding them out.

'I'm *never* singing "Sunglasses" again.' I shiver once more at the thought of me in the pyjamas and kilt on the internet.

Ignoring me, Rose hums the tune to herself. We end up singing it side by side, in front of the mirror, with me in the John Lennon glasses and her in a white-rimmed sixties pair, and a battered straw hat for good measure. It's always like this when she comes round. She slows me down hopelessly. But she knows I love it really, whatever I say.

When I'm finally done with sorting, Mrs Venning kindly puts the shrug and beads in a bag for us, and we head for the bus that takes us out of town. It winds down the station road to where the houses run out and the fields begin. This is where Rose's grandparents have their farm, with Mum's cottage a few houses further along.

21

'D'you want to come in for a bit?' she asks.

'Nah. I'm busy. Things to do. People to see.'

She knows I'm joking. We always end up at each other's houses over the weekend, and often on weekdays too. Rose and I are a soulmate thing.

You know how sometimes a new person comes to school who's good at everything you're good at – and mostly *better* than you? Well that was Rose, two years ago. Everyone assumed we'd hate each other, and that maybe I'd be her worst enemy, but that's not what happened.

Rose was the first girl I'd met who loved all the same things as me. We were both into drawing, music, makeup ideas, books and films that made us cry. We shared a longing for sunny beaches and round-the-world travel. We clicked instantly. She could quote from Stevie Smith, my favourite poet, and like me, she kept a scrapbook full of pictures of far-off places she wanted to see one day.

Sure, she came from London, and had seen more of life than me. She had more interesting dress sense, and preferred sophisticated jazz to Abba and Beyoncé. She played classical guitar, while I played Fruit Ninja, and her room was nicer. But she was never grand about it: in fact, she was the opposite – humble and sweet. We never got bored hanging out together. I used to miss her when Nell and Jodie came over to do the Powerpuffs, so soon she came too. She thought we were crazy, but she joined in anyway. The idea of not hanging out with her when I could is just . . . odd.

The back door to the farmhouse is always open in the daytime. We let ourselves in and go up to her room.

'Did you want to share my notes on *Frankenstein*?' Rose asks, referring to an English homework I haven't quite finished. OK, haven't quite started. The whole phone thing really messed up my homework timetable.

'Oh God, yes. Thank you.'

I sit at her ancient computer while she goes to the record player to put on some jazz from her mum's old vinyl collection. The room fills with the sound of piano and strings, then the warm, mellow voice of Ella Fitzgerald. I don't even need to check the album cover: it's the *Cole Porter Songbook*. It was recorded in the 1950s, and was one of Rose's mother's favourite albums. Their record collection was one of the few things she inherited from her parents when they died. The *Songbook* is utterly seminal ('highly influential in an original way' – I checked in the dictionary) and we both know every note of every song.

As Ella sings, I mouth the words of 'Every Time We Say Goodbye'. Rose stares silently out of the window. I sense that her blue mood is suddenly on her again. It hasn't really left her since the end of the holidays, and it's so unlike Rose to be down for long. I wonder if she's totally forgiven me for going off to see Dad somewhere exotic and abandoning her all holidays. Or else it might be a side-effect of jazz that hasn't rubbed off on me yet.

'Rose . . . it's not Vegas, is it?' I ask, just to be sure.

'What?' she asks, looking round, distracted.

'The whole . . . whatever it is that's bothering you.'

'No,' she sighs. 'It's not Vegas. Believe me, you can keep Vegas. Did you find my notes?'

'Yup. Got them. Sent them to myself. I'll work on them later. You're a lifesaver.'

She smiles modestly. It's good to see a smile on her face; at least that blue mood hasn't taken her over completely. She goes back to looking out of the window, though. Meanwhile, with the computer in front of me, I can't resist a quick look on Interface. I go straight to our entry on Killer Act.

62 votes. 63. Who is *doing* it? Is it all the same person, madly clicking 'Vote here'? I try out a vote myself, to see what happens. When I click 'Refresh', the vote button disappears. As I suspected, you only get one go.

A new comment has appeared. I check it out.

The fat girl's good at guitar.

Whoa! What? The *fat* girl?

Instinctively, I shift around so Rose can't see the screen. It's true, she has a larger frame than average, but so what? Rose is gorgeous. She's 'eclectic' (her word) and unique. I hate it when people are just plain rude on the internet. I bet nobody would dare say that to her face. They certainly wouldn't if I was around.

I check the page. Is there some way of deleting comments? I can't see one. Or reporting them? No, not that either. Without thinking, I start typing.

Who do you think you are?

But then I *do* think. You don't want to get in an argument online. They can be nastier than the face-to-face ones and just make things worse. However, another thought occurs to me. Whoever uploaded this video may be reading the comments. Maybe *that's* why she did it, or he did. I decide to play nice. I ignore the comment about Rose – with great difficulty – and write one of my own.

Ha ha. Please may I have it back now?

My username is SashaB: not too difficult to work out it's me, or what I want. Which I do, desperately. I need that phone!

Now all I can do is wait.

A Million Reasons Why

O n Monday, back at school, we're all on the lookout for the Mystery Uploader. Jodie and Nell are in one form room, Rose and I in another. Jodie holds a conference in the locker rooms before we go our separate ways.

'It'll be somebody shifty,' she says, 'who gives us strange looks or a smug smile. He'll definitely be watching us, to see if we've noticed. Before he enacts part two of his plan.'

'What part two?' Nell asks nervously.

She shrugs. 'I couldn't say. Who knows what he could be capable of?'

'Maybe he *did* see that video of you in the leotard and he's nefariously entered you for *Strictly Come Dancing*,' Rose says, smiling at me.

'Oh, fabulous,' I sigh. 'This is still funny for you. It wouldn't be so funny if you'd been the one in the kilt, shimmying your little butt off.'

Rose laughs. She sounded great on guitar, and looked it too, in her full-length dress. Sitting down. She has no idea.

We scan the crowd in the corridors and our form rooms, and, frankly, if Jodie's right, the Mystery Uploader could be anybody. Everyone at St Christopher's seems to give us either strange looks or smug smiles or both. By lunchtime, Jodie's pretty convinced that at least half our year are in on it. Nell's a nervous wreck and I'm pretty close myself. Rose has to take notes for me in History, because I just can't concentrate.

Then, back in our classroom, I'm rootling around in my school bag for a biro and suddenly there it is: my beautiful iPhone, still in its sparkly turquoise cover, nestling in its little pocket as if it has always been there. Is it a mirage? Is it a joke? Did he or she read my comment last night? Is this the reply?

I turn it over and over, checking for signs of damage, but there are none that I can see. Rose, seeing me holding it, rushes over to me with a shriek of delight. When I turn it on, my emails are still intact. So are my messages and my Interface page. Nothing has changed. Nothing embarrassing seems to have been sent, done or used, apart from that one video.

Still only that one mean comment about Rose, which was half nice anyway: it did say she was good at guitar, after all.

Plus one saying:

The fit bird in the skirt has great legs.

And one saying:

Hotlegs is Sasha Bayley, Year 11.

75 votes. 76. 77.

This is what it says on the home page of Killer Act on Interface:

Do you have the talent? Are you a future star?

Now in it's 3rd year, the most exciting competition for teen talent is back – sponsored by Interface, the fastest-growing social network in the world.
You can be any kind of musical act – singer, dancer, band, rapper. You just have to be 18 or under, still in full-time education, and unsigned.

Upload your video and get your friends and fans to vote.

The 100 acts with the most votes will get the chance to audition for the LIVE TV FINALS!!!!!!

In March, the top 9 acts, as chosen by our team of internationally successful star judges, will compete ON LIVE TV IN THE UK AND STREAMED LIVE WORLD-WIDE, for the prize of a contract to advertise Interface for a year, worth
£100,000!!!!!!!

Want to be the face of Interface?
Then upload your video now.
KILLER ACT. CAN YOU KILL IT?

It's October and the competition has already been running for six weeks. The deadline for votes is in December and there are currently over 2,000 entries, from right across the UK. Last year, the winner was a drummer called Shady from Inverness. Since then, he's played on several TV shows, guested with two international rock groups, made an ad for Interface which pops up several times a day on the web, and got over half a million fans on his Interface page. Killer Act is a serious competition. The final is televised across the UK and streamed online worldwide. As Shady's shown – if you win, it could change your life.

This year, the leading acts all have over 1,000 votes already. Call of Duty, from Castle College, are way down the list with 357. Not that I'm checking on an hourly basis. OK, I am, now I've got my phone back. But so is Jodie, even more than me, and so is Nell. Only Rose doesn't bother. Mostly because I tell her the latest count several times a day anyway, but also because she usually ignores social networking in favour of 'real people' and 'actual conversations', and finally because she noticed the misplaced apostrophe in 'it's 3rd year'.

Yeah. Of all the information on that page, *that's* what Rose focused on: the apostrophe. As a result of which, she has no faith in Killer Act at all.

85, 97, 109 . . .

In the course of the next week, a couple of people in

our class spot the video and send the link to their friends. Not that we are talking about it to anyone. We're still really, really nervous about everybody knowing that we revert to our inner six-year-olds on a regular basis.

I think it might be worst for me. Do you want to know the real secret about my dad? When he left, it was because he wanted to be an Elvis impersonator in Vegas. Seriously. It took him years to make it. Years of not being in touch – until last summer, when he invited me over, out of the blue. I think it was his latest girlfriend's idea for me to go, and actually it was fun, much to my surprise. Dad wasn't bad as a performer, but it's hardly something you brag about. It's bad enough being the child of a novelty act: I don't want to be one myself.

However, as the news of our video spreads, people don't seem to mind about the boa, or the pyjamas. In fact, if anything, they seem to like them. Over the days that follow, increasing numbers of people nod and smile at us in corridors. When Jodie overhears our French teacher humming the tune of 'Sunglasses' while he sorts through some textbooks, she is officially FREAKED. OUT. A week later, the Head has it as her ringtone. I'm not kidding.

And the votes keep rising.

205, 207, 323 . . . 350, 370, 410 . . .

We start hanging out in the school library at lunchtimes, where Rose works as a monitor. It's good for checking ourselves out on the computers, because the screens are bigger there and we can surreptitiously try to see if anyone nearby is voting for us, to explain the crazy numbers.

'I've created a band page for us,' Jodie announces one

day in early November. She brings up Interface on the screen in front of her (which is supposed to block social networking sites, but honestly, there is SO much we could teach our IT department, if they asked).

'There we are. See? Sam helped me.'

There's a page with an enormous banner across the top, with a picture of us all in our glittery finery. Jodie's brother, Sam, must have done that for her – he's a sixth-form computer nerd, so he'd know all about things like grabbing still pictures from video. Jodie sighs.

'The only problem is the name. I had to use the same one as on Killer Act. Of all our names, why did Mystery Guy have to pick the Manic Pixie Dream Girls? I liked the Powerpuff Girls.'

Two Year 7s look at us, annoyed because we're disturbing their study time, but as Rose is currently in charge of the library there's not much they can do.

I agree with Jodie. 'And more to the point, how did Mystery Guy even know *what* we called ourselves? We didn't say it on camera, did we?'

'Nope,' Jodie says.

We all shiver slightly. Are we being *bugged*?

'We might have said it on another video, though,' Nell suggests brightly, keen to find an alternative to the bugging theory. 'I'm sure I did it at least once. I might have said that name, because it was the stupidest. Why'd you pick it, Rose?'

Rose blushes.

'It's a literary device. A trope.' She catches us staring at her. 'A . . . *thing*, I promise you. Look it up on Wikipedia. It's a name they give to all those girls in books and films who don't quite seem real. They're just these kooky creatures who the hero wants to find, or rescue or be like. Jennifer Aniston plays them all the time. We were talking about it in book club. I just thought it sounded funny.'

'It does,' Jodie grumbles, 'and now we're stuck with it. Imagine them announcing *that* at the Grammys.' She rolls her eyes.

'We're not going to the Grammys,' I promise her, laughing.

'We might,' she retorts. 'A boy in sixth form has already asked us to do a gig at his birthday party. Well, half a gig, anyway. And if we carry on at this rate, we could make the Killer Act top 100, you know. Then we could be on TV.'

Rose and I shake our heads sadly at her insane optimism. Nell practically chokes on a Starburst.

'Really? Aren't we way behind everyone?'

Jodie pouts. 'Not *way* behind. Slightly. We're catching up fast, haven't you noticed?'

Then I suddenly think of something.

'*Which* boy?' I ask.

'Hmm?' Jodie says.

'Which boy in sixth form has asked for us?'

She checks the details on the page. 'Er, someone called George Drury. My mum knows him vaguely. They have a big house the other side of Crakey Hill with an awesome party barn. We'd be performing in there and we'd get £100. Paid money for a gig! £25 each! Are you OK, Sash?'

George Drury: the boy who had a crush on me last summer. I had a feeling it might be him.

'Fine,' I lie.

Was this whole video thing just some trick to get us to

play at his party? And if so, why? And what is he going to do next?

'Who else is playing?' asks Rose. She sounds edgy too, picking up on my nerves somehow.

Jodie grins.

'Call of Duty. George is a friend of theirs. They do the first half, we do the second.'

All the laughter abruptly disappears from Rose's face. So does the colour. She shakes her head.

'We can't.'

'Why not?' I ask gently, concerned for her, and confused. I mean, I can think of a million reasons why not, but they only affect me.

She pauses for a while to think, then gives a nervous, high-pitched laugh.

'This is getting ridiculous. We've never sung live before. They do it all the time.'

'But people *like* us,' Jodie insists. 'Mrs Richards has our song AS HER RINGTONE. And we get to go to a George Drury party. They're famous. We'll get a million cool points and everyone will want to friend us. Please please *please*?'

Rose hesitates, looking increasingly panicked.

'When I joined, you made me promise to keep the band a secret, remember? That was the point.'

'Yeah, but that was before we got a million trillion votes,' Jodie pleads. 'It's different now. You'll be fine. Just think of all the boys who'll want your number.'

Rose shudders. 'They won't,' she whispers in a tiny voice.

'Oh, they will,' Jodie grins. 'Trust me.'

I hate to see Rose like this. She's so interesting and fun

in private, with us, and so shy in public. She's been like this ever since I've known her. People don't know what they're missing.

'You'd have us,' I promise her. 'We'd look after you.'

She bites her lip.

'Nell, what do you think?' she asks.

'You do whatever you want, Rose. I don't mind.'

Kind, sweet, unhelpful Nell. I say I'm happy to do the gig. I don't want to let anyone think I have a problem with George Drury (because I so do). Rose hesitates some more. It's obvious she doesn't want to do it, but she can't face letting us down.

'OK,' she says eventually. 'Whatever you want.'

'Great!' Jodie says, patting her on the back. 'I'll let George know.'

Seminal Leotards

550, 620, 901 . . .

I've never told anyone about the kiss behind the speaker stacks at the festival last summer. I'd noticed George looking at me a bit, but then I'd been staring too. He's six foot tall and plays football for the county Under-18s team. He is definitely not the ugliest boy in his class.

His girlfriend, Michelle, was off buying him beer at the time. I asked him what time one of the gigs was starting and we got talking. He seemed very friendly and yes, there was a kiss. I was too shocked to stop him.

Pretty quickly though, he remembered where he was, and who I was – or rather, who I wasn't – and he brushed past me as if nothing had happened. I tried to forget the whole thing, although I have to admit I haven't done a very good job of it. Even while I was in Vegas for that whole summer, staying with Dad, I still couldn't get the kiss out of my mind. Every time we sing 'Sunglasses', I think of George. Now we're about to be in his house.

Why did he ask us? Was it purely coincidence, or was it something to do with me? Was he connected to my phone disappearing? I have such a bad feeling about this.

Rehearsals are a disaster. We've never actually rehearsed before. We've just been dressing up, or doing makeup tutorials, or playing computer games, and ended up accidentally singing. And we always ended up accidentally singing whatever Jodie happened to be playing, because it didn't really matter. And Jodie always happened to be playing something poppy and preferably cheesy, because she has, as Rose says, no musical taste AT ALL, but nobody minded.

Now it matters. Now we mind.

Well, Nell doesn't mind. Nell will sing anything, and look gorgeous doing so, and sound it. Nell's real passion is animal husbandry (which I always used to tease her was marrying animals, but so isn't), and if it's anything to do with the ethical treatment of animals she'll argue with you to the death, but if it's music, she doesn't really care. However, Rose's real passion is music, and she cares a lot. If we're going to do this at all, she wants us to do it properly.

Jodie wants Abba; Rose wants Alicia Keys. Jodie wants Britney; Rose wants Amy Winehouse. Jodie refuses to do anything by her because her life was 'so so tragic'. I don't know what *I* want – only that I don't want this stress. The whole point of the band was to relax, and this is definitely not relaxing.

In the end we pick song titles out of a hat. I don't know how she did it, but all the choices are Jodie's anyway.

Turns out that's the least of our troubles.

Nell's dad delivers us to the house a couple of hours before the party. When we meet George, his eyes hold mine for a split second longer than the others. He's remembering, I know he is. For a moment, he seems wary, but then he switches into a different mode: cold, distant and polite. He flicks his eyes past me, as if I hardly exist. I wish, suddenly, that I *had* told somebody about him, because then I could explain how crushed I feel. Which is crazy – because I *wanted* him to pretend it never happened, same as me. Even so, the crushed feeling persists.

I wait with dread for the others to notice my downbeat mood and ask me about it, but as George shows us where we'll be playing and changing, nobody does. Slowly I realise that, for their different reasons, they're all feeling worse. Nell's terrified she'll forget the words. Jodie's excitement has turned to pure fear, and even though Rose couldn't sing a bum note if she tried, her shyness is making her physically shake with the effort of imagining a hundred people packed into the barn at the end of George's garden, all watching us and listening to every note.

I make the mistake of thinking about it too. In two hours, a hundred cool sixth-formers will arrive, cool sixth-formers who could kill us on Interface with a single well-armed putdown. And all we have between us and them are three glitter belts, a silver waistcoat and a couple of moth-eaten comedy hats. We are *crazy*.

'I don't think I can do this,' Rose says, slipping into her costume in George's parents' bedroom, which we've adopted as the Manic Pixie Dream Girls' changing room. 'I know I promised, but . . .'

We've checked out the barn, done the sound check (where we rivalled Alvin and the Chipmunks for squeakiness) and we're supposed to be performing in forty-five minutes. Rose looks wonderful in a stripey black and white dress with the silver waistcoat. But her face is whiter than the dress, and she has thrown up twice in the ensuite.

'Just try,' Nell says gently, rubbing her back. 'You know all the notes. You look amazing. Don't worry if you can't sing when we get there. We'll cover for you.'

Meanwhile, Jodie is applying her makeup for the third time, because her hands are shaking so much she can't get her lipstick straight and she keeps poking herself in the eye with her mascara.

'All those girls . . .' she says. 'Did you see them?'

Indeed we did. Before we came upstairs to change, we watched a good portion of our sixth form arrive, dressed up in tiny, body-hugging dresses and skyscraper heels, with lashings of lipgloss, and enough hair products to launch a major salon. Most gorgeous of all was Michelle Lee, George's girlfriend, who could happily body double for Cheryl Cole if she ever needed the job. She kissed me on both cheeks when she met me. I wanted the ground to swallow me up.

In less than an hour they'll all be crammed into the barn, watching us muck about onstage, sounding like woodland animals on helium. At least I won't be in my pyjama top tonight – I'm wearing my best party dress under the glitter belt – but that's not much of a comfort.

'Just think,' Jodie announces, looking nauseous, 'whatever happens, we'll be able to say we played a professional gig at one of George's parties. Nobody'll be able to take that away from us.'

'Nobody'll want to,' I squeak.

'We just have to take it one song at a time,' Nell says, squinting at herself in the mirror. She has the big advantage that she can always take her glasses off onstage, at which point the crowd will become a vague, bouncy blur. Maybe I could put them on, which would blur the crowd for me too. The thought cheers me up slightly.

Nell's right, though: positive thinking. I admire her attitude.

'Come on,' I say, adjusting the straps on my platforms. 'We're here now. What we need is some sort of band ritual. Stand over here, everyone. Put your hands in the middle. Repeat after me. I faithfully promise . . . on the spirit of . . .' Damn, I've run out of inspiration already. 'Of what?'

'Of the seminal leotard?' Rose suggests, through chattering teeth.

'Of the seminal leotard,' I agree gratefully, 'that I will have fun tonight.'

Still shaking, they faithfully promise. Outside, the barn is already jumping to the sound of Call of Duty. If I could be at home right now, wrapped up in my duvet and playing Fruit Ninja, I totally would.

When we get to the barn, the Castle College band are already halfway through their set. We slip in through the open door and stand near the back, watching them over the heads of the crowd.

They're very good, there's no denying it. The band is made up of three boys and a girl, sixth-formers like George. There has always been rivalry between their school and St Christopher's, and Castle College always wins. They have more playing fields, better players, grander music facilities, more teachers, richer parents. That's one of the many reasons why it's so amazing that we've recently overtaken Call of Duty on Killer Act.

Watching them now, I can't make sense of that at all. The drummer at the back is short and wiry, but all three of the others could happily pass for models at Abercrombie, including the two boys at the front – both on guitar. They look alike, with the same floppy hair and high cheekbones, and the same lazy smiles. Over their jeans and T-shirts, they're both wearing open red military jackets with lots of gold embroidery. Mrs Venning could sell those for a fortune. They make the boys look super-posh, and very intimidating.

Scariest of all, though, is the girl who plays bass. She has a huge shock of tawny blonde hair, perfect skin, a tiny body – dressed in a black PVC mini and a leather jacket with the sleeves ripped off – and the same powerful attitude as the boys, leaping around the stage and glaring at the audience, daring them not to have a good time.

Luckily, everybody's having the time of their lives. The band are in the middle of a song they wrote that seems to be called 'It's Not About You', given how many times they roar out that line at the crowd. It's got most of the boys moshing in a self-made pit, while half the girls are practically throwing themselves at the singer. He's soaking up the attention. Every time he glances out at the crowd, the girls at the front actually scream.

'God, that boy is up himself,' Jodie shudders from beside me. Even she can't help doing her moves to the music, though.

'He's called Ed,' says a girl in front of us, looking round, beaming. 'Ed Matthews.' She laughs and shows us her wrist, where the letters E and M are intertwined in twirling blue.

'That's not a real tattoo, is it?' Jodie asks, amazed.

The girl shakes her head. 'But one day . . .'

Jodie rolls her eyes.

I'm torn. The military jacket thing is very posey and irritating, the screaming and fake tattoos are just plain embarrassing, but the boys are . . . interesting, bordering on hot. Something happens when I'm surrounded by music. All my emotions are intensified. It's why gigs and festivals are so dangerous for me. However, I refuse *ever* to sink so low as to be a screaming groupie. And besides, my stomach is performing somersaults at the thought that we're about to go onstage in just a few minutes.

I look around to the others for support, and notice that Rose has disappeared. Nell mimes being sick and points to the doorway, looking worried. I nip out straight away to find Rose.

She's leaning against the side of the barn with her eyes closed.

'Are you all right?' I ask, although it's obvious she's not.

'I'll be OK,' she says, breathing deeply. 'Just leave me. Please?' I go to her, but she waves me away. 'Honestly. You

41

go back. I'll join you in a minute.'

I don't like to leave her, but I know that when I'm feeling unwell the last thing I need is people fussing over me, so I promise her I'll be back soon.

In the hot, sweaty barn, Call of Duty bring their set to a crashing close with a hard rock version of 'Happy Birthday' to George. The barn erupts into rowdy, storming applause.

'Sorry guys – that's all from us tonight,' Ed Matthews calls out over the noise. 'There's another band on in a few minutes. Some strange name. Massive Pixie Dreamboats or something? Where did you find *them*, George?' He laughs. 'Anyway, they made one video, so . . . well done to the Dreamboats. Meantime, it's not too late to vote for us in Killer Act. We need every vote and your vote counts, OK? And your mum's. And your auntie's. And if you're very lucky, I'll give you a little kiss to say thank you.'

Several girls in the audience shriek at the idea of it. Jodie and Nell are still hovering by the door. Jodie turns to catch my eye and looks as if she's about to combust.

'DREAMBOATS?' she shouts at me, above the screaming.

'He's just jealous,' I yell back.

'One video?'

'Well, we—'

'We are going to Take. Them. Down.'

'Right,' I nod.

Although how we're going to do that with one girl being sick in the garden, one who can hardly see through her steamed-up glasses, one about to explode with fury and one girl whose sole ability is jiggling around in a mini kilt, I'm not exactly sure.

With a fifteen-minute break between the boys and us, the crowd stream out into the night air for a bit of a break from the sweaty atmosphere and the chance to stock up on drinks from the bar in the living room. Ed Matthews saunters off, grabbing a bottle of water from one of the eager girls clustering round him. He comes straight down towards us, by the door, and flicks us a hostile look.

A bit heavy, I think. All we did was enter a competition. We didn't even do *that*, actually – somebody else did it for us.

As he passes us his lip curls.

'Are you ready to take on our crowd then, Dreamboats?'

We have never done this before. So no, we are absolutely not. Not even close.

'Sure,' Jodie says, through clenched teeth. 'Any time.'

'Great. And if it doesn't work out, we always need more backing singers. Hotlegs here would be perfect.'

He winks at me, takes a swig of his water, and moves off into the night.

IhatehimIhatehimIhatehimIhatehim.

Outside the barn, Rose looks a bit better.

'How did it go?' she asks.

'They were OK, I suppose,' Jodie growls.

We chat for a while, until George arrives to tell us it's time for our set. Rose puts on the bravest face she can. 'Shall we go?'

We head for the stage – which is empty by now – shouldering our way through the returning crowd. Jodie sets up the backing tracks. We find our places and check the mics. In the middle of the room, I spot the girl from

Call of Duty high-fiving various people and laughing.

The audience is noisy, happy and not interested in us – still coming down from the buzz of listening to the band as they gradually filter back in from the house. Nevertheless, George steps to the front of the stage and gives us a quick introduction. Nobody listens. Nobody cares.

Jodie starts the backing track. Our first track is 'California Gurls' by Katy Perry, which Jodie says is a classic anthem to get everyone in the mood. It sounded OK when we rehearsed it the last time; even Rose had to agree. Now, however, our voices are somehow lost in the general hubbub of party chatter. Call of Duty girl doesn't seem to have noticed we've started, and the general noise levels don't vary throughout our rendition of 'Party in the USA' by Miley Cyrus. (Actually by Jessie J, as Rose pointed out to us earlier, and only *sung* by Miley Cyrus. Not that the audience would be that bothered about who wrote the song; I'm not even sure they're aware we're singing it.)

Mortified, we carry on. Was *this* what George wanted? To humiliate us? Did he know this was going to happen?

'Shall we stop now?' Nell asks, when we're almost done with Miley.

'Yes, let's,' Rose agrees gratefully.

'No,' Jodie says with a quick shake of her head. Fury and pure stubbornness are pushing her on.

'Just one more?' I suggest, as a compromise.

Unwillingly, the others agree.

And then, suddenly, everything goes black.

A socket behind us pops, with a flash and a little puff of smoke, and the barn is plunged into darkness. For a moment, the sudden silence has a volume of its own, then the crowd starts to laugh and boo.

'Come on, George! Sort it out!' someone shouts.

After a minute of fiddling, a couple of lights come back on – but they turn out to be two spotlights, shining right in our eyes and preventing us from seeing the crowd at all. The mics and speakers stay firmly mute. We're stuck onstage and now everyone must be looking at us. Finally. If not exactly in the way we hoped.

There are a few laughs from the crowd, who seem to have spotted us for the first time.

'Oi!' a boy shouts from near the back, 'aren't you the "Sunglasses" girls?'

'Yeah!' someone else shouts. 'Sing us your song, then.'

Oh wow, so they do know who we are. Not that it helps.

'But we can't,' I shout out. 'No sound.' I point behind us and shrug.

The crowd are in a strange mood, though. Good-humoured, but not really listening to us. They start up a chant: 'Sun-glass-es, Sun-glass-es, Sun-glass-es.'

Nell looks at me helplessly. I look at Jodie. She looks at Rose. Rose looks astonished. Meanwhile, the chant goes on.

'We've got to do something,' Jodie says.

A tall figure pushes through the crowd, which parts to make way for him. It's one of the boys from Call of Duty – not Ed, the singer, but the other Abercrombie type – clutching an acoustic guitar. He stands in front of the stage and holds it up towards me.

'I always bring one, just in case. Maybe one of you could play?'

He glances at Rose. She stares blankly ahead.

'Will you?' I ask her.

She says nothing, and seems rooted to the spot.

'Anyway, take it,' the boy says, handing the guitar to me.

I take it. It seems very kind of him, when we've overtaken his band on Killer Act and he could easily just watch us squirm. Nell gives him her cutest smile and even Jodie looks cheerful. He blends back into the crowd and I hand the guitar to Rose. She looks at it like it's a hologram, or a unicorn. I worry that she might be sick again – here is *not* the place. But she looks more confused than anything.

'You could play it,' I suggest.

She looks out at the audience, then back at the guitar. Focusing on it seems to help – taking her mind off what's happening. There's a strap, which she puts over her shoulder.

'Promise me you'll sing,' she mutters. 'Promise me.'

'I promise.'

She closes her eyes and strums the strings. It's funny: the thing that would terrify me most – playing an instrument in public – is what seems to calm Rose down. She tries a few notes, opens her eyes and suddenly she's a different girl. She looks OK now. In fact, she looks better than she has for ages. I think she's gone beyond fear.

There's a lot of shushing in the audience. Now the crowd are curious.

'Are you ready?' Rose asks quietly.

Jodie shrugs. 'Go for it.'

Rose strums the first few familiar chords. She plays flawlessly, as if she's been playing it all her life. We gather near her, squeezing into the spotlight. From here it's warmer, safer, and harder to see the crowd. After eight bars, we begin.

'I put my sunglasses on
My yellow sunglasses on
And I think of you and the things you do
And it doesn't matter any more because . . .'

Several people in the crowd join in at this point:

'I've got my sunglasses on . . .'

Our voices are wobbly at first, but we quickly find the harmonies. After all our years of singing together, we know each other so well. And the crowd below us are quick to swell the noise.

They know the song! And they seem to like it. Rose was right about it being catchy. Were these some of the people who voted for us after all? Cool sixth-formers and their friends?

Gradually we stop being a bunch of terrified girls and we start being a band. The things we love – being silly together and singing in harmony – they're OK. We look down at the crowd and behind the lights I can just about make out the bobbing heads of a hundred cool partygoers, all singing along to a song we wrote, laughing at our words, swaying to our tune.

I try and keep my voice low. I know I'm the 'truckful of gravel'. But even so, we sound good. We really do – you can just tell. Singing in secret was fun, but singing here, now, is a million times better. I almost wish I still had my feather boa to wave around me. The wonderful feeling builds and grows. By the end, like me, Nell is beaming. Jodie looks happy enough to light up the whole barn and Rose – well, Rose is glowing. I think she's almost forgiven Jodie and me for making her do this tonight.

As soon as we finish, Rose turns to the rest of us and tentatively plays the opening bars to 'I See The Light' by Roxanne Wills – the other song Jodie chose. I didn't even know Rose knew it on the guitar. However, she makes it seem easy and, as we practised, she sings the first verse alone. Her voice is gorgeous: mellow, and smoky, warm and strong.

Jodie's made us sing the words so often that when my turn comes to sing the second verse, I do it without really thinking. The nerves have gone. When we get to the chorus, once again everyone joins in. A hundred chanting voices, a hundred smiling faces. The music lifts me up, up and over the crowd. It's like learning to fly and never wanting to land. It is absolutely the best feeling I've ever had. Looking across at the others, I can tell they feel the same. We're all floating, flying, soaring.

As my eyes begin to adjust to the bright lights in our faces, I glance down into the crowd and see a sixth form boy in the front row, sandy-haired and pale-skinned, filming us on a camera phone. He stands out because he's not so much happy as mesmerised. And he's staring right at me.

I recognise him from Jodie's house, because he hangs out with her brother Sam a lot. His name is Elliot Harrison. He's a bit of a computer nerd, like Sam, and generally avoided by all but the super-geeks. His stare has a strange intensity and the steadiness of his hand contrasts with the general movement among the crowd as he holds up the phone to film us.

In the midst of all the fun we're having, it flashes over me with absolute certainty: Elliot is the person who stole my phone. For some reason, he has an unhealthy interest in the Manic Pixie Dream Girls.

He started all this. He made it happen. He uploaded the video.

Whatever It Takes

I stare at Elliot; he stares at me. But by the time we get to leave the stage, he's disappeared. Anyway, we're surrounded. Suddenly everyone wants to say hello, or fetch us drinks, or get our numbers. George comes over, smiling his face off. He insists we have to meet all his friends. When we pose for photos, he drapes his arms round me and Rose. And now it's OK: I'm not just a girl – I'm a singer in a band.

This, I think, is what it must be like to be a rock star. The buzz lasts for the rest of the party. It even survives the journey home, in the back of Nell's dad's ancient Volvo, squashed up against our costume bags.

There's hardly any talking. Nell quickly falls asleep, but the rest of us are busy reliving our moment in the spotlight. It's not until we're nearly back in Castle Bigelow that I remember to tell Jodie and Rose about my big discovery.

Jodie yelps so loudly it wakes Nell up.

'What? What?'

'Elliot Harrison is a weirdo phone stalker!' Jodie yells at her.

'Who? How?'

'Sam's friend. Sasha just worked it out.'

Nell still looks pretty woozy. It takes a while to bring her up to speed.

'So what shall we do about it?' she asks, when she's eventually awake enough to wonder.

'Confront him,' Jodie says. 'At break time tomorrow. Together.'

'Are you sure?' Nell's dad asks. 'Is he a boy at school? He sounds a bit . . . alarming.'

'Oh no, he isn't really,' I assure him. 'It's just the way Jodie describes him. We'll be fine.'

First thing next morning, I check our fan page. Someone has uploaded another video of us singing last night, and that person must have been standing exactly where Elliot was standing. It was totally him.

At break time, we meet in the main corridor to track him down. However, on the way to the sixth form common room we have to stop to sign three autographs, pose for photos with people who were at the party last night and couldn't make it to us through the crowd, and record a quick a cappella duet of 'Sunglasses' for another person's ringtone. It slows us down quite a bit, but we find him with five minutes to spare.

He's standing near the vending machines, looking at something on his phone. He doesn't see us coming until it's much too late to escape. We crowd round him, Rose and me on one side, Jodie and Nell on the other.

'Elliot Harrison, you have some explaining to do,' I begin.

He looks panicked. He may be a sixth-former, but it's four to one and we can be pretty intimidating if we're angry. He tries to deny it, but with four of us challenging him, he can't hold out for long. The evidence of the second video is the final straw. He turns to Jodie, with as much defiance in his face as he can manage.

'I was doing World of Warcraft with Sam and we heard you talking to her' – he indicates Nell – 'about these videos. They sounded funny. We wanted to see them. That's all.'

'So you stole Sasha's phone to watch our videos?'

He looks super uncomfortable. 'Not stole. Borrowed.'

'And then you thought you'd just put them on the internet?'

Jodie is marginally taller than Elliot, and infinitely scarier. He cowers down.

'Not all of them,' he says defensively. 'Look, we weren't going to do anything. But the Sunglasses one . . .'

'What about it?' Jodie demands.

'It was good, OK? Special.'

'Thanks,' Nell smiles. Jodie glares at her.

'We liked the song,' Elliot mutters. 'Well, *I* liked the song. I thought people ought to see it so I put it up for you. As a favour. OK?'

'No! Not OK!' Jodie yells.

'A favour? You stole our video as a *favour*?' I storm at him.

He sighs as if I'm being stupid. 'Not stole. Shared. I gave your phone back, didn't I?'

'But what if everyone had hated it?' Rose asks, quietly, from beside me.

'They wouldn't.' He looks at us with that same steady stare as last night. 'They just . . . wouldn't.'

He blushes, then looks angry and miserable, as indeed he should. Weirdo stalker.

'So it was you and your geeky friends who voted for us,' I murmur, trying to make sense of it all.

'Ye-es,' he agrees, shifting about and not meeting our eyes.

'That doesn't make sense. How do you explain us getting so many votes? There aren't *that* many geeks in school.'

He twitches nervously.

'I . . . It just . . . snowballed.'

For a moment, he looks up and I catch a flash of something behind his eyes. There's something else: something he's not telling us.

'Snowballed how?' Jodie challenges.

He stares back at the floor.

'I don't know. It's a totally weird phenomenon. You should be pleased, anyway. I only—'

'Only what? *What*, Elliot?'

But the bell goes, loud and insistent, cutting off all conversation. A crowd of people rush by on their way to the next class and Elliot takes his chance to join them and escape.

By lunchtime the new video has loads of comments saying they like us. Not just from people we know at school, but others too.

You were awwwwwweeesoooooome!

Loving you guys so much!

Girl in the hotpants – can I have your number?

1500, 1750, 1999 ...

Now the numbers start to rise in even more rapid leaps. We overtake Call of Duty by hundreds of votes and there doesn't seem to be a single person in school who doesn't recognise us. Three people want us to play at their Christmas parties, and we say yes to all of them, even the cheeky girl in Year 7, because we're so grateful to be asked.

By the first of December, there's a new number at the bottom of our entry: 97th. Temporarily at least, we've made the top 100 on Killer Act and the competition still has two weeks to run.

So what exactly do we have to be angry with Elliot about anyway?

On the last day of term, they announce it in the local paper.

BIGELOW GIRLS MAKE TOP 100

A girl band from St Christopher's School in Castle Bigelow has made it into the finals of a national online school talent competition.

Out of thousands of entries, Sasha 'Hotlegs' Bayley and her band, the Manic Pixie Dream Girls, have reached the top 100 of Killer Act, and will be attending auditions in January for the live TV finals, which will be broadcast in March. The local girls had an online hit with their song 'Sunglasses', and reached an impressive 3,897 votes.

Killer Act is sponsored by Interface, the social networking company that was recently valued at over £600 million($1 billion).

Jodie is not thrilled about the 'Hotlegs' bit – not at all. But she decides to forgive me: it was hardly my fault, after all. She's already thinking about our audition piece.

My biggest concern is Rose. She's our best asset – our most reliable singer, and the only one who can play an instrument. But I saw how she was before George's party. I never want to see that pale, haunted look on her face again.

'Are you sure you'll be OK with these gigs?' I ask her one evening at my place, when it's just the two of us. She's picking out a tune on her spare guitar, the one she keeps in my room.

'I think so,' she says, strumming thoughtfully. 'Last time wasn't as bad as I thought it'd be. In fact, it was pretty good by the end, wasn't it? And as long as I've got this,' she pats the guitar, 'I should be fine. Sorry for letting you down like that last time.'

'But you didn't!' I assure her. 'You were fantastic.'

'It turned out OK,' she admits modestly. 'But you practically had to hold me up.'

'Whatever it takes,' I grin. 'Anyway, performing for a

crowd is good practice for when you're famous.'

She laughs and changes the subject by trying out 'Sunglasses' in a series of different keys.

The Christmas holidays are the best we've ever had. Not only do our gigs go really well, but we get invited to what seems like every party in Castle Bigelow. Our Interface pages are full of good-luck messages and new friend requests. And Mum's café is constantly busy with people wanting to congratulate her, and me, and anyone who knows us.

As Jodie points out, it's a sad reflection of how little there is to do in Castle Bigelow if you get to be a celebrity by coming eighty-fifth in a competition. But as we sing 'Sunglasses' for the hundredth time to a roomful of happy partygoers, who all know the tune, I can't say I care.

La La Big Number Scary

Auditions for the live shows take place over three weekends in January. Ours is the final Sunday, and we're in the last twenty acts they'll be seeing. The venue is the Interface headquarters, a multimillion-pound complex just off the M4, where lots of computer companies have their HQs. We looked it up online. It's very modern and grand, with several large, eco-friendly buildings set among lawns and woods, and even a lake. They'll be filming us in this amazing conference centre behind the main building, which looks like a series of spaceships parked around a large wooden tepee.

When we arrive at seven a.m., as requested, it's not even light. We're squashed into Nell's dad's Volvo again. He's taken to calling himself the band's taxi service. One thing I've discovered about the music business: it's tricky if you haven't got transport.

The tepee looms ahead of us through the gloom. Signs point to places like 'Pathfinders', 'Eat' and 'Vision'. The tepee itself is called 'Meet', and we follow the road to it, sitting in a slow queue of cars all disgorging nervous-looking teenagers and their even more nervous-looking parents, who give them quick hugs before watching them go inside.

In the reception area, a young man with a clipboard comes over to us and introduces himself as Rob. He ticks off our names on his list and waits while we sign various papers that he explains are 'standard TV release forms'. These allow the TV company to use any footage of us they like, and prevent us doing . . . a bunch of stuff we don't have time to read about but hope won't be a problem. With a queue of people forming behind us, we all sign as fast as we can.

Once a group of about ten of us have signed, Rob accompanies us all to a cavernous space at the back of the centre, which is where all the auditionees will be relaxing and practising.

'Make yourselves at home,' Rob says. 'The facilities are at that end.'

He points to a door marked with signs to the toilets. I get the feeling we're going to need them quite a lot.

'Oh, and people may be filming at any time,' he adds. 'They'll use it as background for the live shows. You know the kind of stuff. Just ignore the cameras, OK? They like to use natural footage. But don't worry, you'll get used to them.'

We check out the other acts. There are some street dancer girls in leotards, with tracksuits over the top to keep them warm, a few boys mooching about with guitars, a string quartet who set up in a corner and start practising together as if they don't know that the whole room is listening (who voted for *them*?), and several people on their own, who sit around looking scared and helpless like us, but are trying not to show it.

Now I am slightly regretting my outfit choices. They told us to arrive in costume, so we did. People seemed to like what we wore on our first video, so we decided to be brave – although I think perhaps I overdid it. We're going to be doing the Roxanne Wills song again, so I watched loads of her videos and somehow decided it would be sensible to appear in a gold spangled catsuit that Mrs Venning had been storing since about 1980. Believe me, that is *nothing* compared to what Roxanne Wills's backing dancers wear, but here, in this room, I feel mildly silly. Knowing I have a pair of gold heels in my bag to change into doesn't help. And a cape. For some reason I thought a cape would be a good idea too.

Nell's back in the sequin shorts, but she's got a tracksuit over them for now. Jodie chose silver leggings and a T-shirt from Living Vintage that says FRANKIE SAYS RELAX. Rose is in a purple dress with draped sleeves – a fifties original – and delicate silver shoes. We're all backcombed to match. No wonder everyone's looking at us. It's a relief when the last people trickle in and they take us all off to the theatre, to explain what's going to happen.

We sit in the audience seats while a tall man in a black

59

polo-neck jumper, with a sleek goatee beard, takes centre stage. When he talks, his voice is low, but somehow you can hear every word he says. It helps that his face is projected onto a screen the size of a small house, just above his head.

'Welcome, everybody. My name is Ivan Jenks. I'm in charge of marketing at Interface, and it's my job to find the next act to advertise our product worldwide. And that act could be you.'

He looks out at us and suddenly flashes us a wolfish grin. Magnified behind him on the screen, it's mesmerising and almost frightening.

'I want you to think about Interface for a moment,' he says. 'We have over half a billion customers around the world, people just like you, who watch us every day on their computers and their tablets and their mobiles. Every day, the advert made by our winner will appear on over a billion devices. Not a million. A *billion*.'

Behind him, the projection suddenly shows an image of a phone screen, flashing up loads of different Interface pages. The screen multiplies again and again, until there seem to be thousands of them. Even so, it's only a fraction of a billion. I can't actually imagine a billion. Not really. If he just said 'Lalalala big number scary' it would have the same effect.

'So we're looking for something very special from the nine acts we'll pick from these auditions,' he continues. 'You've got to stand out. The judges know what it is we're looking for. Listen to them. Learn from them. Even if you don't get through, you're about to get the best masterclass in the music industry that you could ever hope for. Now let me introduce the judges. Linus, come and join us.'

A short, broad man walks onto the stage. He has close-cropped hair and a lined face and is dressed in a open-necked shirt and baggy jeans. He's nothing much to look at, but when he opens his mouth to smile, his teeth are so white it's as if they belong to another person. TV teeth. We all applaud, although I can't say I've ever seen him before. Ivan introduces him as Linus Oakley, a big-time music manager. But we've never heard of him, so we'll have to take Ivan's word for it.

Next is Sebastian Rules, the rapper and producer from London. We certainly know him, as he's been in the charts a lot recently. He's taller and much younger than Linus, dressed in a razor-sharp grey suit. Jodie nudges me and points at it.

'His own clothing line,' she mouths, impressed. Jodie yearns for her own line one day. She's even designed the logo.

'Does he do his own perfume, too?' Rose asks, nudging me gently.

Jodie nods happily, not noticing the nudge. Rose and I share a smile. Jodie's ultimate definition of success is having your own perfume, whereas Rose's is mastering advanced Spanish guitar, or having a megastar songwriter like Paul McCartney tell you they love your stuff. Nell's is working at London Zoo. Right now, mine would be making it to the loo in this catsuit without any major catastrophes.

Finally, Ivan announces the third judge, and Jodie and I squeal with excitement. It's Roxanne Wills: the singer whose song we've chosen for today. She's a megastar from Florida – a great singer and a fabulous dancer. She's one of our all-time heroes and it can't be a coincidence that we're doing her song. It just can't. It's got to be a sign, surely?

We're not her only fans, though. When she comes on, the applause is deafening. People stomp their feet and whistle. She stands onstage now, waiting humbly for the noise to die down, looking incredible in a mock-croc mini-dress and five-inch heels. It's weird to see her in the flesh, after years of only seeing her in magazines and on video. She looks smaller, slighter. But when she eventually grins, her smile is enormous.

'I just wanted to say,' she says, stepping forward and talking breathily into the mic, 'that I feel so proud and humbled today to be a part of inspiring the next genera-tion of music makers on Killer Act. I want to send my good wishes to each and every one of you.'

I feel her look straight at me as she says it, and it's like getting a jolt of electricity. She's right there, so close: I could almost touch her. Beside me, Rose raises an eyebrow.

'Patronising, much?' she whispers.

But I don't care. Roxanne's good wishes are good enough for me.

The judges stay where they are, while we go back to our original waiting room, ready for the auditions to begin. It's the start of a very long day.

After a while, a couple of men in T-shirts arrive with shoulder-mounted TV cameras and wander around, filming conversations. Everybody tries to look interesting and suddenly I can't think of anything to say. Meanwhile, the waiting is endless. First the street dancers are taken off to see the judges, then the string quartet. Our wait continues.

At twelve o'clock Rob finally calls us, but it's only to

see a group of three producers, all sitting in a small airless room with about five empty coffee cups on the table in front of them, who want to talk about our 'journey'. Nell is five minutes into describing the traffic on the motorway before the bearded guy at one end of the table explains that they meant 'Your journey to the competition more broadly. What made you want to sing together?'

Oh. That journey. Our backstory-type-thing. We talked about this before we got here, and agreed not to talk about Rose's parents (she hates it), or my dad (you must be joking), or our sad addiction to Abba and Kylie. Instead, we tell them about Jodie, Nell and me meeting in primary school, and Rose joining us later on. We mention how 'Sunglasses' was the first song we wrote together and, no, we haven't done anything since. God, we sound dull, though. We're even reduced to Jodie talking about Rolo, her ancient pony (on the basis that animal stories are cute), and Nell telling them about her plan to be a vet. The thing is, we're just a group of girls who ended up singing together by accident. We haven't really *got* a backstory.

'And what made you decide to enter Killer Act?' the bearded guy asks, looking a bit desperate.

'Oh, we didn't,' Nell says cheerfully. 'One of our friends did it for us.' I glare at her. 'Er, not a friend, actually. Just someone we know,' she amends.

'But we're really, really glad we made it,' I add, trying to move the subject away from weirdo stalker types.

It's too late, though. To my frustration, they seem to like the story about the friend, especially when they ask for more details and Nell admits we didn't know who it was at first. Our agony when my phone was stolen sounds quite entertaining to the producers, as does the fact that we entered the competition so late, but gathered votes so fast. Even that, though, is only *quite* entertaining. In the end they all nod without looking up at us and tell us we can go.

Part one of the audition: probable fail.

Next is Bert Blackwell, the musical director. We meet him in a large, airy room containing a grand piano, several instruments stacked neatly against the wall, and another TV guy wandering round with a camera.

'Hi,' Bert says, welcoming us in. 'I've seen your video. My job is to find out how much talent you really have lurking there. The video's part of the story, but we want acts with real potential. Let's see what you can do.'

OK. No pressure, then.

He's gentle, but very organised, and a brilliant pianist, sitting at an electric piano with a vast array of buttons above the keyboard. We sing 'I See the Light' for him, first together, then individually. Then he gets us to sing a range of phrases from different songs. It's quickly obvious – although it never was to us before – that Jodie has the loudest voice, but can lapse into a bad American accent if she's not careful. She promises to watch it. Nell is the quietest and needs to project. When she's by herself, she gets so nervous you can hardly hear her. But if she breathes properly, as Bert suggests, her beautiful tone shines through.

When it's my turn to sing, I instantly stop at the sound of my husky voice in the mic.

'What's the problem?' Bert asks.

'It's just the gravel,' I say apologetically.

Bert frowns at me. 'Gravel?'

'My old choir teacher said I sounded like a load of gravel being poured down a hole.'

He smiles. 'I see what she meant. But I suppose she didn't think to mention that can be a good thing? Not for choirs, maybe, but for rock songs. Try this.'

He plays a few bars of 'Hey Jude' by the Beatles.

'Do you know it?'

Of course I do. Dad taught it to me in my cot, practically. Plus, Rose and I often sing the Beatles together. In fact she can't help harmonising with me when I hit the chorus.

'Not bad,' Bert says, watching me closely, 'but you need to be careful of the high notes. You tend to go flat.'

'I know,' I admit. I don't have the natural talent of Rose or Jodie. I love to sing, but there is no way I will ever be Paul McCartney.

'Loosen up,' Bert says. 'Enjoy yourself. Believe it or not, that will help.' He smiles enigmatically and makes notes on a clipboard.

'Right, Rose,' he says eventually. 'You last. I did some research and I notice from your Interface page that you like jazz. Shall we try some Nina Simone?'

He starts the introduction of 'My Baby Just Cares For Me', which is one of Rose's favourite songs of all time. All the way through the opening bars she just stares at me. Her eyes say clearly, *He did some research on my* Interface *page? Who is this weirdo?* She only has a personal page at all because we did it as an exercise in ICT.

She looks nervous, but she knows the song so well and Bert plays it so expertly that when the time comes, her voice seems to take off, and there it is again: that warm, jazzy tone we heard at George's party. To me, it sounds as if she's got the best voice of all.

'That was lovely,' Bert smiles when she's finished. 'You have impeccable timing. And a real gift. When you're in your comfort zone, you definitely stand out.'

Rose shifts around, super-embarrassed, staring at the floor.

I give her a squeeze, while Bert makes more notes on his clipboard.

'That's it. You can go now. Good luck with the judges.'

What exactly was he writing on that clipboard? It was a lot.

'You were amazing,' I whisper to Rose as we leave.

She shakes her head. 'Not really. It's just a good song, that's all.'

Outside, Rob greets us with a grin. 'That go OK?' he asks, not waiting for an answer. 'They're ready for you now, you'll be pleased to hear.'

Rob introduces us to a woman I've seen popping in and out, always looking busy. She's dressed in smart grey jeans and a soft black jacket, with sharp brown eyes and blonde hair scraped back into a bun.

'This is Janet,' Rob says. 'She's the floor manager. She'll take care of you.'

I notice Janet's radio mic, and the tired look around her eyes. We're among the last to be seen. It's almost evening already, and she must have arrived here, like us, long ago. Nevertheless, she gives us a smile.

'This way.'

'Good luck, everyone,' Nell whispers.

As we troop behind her towards the theatre, where the

judges are, I think about the musical director's last piece of advice: *Loosen up; enjoy yourself.*

Yeah, right.

Catsuit Girl

We creep through the wings, onto the main stage. The judges are sitting at a table facing the stage, just like we imagined, each one spotlit for extra, nerve-racking effect.

Linus Oakley sits stiffly in the middle. To his left, Sebastian Rules is so relaxed in his chair he's practically horizontal. But it's Roxanne Wills who really gets our attention. She's got one camera zoomed in extra close on her face as we walk in. Perhaps it's not just in my imagination that we have some sort of connection. Perhaps, somehow, the TV people sense it too.

'How are you?' she asks, in a low, husky voice.

We mutter that we're fine – which is code for the fact

that we're sick with nerves and we still can't quite believe we're here at all.

Linus checks the notes in front of him. There are lots of them. I think I recognise some of Bert's upside-down scrawls from our meeting with him just now, but I can't be sure.

'You got your backing track ready?' Roxanne asks.

We shake our heads. After our success at George's party, we've decided to pare things back.

'It's just us and the guitar today,' Rose explains, after a cough to clear her throat.

'And we're doing one of your songs,' I tell Roxanne. I sound as if I'm being strangled. Roxanne ignores my nerves and beams delightedly.

'OK,' Linus calls out, checking that the cameras are in place. 'Off you go.'

One of the stage hands comes on, as we requested, with a stool for Rose and her guitar. She sets herself in position on the right-hand end of the group with the guitar in her lap. At this moment, I remember that we didn't say 'Seminal leotards'. We meant to, but we got so distracted by following Janet. Too late now. Rose taps her guitar and starts to play the opening chords of 'I See The Light'.

Oh. Utterly. Wow. This moment is really happening. I am about to sing Roxanne Wills's lyrics. TO Roxanne Wills. In a theatre in a space-age HQ. Surrounded by my best friends. Dressed in a catsuit. It's bizarre, certainly, but possibly in a good way.

We've practised a thousand times, and we know the song backwards. We've tried to recreate the feeling we had when we sang it that time at George's party, after

'Sunglasses'. We launch into our harmony on the second verse and, as far as I can tell, we sound OK. Certainly not a disaster. In my dreams, I've pictured the judges leaning in towards us and singing along, like the crowd did then. Maybe even some of the camera crew and producers. Wouldn't it be wonderful if everybody . . . ?

'*Stop!*'

I'm startled out of my daydream. Linus is holding his hand up. He looks frustrated and almost angry. In the silence that follows, the sound of my heart beating is deafening. We don't look at each other. We don't dare.

Linus sighs. He must see the crushed look on our faces, because his scowl fades slightly.

'It's not *terrible*,' he says, 'but it's not working. What d'you think, Roxy? It's your song.'

Roxanne purses her lips. 'Oh, I don't know. You're cute, girls. But it needs . . . something.'

Linus and Sebastian both nod.

It probably needs a group of girls who've done more than four live performances, to be fair, and who don't normally just muck around in each other's bedrooms singing in their pyjamas. I guess I was getting carried away just now.

'Try losing the guitar,' Linus calls.

'No!' Rose exclaims. The sudden fear in her voice startles me. 'But I need it!' she stutters more quietly. 'Without it we can't—'

'Sure you can,' Linus says. 'We've got the track for that, haven't we?'

He looks at Janet, the floor manager, who's hovering near the wings. She presses her headset to her ear, listening for instructions coming from the control room at the back of the theatre. Ivan Jenks is sitting up there, watching us all and controlling what's happening. Janet nods. She comes over to collect the guitar, which Rose hands over reluctantly.

'OK,' Linus instructs us. 'Now stand all together. I see you as a girl band. I want to see you moving, like catsuit girl did in your video. I loved the video, by the way.'

Right. So he loved the video. That's good. Bert mentioned the video too. Girl band: we can do that. Perhaps I wasn't getting too carried away.

'I refuse to jiggle,' Rose mutters to me through gritted teeth while they quickly sort out the backing track in the wings.

I give her half a smile.

'Oh, come on. It's not jiggling, it's dancing. You'll enjoy it.'

'I won't,' she says, grim-faced.

I sigh. I wish she wouldn't be so down on herself, or us. I know it's hardly Ella Fitzgerald, but it's supposed to be a masterclass and they're giving us advice.

'Just do it a little bit, *please*,' I whisper.

'I hate it. You know that.'

Poor Rose. She does. Not that she can't dance: she just doesn't enjoy it.

Nell and Jodie get into position. Rose huffs discontentedly, smoothing down her skirt with restless hands. I try and relax my shoulders so I can get into the mood to impress the judges. If they want jiggling, they can have jiggling. Actually, this is what can help me 'stay loose', like Bert Blackwell suggested. I try to imagine myself back in my pyjamas, the way I was for the original video. It seems to work.

71

The track starts. I know I haven't got the best vocals, but as we sing I try and remember some of Roxanne's moves from her video of this song. I have a go at a simplified version and to my left, I can see Nell and Jodie doing their best to follow. To my right, Rose is just about swaying from side to side, but that's it. This is hardly team spirit. I pirouette. I move my hips. It's a fun song and it needs some fun presentation. I know Rose isn't a huge fan of Roxanne's music, and I'm sorry about the guitar, but I wish she'd at least try.

At the end, I crowd in with Jodie and Nell, panting, to see what the judges thought this time. Rose stands a little apart.

Roxanne beams up at us and claps her hands.

'That was cool. I really liked that. I *love* you girls.'

Oh. Wow. I mean, *wow*.

At the end of the table, Sebastian Rules shrugs and spoils the moment slightly. 'You're OK. It was better. Still not really working, though.'

'I'd like you to try it again,' Linus announces. 'One more time. Give it all you've got. You,' he says, 'the girl in the catsuit. Move over there.'

He makes me swap with Jodie, so I'm between her and Nell, with Rose still on the end. As we shuffle around, Jodie stares at me, her mouth a round O. I think she's thinking what I'm thinking: despite what Sebastian said, there's no way they'd be giving us this much attention if we didn't have a serious chance.

Two more minutes and forty-five seconds. Nell, Jodie and I give it everything, all over again. Rose holds the tune for us and even jiggles slightly more this time, although she doesn't appear to smile. The harmonies go to pieces a bit by the end, but overall, I'm pretty sure, to quote Jodie, that we did not 'totally suck'.

When we finish the song, there's a silence. A long silence. The kind of pause they love in talent shows, when they allow your heartbeat to get so fast you think you might need medical attention.

Two of the judges are leaning forward this time. Linus and Roxanne. The silence continues.

Nell sneaks her hand into mine, and I squeeze it, holding out my other hand for Jodie. I can't see Rose properly, at the end of the line, but I assume she's holding hands with Jodie too. We watch and wait. The nearest camera moves in to focus on Linus. He lets a slow smile gradually play across his face.

'Well, yeah. OK. That worked.'

Did he really say that? Nell squeezes me again and squeals under her breath. Jodie grins a totally un-Jodie, un-cool grin.

Then Linus pauses again, and his smile starts to fade. Oh no. I can feel a 'but' in the air. This is definitely one of those pauses that ends with 'but'.

But what? After all that. Did he notice that I was flat? I know I was, in certain places.

Linus taps his pencil on his yellow notepad.

'I see you as a trio,' he says. 'Like the Sugababes, or Stooshe – but younger. You look like a dream, you've got some crazy energy and . . . how old are you? Fifteen? Sixteen?'

We nod.

'Yeah. You're young. You're hot,' he continues. 'But like I say, as a trio. I think one of you . . . has a voice that just doesn't work with the others. It throws everything out.

73

And the dance moves aren't working.'

As he says it, my heart slows down. It feels like it's contracting into a tiny ball. Oh God. I was flatter than I thought. And I got so close and loved it so much and all the time I must have sounded ridiculous, and probably looked it, too. *Catsuit girl.* I can't bear to think that I've let everyone down.

'The thing is,' Linus adds, 'I think you're going to have to make a choice. The band, for me, is you, you and you.' He points with his pencil. 'Like that, you could go through to the final nine. I'd send you through right now. But as you are . . .'

A camera moves in to do a close-up on his face, and then Roxanne's. She looks shocked for a moment, then she nods reluctantly. She stares at her multi-ringed fingers for a moment, while she works out what to say. At the end of the judges' table, Sebastian shakes his head.

I look along our line. Beyond Nell, Jodie is squeezing Rose's shoulder.

Rose?

Wait. Me . . . or Rose?

Rose wasn't flat. If anything, her voice was even more gorgeous in this big auditorium. But a camera is closing in to do a special close-up on her face.

How did her voice not fit? It doesn't make sense. But it's happening.

Rose.

This is wrong. Rose is our best singer. I look across at her, but her face is a blank wall. She doesn't seem surprised at all, but I'm astonished.

Rose?

Meanwhile, Roxanne smiles for the nearest camera.

74

'Oh, Linus. You're so mean! I remember when I was growing up, how close I was to my girlfriends. You can't do that to a girl!'

She smiles again at Linus, but he isn't smiling back.

'So? D'you agree with me or not?'

Sebastian leaps in with his opinion.

'You're such a doofus, Linus. I totally disagree. Let them stay together. I don't think they'll go that far, if I'm completely honest. But splitting them up like that? School friends? That's just perverse.' He shrugs.

Linus grins at Sebastian. It's clear he loves a fight.

'Not just schoolgirls,' he counters. 'I think they've got a look. Think the Spice Girls, remember? Or even Destiny's Child.'

As soon as he says Destiny's Child, Jodie squeezes my hand so hard I think she's going to break it. Beyoncé's old band: home to my other favourite pop star, apart from Roxanne.

'Roxy?' Linus says. 'It seems you might have the casting vote.'

Roxanne takes a deep breath and smiles wryly for the nearest camera.

'Oh God, this is So. Hard,' she complains. She looks up at the four of us. 'I mean, it's tough, girls, but I guess Linus has a point. We're here to deliver the good news, but the bad news too. The bad news is that sometimes a group just doesn't fit the way you hoped. But the good news is that the three of you could really make it as a trio. I see that in you. I do.'

She beams at us like what she just said is a good thing. But a trio is not good. Not when there are four of you.

She didn't seem to think that before. What happened?

75

What went wrong?

'Guitar girl,' Linus calls out, making me jump. He checks his notes. 'Er, Rose, right? . . . This is tough on you, I know. What do you think?'

Rose Ireland. The 'stand-out' girl who could sing all of us off the stage without even thinking about it, never mind playing the piano like an angel and the guitar like a dream.

She dips her head forward to the mic in front of her and says in a clear, low voice: 'It's a band decision. I'll do whatever the girls want to do.'

Jodie steps forward.

'Er, I think we'll stick together,' she mutters.

Nell and I nod. I mean, obviously.

At the judges' table, Linus shrugs. 'OK. But I want you to think about this. It's all nice and lovely if you all stick together and I'm sure you'll be an OK school band. But I don't think you get it. I'm not just talking about making the final nine here. I could make you into recording stars. I'm serious. Take fifteen minutes. Think about it.'

fifteen Minutes: Part 2

final nine. Recording stars. No Rose. My head feels as if it's about to explode.

Shell-shocked, we're led out of the room by Janet, who's busy radioing details of what's happening to the central control centre. She pauses in the corridor outside and turns to us.

'We've got a room nearby. You don't mind if we bring the cameras in, do you?'

We shake our heads without really considering it. We're used to the lenses, lights and cables by now. Besides, we have more important things to think about.

I walk quickly down the corridor to catch up with Rose, who's stormed ahead of the rest of us.

'Are you OK?' I ask.

'Sure,' she mutters gruffly. 'Of course I'm OK. It's only a competition.'

She glares at me briefly, then looks away. Her cheeks are burning. She won't let me put my arm through hers. Instead, she wraps her arms around herself.

'I could see this coming,' she goes on. 'I knew I was crazy to come here.'

'But you're not. You're amazing. You know it.'

She just glares at me and shivers.

Janet tries a couple of locked doors, then finds one that opens onto a small, airless meeting room, with four chairs set around a white-topped table. We each take a chair.

'You have fifteen minutes,' Janet says, glancing at her watch. 'Actually, twelve now. But wait until I get the cameras before you say anything, please.' She disappears into the corridor, already barking instructions into her head mic.

For a moment, we do as we're told, sitting in silence, until I really can't bear it any more. I'm not going to sit here saying nothing just because the cameras aren't here yet. Honestly.

'That man! I can't believe he'd try to split us up. We wouldn't be the Manic Pixie Dream Girls if it wasn't the four of us.'

'It's fine,' Rose says crisply. 'Don't worry about it.'

All the blood seems to have drained from her face, apart from two bright pink spots on her cheeks.

I try to put a hand on her arm, but she pulls it away as if it's been scorched. I've rarely seen her like this, and she's never been so harsh with me before. Is she blaming me for dancing? It's not really my fault if I can 'jiggle' and she doesn't want to. There are a million things she can do and I can't.

There's a long, awkward silence. Eventually, Rose breaks it. Her voice is flat, and she won't look at any of us, not even me.

'Look, it's clear they want you three,' she says. 'And to be perfectly honest, I hate the stupid song, and I hate the stupid dance moves, and I couldn't do it anyway.'

'Of course you could!' Nell says. 'You were brilliant just now.'

Rose gives us a cold stare. This isn't like her at all. I don't understand.

'I'm holding you back. Just forget about it. It's only a stupid show. You do what you want to do.'

There's a knock on the door and it opens to reveal a cameraman and a sound recordist, with a fluffy mic held high on a boom.

'Don't mind us,' they say, moving in and setting up in the corner of the room. Janet hovers in the doorway.

'Right, girls,' she says, checking her watch. 'You can talk now, but you've only got about ten minutes left, I'm afraid. Then they need you back in the theatre for your decision.' She smiles anxiously.

Rose is already on her feet. 'I'm coming with you,' she says to Janet, pushing her chair back. 'It's easier for them if I'm not here.'

Janet looks uncertain for a moment. She's obviously considering the TV value of 'decision with Rose in the room' against the value of 'decision without Rose in the room'. But Rose doesn't give her the chance to make up her mind. She's already out of the door, and she doesn't look back.

Left alone together, Nell, Jodie and I stare at each other in silence for ages.

Jodie's the first to speak. She looks utterly dejected.

'Well, that was a waste of time. I never thought we'd get so close, though.'

'Yeah,' Nell sighs.

'I know,' I say. 'Except . . .'

They both stare at me. I wasn't supposed to say 'Except'. But now it's out there.

My God – why did I say 'except'?

'Except what?' Jodie asks.

Everyone's looking at me. My thoughts are a jumble.

'Well, Rose really didn't want to be here, did she? She's always been shy. I know it's crazy, because her voice is fantastic, but think about it. She didn't really want to do George's party, until we made her. And she hates dancing.'

It looks like dancing is part of the deal, and thinking back, I enjoyed that last version we did so much, when we could put in some choreography. To be perfectly honest, it was the easiest it's ever been.

Jodie nods slowly. 'I suppose so.'

Nell bites her lip. 'I never pictured us as a trio.'

I nod. Neither did I. Now, though, for a moment, I do. Three months ago, we were just a bunch of girls, singing stupid songs in our bedrooms. Now, thanks to Elliot Harrison, we could be on live TV, being watched by millions of people. It would only be for one night – two, if we made it down to the last three acts. I don't believe what Linus said about making us recording stars. But would two nights on TV be so terrible?

Rose seems to think it would be OK. Think of all the rehearsing we'd do . . . the costumes . . . the professional advice. I never, ever thought I'd get this chance. Rose is the one with the talent. She's always outshone me. She can make it any time . . . but this could be the only chance I ever get.

What if someone gives you a winning lottery ticket and you just hand it right back? What then?

'Five minutes!' Janet calls through the closed door.

'You've gone very quiet, Sash,' Jodie says. 'What are you thinking?'

I screw my face up. This is all too complicated. 'Maybe we could just *ask* her,' I say. 'You heard what she said. She seemed happy for us to be a trio. Could we maybe just do the TV bit without her?'

'Wouldn't she be upset?' Jodie frowns.

'Well, like I say – we'd ask her. We'd get back together afterwards, obviously.'

Nell says nothing. She picks at a loose thread at the bottom of her shorts and looks unhappy. But she doesn't disagree.

'So, what do you think?' I say, watching both of them.

'Yeah, I suppose,' Jodie shrugs, looking very uncomfortable for a girl who so badly wants to be famous that she's already designed the perfume bottle for her fragrance range.

'I don't know,' Nell mutters, dislodging a sequin from her shorts and looking almost tearful about it. 'Whatever's best for Rose.'

'Time's up!' Janet announces from outside, before flinging the door open. 'Ready, girls?'

No. No, absolutely not. Did we come to a conclusion?

What did we decide?

We file out into the corridor, with the camera still filming us from behind.

'You'll tell her, right?' Jodie says.

Tell her what?

Jodie sees my panicked expression.

'Ask her, I mean. What she thinks. Remember?'

OK. We said we'd ask her. My mouth is dry. Rose didn't want to be in the band, she said so. I'm just going to ask her if it would really be OK to do this bit without her. She can always say no. In fact, I half wish she would, so we all know where we stand, and then we can just go home and forget about it. And I wish there wasn't a camera in my face, and that I could hear more than the sound of my blood pumping in my head.

'Shall we go?' Janet asks.

'I just have to talk to Rose quickly,' I explain.

She nods. 'Sure,' she says. 'She's right over there.'

Rose is waiting at the end of the corridor, with Rob. The colour is back in her cheeks now, just a little. As we walk towards her, Jodie squeezes my arm good luck. I feel sick. But I'm just talking about the TV show. It's not as if we're breaking up the band or anything.

Jodie and Nell fall back. I go forward. I suppose it has to be me.

'So?' Rose asks.

'Er, hi.' The hostility radiating off Rose – which I still totally don't deserve, by the way – isn't helping. 'We were just wondering . . .' My voice will hardly come out. My throat isn't working, with all the stress. 'We were wondering if you really meant it. About not joining us? Because if the three of us went ahead and got through then you could come back in the band afterwards and . . .'

'Afterwards?'

'Yes.'

'When you're not on TV any more?' she checks, coldly.

'Well, yes . . . and . . .'

'Sure.'

'What?'

'Sure.'

'Really? I mean, do you really not mind if we—?'

She looks at me haughtily. It's not often that I remember how much taller than me she is, but now is one of those times.

'I'm out of the band, don't worry. Say hi to Linus for me.'

'But—'

Standing there, I watch the blood run out of her cheeks again. Her eyes look searchingly into mine, and then . . . nothing. A rigid, blank stare. She moves past me, down the corridor, and I watch her disappear round a corner.

What have I done? I call out her name.

'Rose!'

Janet steps forward and puts her hand on my arm.

'Let her go,' she says gently. 'It must be hard for her.'

Janet's right. Rose needs a hug. But who will give it to her if I can't?

Wait.

Did we just dump Rose from the band? Did *I* just dump her? I can't believe I did that. It's not what I meant at all.

'Rose!'

But she's gone.

Broken

There were other things I didn't think about. The look on Sebastian Rules's face when we told him our decision, for a start. The other judges were pleased, but Sebastian's sneer stayed imprinted on my mind for a long time. Another was the fact that we had to share a car with Rose for an hour and a half on the way home, and she didn't say a single word to us all the way.

It was Jodie who reminded me of the worst thing of all: what if we win? I have to say, the possibility hadn't crossed my mind, but what if we actually win and our act goes on a billion screens and makes us famous? It would be just the three of us, without Rose. How could she come back in the band then?

On Monday, Rose is not at school. She officially 'has the flu'. I call her granny, Aurora, who says she's in bed.

'Is she OK?' I ask. 'Can I come round?'

Aurora hesitates.

'She asked not to see you, Sasha. Not for a couple of days. I'm sure she'll be fine.'

She's never done this before. Not even when she had real flu. Not being able to see her is shocking.

'I don't get it!' I complain to Mum, as we're preparing supper. 'She's my best friend. It's all about singing in public and she never *wanted* to sing in public in the first place. We had to make her. Why is she taking it so badly?'

Mum stirs the soup in silence.

'Why, Mum?'

'Do you really need me to answer?'

I sigh. 'She could always have said no,' I point out. 'We gave her the option.'

'Uh huh,' Mum says.

In the silence that follows, I imagine if it had been the three of *them*, asking *me* if I wanted to stay or go. If you have any pride at all, there is only one answer to that question. Now, too late, I realise it wasn't really an option at all.

Two days later, we get the official news from Ivan Jenks: we're in the final nine. We'll be filming on national TV in March: three live finals on consecutive days at the start of the holidays, showcasing three acts each. The public will vote and the winner from each night will go into a grand final on the fourth and final show. The performances will also be streamed live to over five million phones and computers in the UK (the billion comes later, when the ad goes out worldwide). Meanwhile, we're going to be interviewed by a presenter called Andy Grey for the backstory bit of our slot, but we mustn't tell anyone about the decision to drop Rose, because they want to 'preserve the drama'.

I don't want to preserve the drama at all. I hate the drama. My best friend isn't talking to me. I want the drama to go away. However, it turns out that we all agreed to do whatever the producers say when we signed all those release forms on the audition day. So outside of home, the drama gets preserved.

Rose 'recovers' from the flu and comes back to class, but still looks under the weather. At school we are heroes. The Head asks us to sing 'Sunglasses' at a special school assembly. Rose plays her guitar, as before, but at a very slight distance from the rest of us. I really don't feel like dancing. However, everyone sings along and loads of people promise they'll vote for us. In our class, nobody seems to notice that Rose still isn't talking to me.

The Killer Act homepage shows nine videos now, under the banner LIVE SHOW PERFORMERS!!! They include us, the street dance group, two rock bands (Jodie fancies all the members), an eleven-year-old opera singer, a boy band, two female soloists, and a ukulele orchestra called Me and Uke. We watch them all, and they're all fantastic. Our video is still the original 'Sunglasses' with the four of us, and me in my pyjamas. Totally preserving the drama.

One day in February, Andy Grey arrives after school with a cameraman to film our backstory slot. Andy will be the presenter on the live finals, and it's a chance to get to know him. We feel as if we already do: he presented children's programmes when we were growing up and I'd swear he was the guy who taught me to count. I still remember him standing cheerfully in front of a screen of bouncing cartoon bubbles, singing 'My ARMS and my LEGS make FOUR'.

Andy still looks like a big teenager himself, with black hair, white teeth, a wide smile, and a gentle West Country burr to his voice that makes us feel at home. We kind of are anyway, because they decided to film us in Jodie's bedroom, which was the tidiest.

Jodie, Nell and I sit on Jodie's bed for an hour, under a shelf full of riding cups and rosettes, talking to Andy about how much we've always loved to sing together. I keep waiting for the moment when Andy will mention Rose, and ask what it was like to lose her, but that doesn't happen. Maybe they're going to try and pretend she was never part of the band. But how could they do that? There she is, on our original video, and on our band page.

That page hasn't changed at all. We don't know what to say on it now. Jodie emails someone at Interface for advice, but they never get back to her.

Meanwhile, we get several invitations a week to do gigs and parties all over Somerset. We can't do them, because now we're a trio and people are expecting a quartet. So we say we're busy rehearsing. The team at Interface have sent us a video – performed with professional dancers – of the song they'd like us to do for our performance. It's an old number by Nancy Sinatra called 'These Boots Are Made For Walkin', and the wardrobe director thinks it will provide a great opportunity to showcase our legs.

We rehearse together, over and over, in Jodie's room, to

get the song right and perfect the routine. The choreography is easy now that it's the three of us – just as I thought. Jodie and Nell enjoy dancing almost as much as I do. But vocally, we sound scratchy and light. At least, I think we do. Andy told us not to worry. He says it's amazing what they can do these days with auto-tuners and post-production. But I miss the warm, smoky tones of Rose.

She still won't talk to me, or see me after school. It's like a permanent, dull, physical ache. Her spare guitar – the one she keeps in my room – sits there in the corner, reproaching me. Several of my eyeshadow palettes are really hers, and she has a lot of my bracelets and books. I don't know what to do with her stuff. We're like some married couple splitting up.

And I still don't understand it, not really. I get her being angry with me, of course I do, but this is worse than anger – it's deeper. I've apologised by phone, text and email, written her a letter and sent her a card. Still nothing. I don't know what else to do.

It's so bad that I can't sleep. Every time I try, I find those fifteen minutes running through my head. Not the first, golden fifteen, when we wrote the song, but the second, black fifteen, when I talked myself into *asking if it was OK if we temporarily dumped her*. Which is what I was effectively saying. The shocked looks on Nell and Jodie's faces. The countdown from Janet outside. All to please Roxanne Wills and a guy with baggy jeans and TV teeth, who I've never heard of. The sheer stupidity of it all.

With a week to go, I drag myself out of bed in the middle of the night, wrap a coat around me over my pyjamas, slip into my wellies and let myself out of the cottage as quietly as I can, so as not to wake Mum. I use my phone as torchlight. According to the screen, it's 12.45 a.m. This may not be my best idea ever, but I simply have to talk to Rose. I walk down the lane and up the path to her house, then round the side till I'm just below her bedroom window.

'Rose! Rose!'

It's hard to shout and whisper at the same time, but I do the best I can. Nobody in the house seems to stir, but one of her granny's dogs comes to the side door and plants her paws on the pane in the middle, staring at me. She's a rescued greyhound called Leila, who knows me well. I go over quickly, to reassure her it's me, and she looks a bit surprised, but ambles off back to her bed by the Aga.

'Rose! *Rose!*'

Nothing. I search round the house and farmyard for something to catch her attention: gravel, small pebbles . . . anything that I could throw at her window without breaking it. In the dark, though, I can't find a thing. I send her a text, telling her I'm outside, but I'm convinced she'll have turned her phone off, or be too fast asleep to hear it.

To my amazement, I hear the sound of creaking wood and rattling glass. Looking up, I see her raising the sash window and staring out, her red-gold hair hanging loosely round her face.

'What on *earth* are you doing here?'

'I had to see you!'

'You see me at school.'

'You never talk to me.'

She looks angry, surprised, frustrated. She rolls her eyes.

'Stay there. I'm coming down.'

Two minutes later, she pulls the bolt on the side door and lets me into the kitchen. Leila raises her head from her dog bed for a moment, then goes back to sleep. Rose stands in her dressing gown and bare feet, hands in pockets, watching me.

'So?'

'I need to know,' I say, searching for the words.

'Know what?'

'Why sorry isn't enough. I've said it so many times. I'm sorry, Rose. It's not the same without you. Please come back.'

'I can't.' She gives me a pointed look.

'You can,' I plead. 'I mean . . . not for the TV thing. Oh God. Linus is crazy, but it's only for one performance. Two at the most. After that. Please.'

I stand in the middle of the kitchen floor, with my begging face on. Rose doesn't look quite so cold and distant as before, but she doesn't ask me to sit down. She doesn't break into a gentle smile and forgive me. Something has changed. Something is broken.

'Linus was only pointing out the obvious,' she says. 'I don't fit.'

'But you do. We don't have to do the dancing. That's not why we got together.'

'It's not about the dancing,' she says, shaking her head at me, like she's talking to a child.

'We don't have to do big gigs. Not after this, anyway. Not if you don't want to.'

She shakes her head. 'It's not that, either.'

'I don't get it,' I moan. 'You're brilliant, Rose. Better than you know.'

'No,' she says, her lip wobbling. 'You *don't* get it, Sash.

90

There were only two people who ever made me feel special. And one of them . . .' She bites her lip. 'One of them . . . whatever.' She can't talk properly. Tears come. She fights her way through them. 'And then there was you.'

We stand there, facing each other, in the cold, moonlit room. Our tears are silent. The only sounds are her gran's old kitchen clock ticking and Leila snoring in her sleep.

'I'm so sorry.'

'I know,' Rose says sadly. 'And I know you didn't mean it.' She moves forward to give me a quick hug, then pushes me back. 'It's good this way. I need to work out . . . some things.'

'What things?'

'What I want. Who I am. I meant it when I said I didn't want to jiggle or sing those tunes. I was kind of hiding in the band. This is good. Really.'

This is SO. NOT. GOOD.

This is terrible. I feel awful. I'm crying buckets. NOT. GOOD. SERIOUSLY.

'You'd better get some sleep,' she adds. 'You'll need it for later.'

What she actually means is goodbye.

There is, however, just one tiny chink of hope. The day before we're due to leave, a plain white envelope is posted through our letterbox, with 'S' written on the front. I open it and a piece of coloured paper flutters out. It's an odd shape – a bit like a leaf that's been partly eaten by a caterpillar. That's all there is.

I show it to Mum.

'What do you think this is?'

Mum holds it up to the light and turns it in her hands for a while.

'I couldn't be sure, but I'd have said it was a cut-out of a leotard. Does that mean anything?'

It feels like a thin ray of sunlight in a darkened cave.

Most people would have sent me an email. Only Rose would think of posting a seminal leotard.

Through The Camera's Eye

T he Manic Pixie Dream Girls have been chosen to perform in the first of the three live finals. Then we'll stay to watch the other shows, with all the other finalists. This time, our mums travel with us. Mum shuts the café so she can be there. With the agreement of Mrs Richards, the Head, we skip the last two days of term to rehearse in a cold, empty studio in South London with the other eight acts. At night, we stay in a hotel overlooking a massive rubbish tip by the river.

As Jodie puts it, staring out at the piles of moonlit steaming rubbish: welcome to the world of Killer Act Live.

It's great to hang out with the other acts, though. We're all equally nervous, all equally obsessed with music, and we quickly form a bond – a bit like soldiers going into battle, some people say. The shared experience seems to pull us all together. It's helpful for us as a group because in rehearsal, our voices still sound thin and reedy. When Jodie pumps up the volume to make up for it, she goes all American again. Nell's practically a whisper. I'm flat every other note. People say it's the cold, and we'll be better on the night. I'm not so sure.

We'll look good, though. At least there's that. The show has a professional stylist, who's brought a whole warehouse full of clothes for us to look through. If it was all of us together, we'd be having the time of our lives.

With the stylist's help, Nell chooses a taffeta party dress with a corset top and tiny skirt; Jodie picks denim shorts and a T-shirt with a diamante skull on it; and I'm in a waistcoat made out of a Union Jack, a bright red mini-kilt and long red socks. We've each been given a pair of vintage high-heeled boots. Mine look Victorian. They have a row of tiny buttons up the front, which a wardrobe girl kneels in front of me to do up, carefully, one by one.

I wonder if Rose will be watching tomorrow. I bet she will, although she'll never admit it. If she doesn't watch us on TV with her gran, she can always do it on her phone. If she knows how. Actually, it would have been funny if we'd won the whole thing together and she'd ended up advertising Interface. She's the only person our age I know who hardly uses it.

The judges aren't there on the first day, but they arrive for the dress rehearsal on the morning of our show. We're waiting in a queue for lunch when I see Roxanne Wills dash past us. She's surrounded by security, but through the burly guards I spot her five-inch heels, a tiny skirt to show off her perfectly toned legs, and miles of spiky jewellery. I rush to catch her up before she disappears into the corridor where the judges' dressing rooms are.

'Roxanne! Roxanne!'

She looks round, confused.

'Oh, hi. Did you want something . . . ?'

Roxanne has been one of my idols for such a long time. Right now, she's the only person I can trust.

'I wondered what you thought about—'

'Hey!' calls a security guard. 'The lady's in a hurry. Step back, please.'

'No, wait, it's fine,' she says to him. She gives me a flash of her starry smile. 'I've got a couple of seconds. What did you want?'

'I wondered what . . . I wondered why you and Linus thought we should be a trio,' I stutter. 'When our friend had the best voice and everything. I mean, you've had such a successful career. What made you think we'd be better without her?'

'Oh, I see,' she says, thinking back. 'Hmm. You were the foursome, weren't you? Well, the thing is, Sandra—'

'Sasha.'

'Sasha. The thing is, Sasha, realistically, I don't think you had a choice. I mean, this is a tough, tough business. We've got to be real here. You know what I'm saying? And it's not all just about the voice. It's about the presentation and the whole package and—'

'But I thought you said it *was* about the voice. Or Linus did, anyway. He said Rose's voice didn't fit.'

Roxanne shakes her head. 'He was being kind, sweetie. Just face facts. Larger girls don't work in girl bands. You know that. And that girl—'

'Rose.'

'Rose. She wasn't just large. She was *large*. She has a great voice, actually. But it would have been horrible for her, and I think she knew that. Linus saw it first, but once it was out there, I had to agree. You were doing her a kindness to let her go, trust me.'

The security guard steps forward and reaches out a hand to Roxanne's elbow. She shrugs to me apologetically and obediently trots along beside him on her five-inch heels, aware that she's late.

I stand there, feeling sick.

*She wasn't just large. She was **large**.*

I thought they wanted us to drop Rose because she was shy, and because of some weird problem I didn't understand about her voice. It never occurred to me she was just . . . *large*.

Nell and Jodie rush up, panting.

'Was that Roxanne again?'

'Did you actually speak to her?'

'What did she say? Did she give you her autograph?'

I ignore their questions.

'Why do *you* think Linus didn't want Rose in the band?'

They stop dead. Nell gasps slightly and goes pink. Beside her, Jodie bites her lip.

'Er . . .' Nell says. She clams up. I watch her shift from foot to foot, just like Elliot Harrison the video boy.

'Was that what you asked Roxanne about?' Jodie asks me.

I nod.

'And?'

I breathe deeply. I can hardly bring myself to say it.

'She said Rose was large. She said that was why.'

I scan their eyes for some sort of shock at the suggestion, but it's not there. They don't look even vaguely surprised.

'We thought you knew,' Jodie says, giving me a crooked smile. 'I mean, it seemed a bit of a coincidence, Linus saying Rose should go when she was the best singer. Don't you think?'

Well, I do *now*. Of course I do. But I never really thought about Rose's size before. I sit down on the nearest step. I can hardly breathe. Sure, she doesn't have a typical pop-star figure, but I thought that stuff didn't matter to people because we were friends, and we could sing. I was so naïve and stupid and wrong.

And Rose knew instantly. *That's* what her strange behaviour was all about. She knew she didn't fit because she was 'large' . . . and I agreed. That's how it must have seemed. Her best friend agreed – the one person she thought she could trust. She didn't get then that I was *jealous* of her, she thought I was just like the others. Now, I think, she's starting to understand that it was more complicated than that. She knows me well enough to realise that I am STUPID, but not mean. Not really. But it's too late.

I don't let Nell take my arm. I can't bear to be touched right now. She pulls her hand away, looking offended. This is how Rose was with me, I realise, after the judges' comments. Too angry and upset to be touched. She just needed me to be there for her. And I totally wasn't.

'I never thought about it . . .'

'Wow,' Jodie says, realising how I misjudged the whole situation. 'Awkward.' She bites her lip.

'Awkward? *Awkward?* If I'd realised I'd never have . . . Oh my God. And I said that we'd take her back after the TV shows were over. I meant to spare her shyness. She must have thought we didn't want her to appear on TV . . .'

'Don't let it get to you,' Jodie says. 'I talked to Mum about it and she said Rose was better off out of it. People can be mean, you know?'

'Yes,' I whisper. Because, like it or not, I am one of them.

Jodie holds out a hand to help me up, but I refuse it. She shrugs and walks off. I walk slowly after her, making sure to keep a good distance between us. Nell trails behind, keeping more distance still.

Four hours later, we're back in costume and ready, waiting backstage while the first act launches Killer Act Live. It's the ukulele players. They sound amazing. Through a tiny crack in the wooden wall at the side of the stage we can just make out the studio audience and the judges, spotlit at their table. Two cameras are trained on them, and two more on the stage. I try not to think of them broadcasting their images to millions of people. They're scary enough as it is.

After the adverts, it's time for the next act: the street dancers. They're aged between eleven and thirteen, and they could frankly be in the Olympics, the way they tumble, balance and leap. They must have been practising every minute since they passed the audition. How did the three of us ever make it this far?

Janet, the floor manager from the auditions, is in charge of us while we wait. 'You know what you've got to do?' she checks.

We nod. We've rehearsed this a dozen times. After the next advert break, we will go onstage and chat to Andy for a minute or two, then watch the background video they've done about us. They haven't shown it to us yet, because they always like to film the surprise on the band members' faces when they see it for the first time. After that, we go to our marks on the stage floor, and then we sing. And, in my case, wiggle about in my kilt for three minutes in front of several million people I can't see.

Seminal leotards. Totally.

The street dancers finish their act flawlessly. The judges tell them how great they are. Advert break. Nerves. Three. Two. One. Janet sends us out. We walk to our marks next to Andy. We're on.

Bright lights shine in our faces. Andy takes a breath and does his best professional smile.

'And finally tonight we have three girls from near my home town in Somerset,' Andy says, in his reassuring, familiar West Country burr. 'These girls entered the competition with their own song, back in October, and became our fastest-rising entry ever! And look at you now! Don't they look *hot,* ladies and gentlemen?'

He gets the audience to whoop and applaud. The judges join in from their spotlit table at the front – Roxanne Wills clapping harder than anyone. We chat for about a minute, as we rehearsed. But all I can think about are the lights shining in our faces. I have no idea what we say. Finally, Andy moves us all a bit further backwards as the lights go down and the screen at the back of the stage lights up with the words 'Manic Pixie Dream Girls'.

'Let's follow their journey from a little bedroom in Castle Bigelow to the heart of London,' Andy says. 'Don't forget, folks, the voting starts after the final act, in just a few minutes. And meanwhile, you can send us your thoughts by tweeting or Interfacing us using the hashtag *killeract*. I'll share some of our favourite tweets and FaceFeeds at the end of the show.'

In the darkness, my heart rate slowly starts to subside. The tape starts with an extract from our original video of 'Sunglasses'. Then there are pictures of our voting numbers rising and rising. There's a shot of us arriving at the auditions, and a little clip of us chatting nervously. To my surprise, there are lots of shots of Rose. It's not as if they're trying to pretend she was never there. That's a big relief. What the camera captures, though, is how uncomfortable she looks. I didn't spot it at the time, but she's constantly smoothing the skirt of her dress and looking unhappy if anyone stares at her. People stared at all of us, of course, because of our crazy outfits, but the camera only shows them staring at Rose.

Then we get to the audition. Now, the camera focuses more than ever on Rose. It captures how desperate she was not to lose her guitar, how much she hated 'jiggling'. It contrasts with how much more confident I am, by comparison, throwing myself into the dance moves. When Rose is shifted to the end of the line, the background music changes tempo, sending a message. The tension builds. Something bad is about to happen.

And that's when I see it for the first time. I should have seen it all along, but I didn't. Nobody will ever believe me, but you have to remember: I've known Rose a long time. She's my friend. All I ever saw was a girl who was better at music than me.

What I see now, through the camera's eye, and with the music wailing to a climax in the background, is three skinny girls on one side, moving in time to the music, and a big girl on the other side. A girl who feels uncomfortable, hating to dance. And her so-called friends all ignoring her and having fun.

Oh no. This is all wrong. All I want to do is stop the tape, but it rolls on.

Linus leans forward: he wants us to be a trio. Sebastian disagrees, but Roxanne says Linus has a point. Rose can sense what's coming. Linus singles her out. I look shocked on tape, but Rose does not. It's as if she knew she was the big girl in the band – the one who didn't fit.

But this is crazy! What about how good she was?

Now we're inside the room, and Rose is already leaving. Of course – they had to miss out the early part of our conversation because the cameras hadn't arrived yet. So there's nothing about us saying we should stick together. Instead, they show Jodie and Nell looking shocked, and me talking them round, saying it will be OK.

As if I chucked my fat friend so we could go on TV.

As if I would do that.

But as I watch the tape it seems clear: I did.

Outside the room, the camera watches from a distance as I approach Rose and talk to her in a low voice. It follows her dignified walk as she leaves me standing.

It doesn't show me calling after her. Instead, the tape cuts to the rest of us reacting as the judges put us through.

We stand there, as a trio, shocked and hugging each other.

And then it stops. I want to die.

So *that* was our backstory. Nothing to do with writing 'Sunglasses', or Nell's plans to be a vet. I just betrayed my fat best friend on TV.

'So here you are!' Andy says, sad and serious as the tape finishes and we're back in the spotlight. 'You've come all this way and it obviously wasn't easy for you.'

Even bright, bouncy, 'my arms and my legs make FOUR' Andy Grey looks as if he's wincing behind his smile.

'I suppose you must have really, really wanted to be here tonight.'

I did at the time. But not like this. Onstage, not looking at each other, we nod and shuffle miserably.

'And how is Rose? Is she watching you tonight?' Andy asks, trying to keep talking over this tumbleweed moment.

'We don't know,' I whisper.

Which, of course, makes it much, much worse, because now it sounds as though we didn't ask and we don't care. Fabulous.

He decides to avoid taking it further. Instead, he smiles his brightest smile again. Ever the professional.

'And now, ladies and gentlemen, with a song from the sixties, we have . . . the Manic Pixie Dream Girls!'

Spotlights create a circle of light, centre stage, where we're supposed to stand. I'm at the front. The audience waits in silence until the start of our backing track. It's time to sing.

Yeah. We shimmy and high-kick our way around the stage in our fabulous high-heeled vintage boots and cute little outfits.

Just the three of us. Without our fat friend, who wasn't there because we dumped her. Obviously.

Toast

'We're dead,' Jodie says, head in hands in the dressing room after our performance. 'We're one hundred per cent toast.'

I say nothing. I'm beyond speech.

'I'm sure they didn't mean it to look so bad,' Nell says nervously. 'They wouldn't deliberately do that, would they? I mean, Linus really liked us.'

'Yeah, right.' Jodie gives her a sarcastic smile. 'The way Rolo really likes apples. He likes chewing them up and spitting them out. Come on, Nell. They always like something controversial for people to talk about, and we're it.'

'Rose is it,' I correct her.

Jodie just stares at me.

'You really don't get it, do you?'

'I do now,' I say. 'Roxanne Wills explained it pretty well.'

Jodie shakes her head.

'Check FaceFeed,' she says. 'See what they're saying about us.'

FaceFeed has taken over Twitter as the forum for comments about what's going on in the world. It's part of Interface, so you can always see the FaceFeed at the side of your page. I get my phone out of my bag and we all gather round it.

Sure enough, #killeract is trending, and a lot of the FaceFeeds are about us.

Hahah! Did you see the three skinny ones drop the fat one? Killer Act was on form tonight. ROFL

Loving the bit where the three skinny witches dropped the only one who could sing. #dropthefatgirl

Watch this clip: 3 pretty girls drop the fat one who can play guitar! OMG

My heart sinks. Poor Rose. Nobody deserves humiliation like this. What have I done to her?

'See?' I say to Jodie.

She glares back at me.

'You think this is about Rose?'

'I'd say it's *all* about Rose, wouldn't you? Pretty much. Or does *everything* have to be about you?'

'Stop it! Stop it!' Nell shouts. 'It's bad enough as it is. Don't fight.'

Janet, the floor manager, appears in the doorway.

'Time to go, everybody. We need you on the stage in five for the final wave.'

I glance at my phone screen one more time before I shut it down and put it away. There's a personal message to me, so I click on it. It's from Nina Pearson, one of the girls in my class.

I had no idea u could be such an evil witch. I hope u lose.

We step forward into the brightest lights, still holding hands. Before we wave goodbye, the judges comment on our performances. Andy asks Sebastian to go first.

'I'm with the ukes. Sorry, Dream Girls and Street Wise. You did a good job, but the ukuleles really nailed it for me tonight.'

Then Roxanne.

'Oh, this is So. Difficult. I loved the ukuleles. You guys are so cute! I think everyone should play the ukulele. And Street Wise, you are A.Ma.Zing. You guys have so much energy! But there's something about the Dream Girls. You've come so far. You looked great! I'm going with the Dream Girls.'

Then Linus.

'This is the hardest part of my job,' Linus says. 'It's up to the public anyway, so this is just my professional opinion. Street Wise, you danced your little socks off tonight. Great routine, but is it a world beater? I'm not so sure. Me and Uke, you gave it your all and it was a fantastic performance, but I don't know how much further you could go. Dream Girls – you were good, but I know you can do better. Off-the-scale better. I think there was something holding you back tonight. You just have to let go and move on. So . . . I'm going to go with the Dream Girls.'

He starts off confidently, but seems surprised when the audience start to hiss and boo. Maybe he hasn't looked at the internet yet. By the end of his speech, his frown lines are deep crevices in his face and I can see he's starting to regret his decision.

As soon as we get back to the dressing room, we check our phones to see what people are saying.

#dropthefatgirl is still trending, but at least Rose's Interface page is full of supportive messages. There are lots of horrible ones on my page – I scroll through them quickly – but the band page has loads of new fans, and I have over a thousand new followers on my FaceFeed, which is insane.

The most reassuring thing is that lots of people have seen the videos of Rose performing that night at George's party and most of the comments say how good she was. The link to the one of her singing the intro to 'I See The Light' must be whizzing around the internet, because already over 10,000 people have viewed it.

Ten thousand!

Meanwhile, #selfishcows is trending on FaceFeed. So is #skinnywitches. #dropthefatgirl is second trend after something about Justin Bieber.

By the next morning, it's number one.

JUDGES TELL TEEN BAND TO
'DROP THE FAT GIRL'

It's even made the papers in the hotel restaurant, where we sit in a corner, having breakfast. Poor Rose. It's everywhere. Every time I see the headline, I think about how the story should have gone: *Judges tell teen band to drop their friend, and they refuse and stick together to live in happy obscurity for the rest of their lives*. Except, of course, then it wouldn't have been a story at all.

'Why do they have to keep calling her that?' I ask. 'I mean, going on and on about how bad she must be feeling, and reminding everyone she's supposed to be fat? Don't they see it just makes it worse for her? God, I hope her gran's looking after her.'

Because it should be me. It should be me looking after her.

'You still don't get it, do you?' Jodie mutters, biting morosely into a croissant and holding the paper up to hide her face.

'Get what?' I ask.

'Forget it.'

It's not until late afternoon that I finally understand. We're back at the hotel, changing into our outfits to be in the audience for the second show, when Jodie comes over to me, holding out her BlackBerry.

'I told you you never got the point, Sash,' she says. 'All this time you've been worrying about Rose . . .'

'Yes. And?'

'My brother sent me this link,' she says. 'He just found it. Watch.'

Her screen is set to show a video clip from a US online entertainment show. A man with slicked-back hair and a broad smile sits in front of a screen saying 'Killer Act Backlash'.

'It's all kicking off at Killer Act,' he says. 'The latest competition to find the new face of Interface in the UK went mega controversial when one of the acts dumped a singer because . . . wait for it . . . they thought she was overweight. Yes! It's really true. Where is the sisterhood when you need it, people? All day, Twitter and FaceFeed have been going crazy with angry fans of the show pouring out their support for the girl, while the others battle it out with the latest finalists for a prize to advertise Interface for a year. Remember this?'

There's a short clip of Shady doing his impression of Animal from the Muppets on the drums. It's a worldwide hit, so everyone will recognise it.

'Well, that's the prize these Dream Girls are chasing. While *some* people have been adding nasty comments about the larger lady,' the presenter continues, 'it's clear that the vast majority of today's teens won't stand for that kind of behaviour. They want the remaining band members off the show, and they're organising a campaign to make it happen. "Talent isn't all about size," says hellokitty582. And, "True friends stay together, through thick and thin. Literally," says Sharon M. Looks like Killer Act is shaping up – geddit? *Shaping* up? – to be the hottest controversy since the *Twilight* breakup. Slap hand, K-Stew. Aw. You know we love you really.'

Jodie arches an eyebrow. 'You see?'

I take a deep breath. I see. I *get it* get it now.

My first thought is relief about Rose. Thank God there are lots of people on her side.

My second thought is that Jodie understands all this stuff way better than I do. It's taken me a while, but I'm there now: #dropthefatgirl is not about Rose being large; it's about us being mean. And we sang a song about boots walking all over people.

Right, well I'm sure that went down well.
Toast.
We are totally toast.

Breathless

On Friday, the second night of Killer Act Live, the ukulele band are announced the winners of our show. It was inevitable. When Andy announces it, I hardly feel a thing.

We sit in the audience with our families to watch three more acts perform. Only two more days to go: one watching the last three acts, and then standing onstage with the other losers for the grand final. After that we can go home, be private, and forget this whole thing ever happened – apart from the bit where I grovel to Rose again, and beg her to talk to me.

After Friday's show, Jodie's mum tries to get backstage to talk to Linus, or Ivan, or Janet, or *somebody* about what's happening to us online, and how to deal with it. After all, it must be happening to them too: Linus was the person who came up with the idea of dropping Rose. He doesn't come out of it much better than we do. Except, of course, that he wasn't Rose's best friend. Anyway, he obviously doesn't want to see us. Nor does Ivan Jenks. Everyone we meet says that the judges and producers are 'busy', or 'tied up'. It's true that when we do catch sight of them, in the distance, they seem deep in urgent conversation about something. One of the TV production runners hustles us out of the building.

'You go back to your hotel and relax. We'll see you tomorrow.' He checks a piece of paper. 'You'll be sitting near the front, so you'll have a good view. Just have a nice day, OK?'

I challenge anyone to have a 'nice day' when they discover (as Jodie does) that there's a new page dedicated to their band called 'I hate the Manic Pixie Dream Girls' and it already has over 28,000 'haters'. Or while they watch a clip of themselves being discussed on the morning news by someone saying they are 'the encapsulation of everything that is wrong with teen culture at the moment – the total focus on fame and body image. It was quite cruel what they did to that girl. I hope they're ashamed of themselves today.'

#dropthefatgirl is trending worldwide now. So is the translation of it into Spanish. And, as far as we can tell (using Google Translate), Arabic and Chinese.

Nina Pearson has messaged me again.

Glad you got it, witch-face. You totally deserved to lose, you loser.

112

This time, something makes me show the message to Jodie, although up to now I've kept all the personal insults I've been receiving to myself.

'Rose would laugh at that one,' I say. 'Tautology. She can't take it seriously when people don't get their grammar right.'

'What's tautology?'

'Repeating yourself unnecessarily. Of course a loser loses.'

I wish Rose were here to raise an eyebrow at Nina's grammar and make the moment a little lighter. But of course she's not, and that's the point.

On Saturday, we arrive back at the studio along with the rest of the audience for the third evening's show. Jodie's dad arrived early this morning, speeding up the motorway to join the trio of mothers and offer his moral support. It's sweet that any of our parents think they can protect us from all this stuff. They can't. But at least they can help take our minds off it. Mr Evans spends ages saying how he could have sworn he saw Rose's granny driving her old BMW up the motorway on the way here.

'What on earth would Aurora be doing in London?' Jodie's mum asks. 'She hardly ever leaves the farm.'

It's actually great to share her mum's endless theories about what Rose's gran could be doing in any county other than Somerset, and her dad's criticism of the build quality of the studio (he's an engineer). It's even good sharing Nell's mum's excitement at seeing the next set of acts.

'I've checked out all the videos and I really think the little boy who sings opera is going to get it. Aiden, is he?

He's wonderful. I always wanted him to win. Apart from you girls, of course. Until . . .'

She stops herself. Until we got voted off two nights ago because of an internet hate campaign. Yeah, that.

'Just wait till you see Roxanne Wills,' she continues, hurriedly, to Jodie's dad. 'She's extraordinary. She looks normal-size on TV, but in the flesh she's practically minute . . .'

Soon, the lights go down and a producer comes on to tell some jokes and get the audience in the mood. When it's time for the show to start, Linus, Sebastian and Roxanne appear in the spotlight, announced by a booming voice over the sound system, before taking their seats at the judges' table.

'*Tiny*,' Nell's mum observes, leaning across to mine. 'Isn't she? *Tiny*.'

There's a strange atmosphere in the studio tonight. The judges look nervous. Jodie leans over from my other side and whispers to me:

'Did you see the look on Linus's face this morning? It was on breakfast TV. Someone stopped him in the street and called him a tired old body fascist. They said people like him were responsible for half the eating disorders in the country. He looked like he'd been punched in the face.'

I sit there for a minute or two, trying to imagine what it would be like to feel sorry for Linus. Nope. Still not working.

Andy Grey comes on to introduce tonight's first act: Lucy, the female soloist. We see her backstory video (a dog saved her life when she was six – yes, animals are cute), and she sings a pitch-perfect pop song. After her, Andy introduces the boy band, What Now, in what feels like a hurry. Backstory . . . act. Backstory . . . act. The acts and the adverts seem to pass by in a blur. Aiden, the little opera singer, comes on and performs a beautiful song in Italian, but when Andy Grey comes back to congratulate him, there still seems to be plenty of time left. Have they rushed too much tonight? Are they ahead of themselves? Could Ivan possibly make that sort of mistake?

Andy stands centre stage and grins into the nearest camera. On the big screen behind him, a close-up of his sincere smile lights up the stage.

'Before we go to voting, we have a treat for you tonight, ladies and gentlemen. Based on your feedback – the literally thousands of emails and messages we've been receiving – we've decided to break the rules and invite one of our earlier contestants back on the show. The judges want to give her a second chance. And I promise, you won't be disappointed. Here tonight, singing a song she wrote herself, is . . .'

He lets the silence linger for as long as he possibly can, but already I know what he's going to say. I reach out and grab Mum's hand so tight that she squeaks in surprise. I wait, and Andy takes a breath to say her name:

'Rose Ireland!'

As the lights go down, a screen slides up to reveal a revolving stage with a grand piano, and a girl already seated in front of it. She's wearing a long red dress, with her hair in a tousled bun and a diamante headband peeping out of it. Nell squeals. Mum squeezes my hand back, but I don't turn to look at her. The cameras will be on us, I'm sure, waiting for our reaction, and I want to seem calm. I don't want them to capture a flicker of the emotions I've been feeling since the moment Andy said 'singing a song she wrote herself' and I suddenly knew it would be Rose.

No point in even trying to feel sorry for Linus: he's brilliant. How can people possibly blame him for being mean to Rose if he's brought her back? We're the only villains now. He and the team will want us to look shocked for the cameras. I won't give them the satisfaction.

Most of all, I don't want people to see how I feel about Rose. How could she not *tell* me? She must have been busy making plans to come all this way to perform tonight, and not a word. She must actually hate me to have kept this a secret, knowing how I would be feeling now: hurt, abandoned, guilty. Above all, guilty. And nervous for her, too. Rose, who hates performing so much without the three of us around her. How have they persuaded her to put herself through this?

And all the time the sound system is playing a backing track of stirring violins, while the cameras get into position, and she nods that she is ready to begin.

She looks different tonight, though. Every hint of shyness has gone. She is calm and serene. If anything, she looks more beautiful than usual. She's on her own and that's OK. I've never seen her like this.

There's a ripple of excited murmuring around the audience. Some applause, quickly extinguished, some whispers, and then a hushed silence. A spotlight picks out Rose's hair, the serene concentration on her face, the soft smile on her lips. She breathes in, she pauses for a moment, she settles her fingers on the keys for the first chord. She plays.

Something has changed.

This is not the girl who stood white and glaring in the corridor. It's not the girl who hung back at the audition and worried about 'jiggling', or who faced me in her kitchen saying she needed to work out who she was.

It's the girl I always knew she could be. The butterfly, escaping from her chrysalis. I shiver as much as anyone else in the audience. This girl is something special, and now everybody knows it.

The tune she plays is sad – bluesy and haunting. Rose's voice is sad too, as she begins to sing the words. I've never heard her pour out so much emotion. I don't think she's ever dared. But I am sure of one thing: she *has* been checking Interface – or Ivan has told her about her supporters. When more than ten thousand people tell you how good you are, it gives you the confidence to sing.

You can hear the gasp around the audience as her voice soars and her song fills the room with its warm, jazzy tones. A *stand-out* voice, as Bert said. One that makes you want to listen to every note. With growing power, Rose lets the sound build and build, as members of the audience are torn between whistling, cheering and wiping the tears from their eyes.

'If you had to leave me
You would leave me breathless
You would leave the pieces of my broken heart
Too bruised and tired to say goodbye . . .'

I doubt they even had to persuade her much to come here. She seems at home, at last. This is what she was born for.

'What's everyone saying?' Mum whispers, leaning across me to check the screen of my iPhone, where FaceFeed is open.

'Give it a chance!' I say. 'She's only been singing two minutes.'

#killeract is trending, but I don't want to miss the actual moment of seeing Rose nail the song.

She sounds as though she's been preparing for it all her life. It's a song she wrote last summer, called 'Breathless'. I recognise the tune as the one she was working on at the end of the holidays. But we got caught up in the competition and I never heard what she did with it, or what lyrics she wrote. I assumed she was shy about sharing it because it wasn't ready. It is now.

After all that build-up, the final verse is quiet, almost like a whisper, although we can still make out every word.

> *'But if you had to leave me*
> *I would let you go without a whisper*
> *So just kiss me once then turn and go*
> *You may hear me breaking*
> *But you will never see me cry.'*

She repeats the last two lines, her voice fading gradually to nothing. Concentrating on the keyboard as she plays the final chords, she doesn't seem to notice the camera moving in for an extreme close-up of the intense emotion on her face. She's there, alone, until the last note fades and she looks up at the audience as if surprised there's anyone watching.

People stand. In twos and threes at first, then whole rows, then everyone. The judges, too. Everyone in the auditorium, almost, is applauding as hard as they can, and many people are crying too. I am watching fame happen, right in front of my eyes.

Take Me Home

n my phone screen, FaceFeed explodes with comments.

Incredible.

Best singer the show's ever had.

The show ain't over until the fat girl sings. Well, she did tonight! #voterose. #breathless

Drop the fat girl? You idiots. I hope those #selfish-cows who ditched her are crying now.

'What's it *saying?*' Mum asks anxiously, trying to peer across me.

'It's saying she's great,' I tell her, shifting the angle of my phone so she can't see it.

At the end of the performance, Linus waits until there is total silence before pronouncing his judgment. After all the excitement he has to wait a long time. While he waits, his expression is triumphant. He's the opposite of the scared, nervous man who was on the news this morning. It's as if he *owns* Rose now. As if he invented her.

'That was extraordinary,' he says, allowing a slow grin to play across his face for the camera. 'Sublime.'

'You are So. Special. Rose,' Roxanne adds, with tears in her eyes. 'I always knew there was something about you.'

Yeah, right. *Not large, but **large**.* Was that the something? Roxanne somehow manages to make *every* moment on camera So. Special. But I'm starting to understand that she doesn't necessarily Mean. What she says. All the time.

Sebastian Rules looks happier than I've ever seen him. 'You rock, princess! You wrote that song yourself?'

Rose nods.

'You got a *career*, girl. A total career. How you feeling about the girls who dropped you from the band? You got anything to say to them?'

I close my eyes. Sebastian is the one whose opinion I now respect the most: he's always been honest, I think. Why did it have to be him who mentioned the rest of us? I wish I could just shrink into a tiny pixel and press 'Delete'.

Rose pauses for a moment and looks out beyond the lights, knowing that we're sitting there somewhere.

'They did what they had to do,' she says, quietly. 'I

don't mind, because this is my music. They made me think about a few things when they let me go.'

'Well, you are one classy lady,' Sebastian says. 'And I think you just made the whole world fall in love with you.'

Rose looks modestly down at her hands in her lap.

'I think you just earned yourself a place back in this competition,' Linus says. 'Because we might just have found our star.'

Afterwards, as most of the audience heads for the toilet queues, I catch up with Nell.

'Did you have any idea . . . ?' she asks.

'No.'

'Me neither.'

'I've got to try and see her,' I say. 'Are you coming?'

Nell looks at me nervously. 'I don't think so, Sash. I don't think she wants us right now.'

She's probably right, and that's why I have to see Rose so desperately. Please can the new Rose not hate me? This is so hard.

I get Mum to wait for me in the lobby and I make my way down towards the backstage area, where Rose must be unwinding and getting changed. A big security guard from the TV company guards the door.

'I'm Sasha,' I explain. 'From the Manic Pixie Dream Girls. I've just got to . . .'

'Nobody enters,' he says, not even looking at me.

'But I was there two days ago. My friend's in there. I just need to—'

'That's what they all say. Night night, sweets. Run along, now.'

His eyes meet mine for a second. They are hard, with a warning in them. The door stays firmly shut.

'Just for a minute,' I beg.

He simply ignores me.

At that moment, Roxanne Wills rushes by, surrounded by her entourage. The security guard stands back to let them through, but he keeps his eyes on me, to make sure I don't join them.

'Roxanne!' I call. 'It's me. Can you let me in?'

She turns and looks at me, then shrugs helplessly.

'Sorry, babe. I'm in a rush here. See you later, OK?'

The door shuts behind her again and the guard stands impassively between me and it. Still, I stand my ground.

'I was just in there!' I repeat. 'Two days ago! I'm part of the show. Well, I was.'

He catches the look of sadness and defeat on my face. For a moment, there's a flicker of sympathy in his eyes.

'Why don't you call her?' he says. 'Your friend. If she says you can come in, I'll see what I can do.'

So I do. I try one more time. I call her number. I text. There is no reply.

The security guy gives me a pitying smile.

'Night night then, sweets,' he repeats.

The big black door stays absolutely shut behind him.

I turn away sadly and go to find Mum in the lobby.

'Take me home?' I ask. 'Now? Please?'

'What, to Somerset?' she asks. 'But we're supposed to stay here for the final. And besides, it's a two-hour drive. We wouldn't be there till after midnight.'

'I know.'

'Well, do you want to say goodbye to the others at least?'

But I don't want to stay here for a moment longer.

Mum sees the look on my face. So she holds out her hand, and pulls me close to her.

'All right.'

Rainbow Coloured Cardigan

It's late when Mum comes into my room on Sunday morning, dressed and clutching a mug of tea.

'I thought I'd leave you. How are you feeling?'

'Fine,' I lie. 'Tired.'

'You looked exhausted. That's why I let you sleep on despite the phone calls. Lots of people trying to get in touch. I told them they could talk to you later.'

'Thanks, Mum.'

'Where shall I put this?' she asks, holding out the tea.

We cast around for a mug-sized space, but there isn't one. I shift a pile of papers on top of another to make some room.

'Sure you're OK?'

I nod. 'I just need to be on my own.'

She gives me her *I'm downstairs if you need me* smile and leaves me to it.

Instinctively, I reach out for my phone and check my messages on Interface. Some are from family, friends and new fans:

How are you, love? Your grandpa and I are thinking of you.

Bad luck in the competition! You were the best!

I always thought Rose was lardy. You looked amazing.

Hiya, Hotlegs. You were soooooo coooooool.

Others are from new enemies:

I hope you die, you selfish cow.

It's God punishing you for being such an evil witch. lol

There are ten times more of these. But even the 'encouraging' ones are weird. How can anyone think they're comforting me by calling Rose 'lardy'? Did they not understand our friendship at all?

I scan through the list, put my phone down and reach for the hot cup of tea. Then I drag myself out of bed. My room is a tip. Worse than usual. At the moment, it's got about ten discarded outfits for Killer Act rehearsals in a heap on the floor, several piles of papers on the desk to do with homework I haven't done, and various little pillars of read and half-read books lined up near the bed. Walking across it is a hazard and it hasn't been properly hoovered for weeks. I'm not entirely sure that all the laundry is clean.

In the middle of the pile of clothes are two of Rose's cardigans. Her gran knits them for her every Christmas. She must have left them here when it was too warm to wear them, or maybe to have one ready to slip into when it was cold. She must have loads of my stuff mixed up with her wardrobe, too – not that she'd have worn it. My clothes were generally too boring for her.

I've always admired Rose's style. Only she would wear a vintage nylon evening dress, baggy jacket and boots to go shopping in Castle Bigelow. Only Rose would combine a lime green midi skirt with one of these chunky, rainbow-coloured knitted cardigans. She was impossible to miss. In fact, she always shone out like a beacon.

I miss everything about her. Now it feels as if I'll never see her again.

I pick up one of the cardigans. This one is a colourful statement in every possible shade of blue, with red beads sewn in stringy patterns around the hem. Her gran was inspired by the ocean when she began knitting this and I think the beads are supposed to be coral. I take it off the pile and put it round my shoulders, gradually easing my arms into the sleeves. It's warm and cosy, even if the sleeves dangle past my fingertips and the hem practically comes down to my knees. Will Rose miss it? I can always give it back to her if she does. Right now, I need it, as the weak spring sun struggles to make it through the gap in the curtains in my room.

My phone rings. It's Nell, with Jodie right beside her, anxious to find out what's happened to me.

'Aren't you coming back?'

'No,' I explain.

'But don't you want to be here for the final?'

'Not really. Have you had a chance to talk to Rose?'

Nell sighs down the line.

'No. She's busy in rehearsals for tonight. I think she's avoiding us.'

'Of course she's avoiding us!' Jodie moans. 'We dumped her. Well, Sasha dumped her. She's just doing to us what we did to her.'

'But we tried to apologise,' I murmur. 'Or at least . . .' Or at least, *I* did. Seeing as I was the one who had the brilliant idea of dropping her, it was only right that it should have been me who tried. I'm still trying.

'Ivan's storming around,' Nell says. 'He was really hoping you'd be here for the show. You know, that bit at the end when we all stand onstage? It'll look odd without you. Please come back, Sash.'

'I'm sorry, I can't. Tell Ivan I'm not well. Actually – I don't care what you tell him. Why are you guys even still there, after what they did to us?'

'Because . . .' Nell says, struggling for an answer.

'Because it's television,' Jodie shouts. 'It's what you do. There's, like, a million people waiting to see us.'

'So they can call us selfish cows on FaceFeed,' I point out.

'You're being a coward, hiding away.'

She's right. She's absolutely right. I should probably be up there, with them, smiling for the cameras, ignoring all the hate. But I can't. Instead, I stick my hands into the pockets of Rose's cardigan and sit staring out of my bedroom window.

At lunchtime, Mum tempts me downstairs for soup and toast. As usual, she has the radio on in the kitchen while she cooks. Some woman who's written a book about the female body image is being interviewed about us and 'what we mean to society'.

'I just think it's absolutely terrible,' she says. 'Girls these days. They're so nasty to each other. You wouldn't believe the things they say on websites and social media. This behaviour by those so-called Magic Pixie Dream Girls is just typical: "If you don't look right, you can't be part of our gang." We really need to do something about it. Women need to stand together. As long as you're eating healthily and exercising, there's nothing wrong with your body shape. We should celebrate everyone, big and small. And we should stop criticising each other all the time.'

Mum stares at the radio.

'From Miss "Women need to stand together",' she says sarcastically, shaking her head. 'If that's not being critical, I don't know what is.'

She looks at me with a sympathetic half smile. I try to smile back.

I doubt Mum knows this, because she mostly only goes online to do food shopping from Tesco, but people are selling T-shirts saying #dropthefatgirl now. You can buy them from several different sites. If you like, you can get them with #skinnywitch on the back.

Back in my room, my phone goes again with a text:

I know where you live, Sasha Bayley. And I'm waiting.

This is different. Breathless. I feel breathless.

At 7 p.m. Mum calls me down to watch the final with her. It goes by in a blur. I can't concentrate. *Who* knows where I live? What are they waiting for? Are they watching me now? Mum can't understand why I keep checking that all the curtains in the cottage are shut tight, or why I flinch every time a car goes by in the lane outside.

On TV, there are several close-ups of Nell and Jodie sitting in the audience, looking pale, holding hands. I feel more than ever that I've abandoned them, but really, what is the point of us being there tonight? Before I came downstairs I checked the 'I Hate the Manic Pixie Dream Girls' page. It was up to 107,000 haters. And 107,000 people who hate you can't be wrong.

When Rose appears onstage for her final number, she is wearing a designer dress I'm sure I've seen in a magazine – blue and green, with crystals shimmering around the neckline. She's back at the piano, playing 'Breathless' one more time. Her makeup, as always, is immaculate, down to the triple flick of her eyeliner. Her hair is piled high on her head. She's not like most girls you see on MTV, but there is no doubt she's beautiful. Especially when she's singing, she has a glow about her.

And then there's her voice. Her incredible voice. The voice that comes out of nowhere and never lets you go.

I check my phone, to see what the world is saying.

#voteRose is trending. So are #Breathless and #dropthefatgirl again. But even those FaceFeeds are mostly from people who really like her. Ivan will be pleased: Killer Act has five of the top ten trends in the UK right now.

At the end of this part of the show, Roxanne Wills comes out to sing her new song, surrounded by sexy backing dancers in neon makeup and not much else. There's a break for a game show, while the world busily votes. Then it's back for the final announcement.

Andy Grey stands onstage next to all the finalists and grins at the camera, enjoying the tension. He asks each of the judges which performance they liked the most. Linus shrugs and says it's impossible to call. Roxanne, in a new dress and jewellery after a quick change, says nice things about everyone, as usual.

Sebastian sneers at them slightly.

'We all know what we think is going to happen,' he says honestly, straight to camera. 'The question is, are we right?'

With that, Andy waits for Ivan Jenks to speak the name of the winner into his earpiece. Ivan lets the moment last for what feels like hours. All the contestants, in their personal spotlights, look down at the stage floor. The dancers hold hands. A background drum roll goes on forever.

'And the winner of Killer Act . . . with a contract to advertise Interface for a year . . . worth one hundred thousand pounds . . . is . . . . ROSE IRELAND!'

The studio erupts. Silver confetti falls from the ceiling. Rose dips her head and bites her lip. She looks pleased but shocked. So many people fake surprise, but Rose wouldn't know how. She's genuinely stunned – despite the fact that half the world, it seems, knew what was going to happen. The other finalists swoop in to hug her. Soon she's surrounded by a large group of emotional people, with Jodie and Nell on the edge of it looking uncertain about what to do. The judges, thrilled and satisfied, go onstage to join her too.

Meanwhile, the producers are clearing the stage and repositioning the grand piano so that Rose can play 'Breathless' one last time.

She does. Just a girl, and a piano, and a spotlight. She gives a perfect solo performance, filling the screen with her emotion, and the room with her stand-out voice.

My best friend just won a national talent competition and the video of her first performance – I just checked – has a half a million hits, and counting.

My *ex*-best friend.

When she sings, *'You may hear me breaking, but you will never see me cry,'* I'm right back in that corridor, at the Interface HQ. It feels as though she's singing it straight at me.

Away From Me Now

The next morning, Interface News is full of stories about Rose. It seems that everyone is talking about her.

KILLER ACT WINNER SET TO MAKE A MILLION
BY CHRISTMAS

TEEN STAR'S SECRET CAR CRASH TRAGEDY

BEAUTIFUL ROSE'S BULLYING HEARTBREAK:
EXCLUSIVE!

I hardly know where to start. Ignoring Mum's pleas to come down to breakfast, I spend hours searching the web, following up the stories. The first one I click to is the 'bullying heartbreak'. Is this *more* about Jodie, Nell and me?

But it's not. It's worse.

Life was not always so rosy for singing sensation Rose Ireland, who has just won this year's Killer Act competition with a sensational performance. Attending the prestigious North London Girls' School in her early teens, she was victimised by a gang of classmates who made her life a misery. 'She used to dread school,' says an unnamed friend. 'They would wait outside the gates so they could mime being sick when she arrived. They said she should get bulimia so she could lose some weight. At lunch, if it was sausages, they'd throw them at her. Her nickname was Sausages.'

Oh my God. So that's why she left London. She never told me. She obviously wanted to forget it and move on. Which is what she had done – until now.

Thinking back, she was teased a bit at St Christopher's to start with – most people are, for one reason or another – but when she started hanging out with us, people stopped paying much attention. She was just one of the girls. We must have been her refuge, until we supposedly dumped her for being 'large'. If I was a stranger reading about me now, I'd hate me too.

Then there's the article about her parents, giving details of the crash in which they died. There are bits about what happened to the bus that crashed, and who else died, that she's never talked about, even to me.

If this *is* all true, Rose would hate the world to know it. When Rose and I were together we just talked about the good things: what we liked, what made us laugh, what adventures we dreamed of. It's weird to be finding out so much about her from the internet, when a few weeks ago she was sitting in this room with me, and I had no idea.

I feel cut off and confused, sad for her and angry too. Why didn't she tell me? Why couldn't she share? What must she be thinking now?

I call her number one more time, but she doesn't answer and her voicemail's stopped working. I'm starting to wonder if she'll ever talk to me again.

It feels as though Rose is about the only person who *doesn't* want to talk to me, though. As the stories about her being bullied increase, and #dropthefatgirl is still trending on FaceFeed, everyone wants an interview with the girls who did the dropping. Mum calls Interface to ask what we should do, but they say that as our contract's over, they can't help us. Meanwhile, journalists call the house endlessly, until we unplug the house phone from the wall.

Two days later, there's a car outside the cottage, with a man sitting inside, in some sort of dark jacket. The car is parked on the verge, right up against the hedges. There isn't really parking space on the narrow lane, so the few cars that pass have to pull out to go round him.

'I don't like the look of him,' Mum says, staring through the kitchen window, but I assume he's a stray motorist, lost on the way out of Castle Bigelow, consulting his sat nav or something. I pop my head out of the door to collect the milk and he calls my name. Surprised, I look up. He's got a camera.

'What's it like to be called a witch?' he shouts across the road.

I stare at him, astonished. It's seven-thirty in the morning and it's like he's just slapped me.

He takes a picture. It's online by lunchtime. I look haunted.

After that, I don't go out.

Nell calls, to say she and Jodie are back from London. Sweet, kind Nell. She asks if I want to do some holiday revision together. But I don't feel like seeing anyone right now.

'Are you OK, Sash?' she asks on the phone. 'You sound . . . strange.'

'Yeah, I'm OK. How about you?' My voice sounds odd to me. Unused.

'Fine.'

Nell sounds strange too: clipped and uncertain. Not her usual bouncy self at all.

'And Jodie?'

'Yep, fine,' Nell says, clearly lying. Nell's the worst liar I know. 'She's riding her pony a lot to take her mind off things. Or at least, she did until someone took a picture of her with a flash and Rolo bolted and she nearly fell off. I saw that picture of you, by the way. I'm sorry.'

Nell saw it. Oh God.

I text Jodie to say I'm sorry about her pony bolting and I expect a long, ranty message back about the evils of the paparazzi, but . . . nothing. So Jodie isn't talking to me either. I suppose she still blames me for not going back for

136

the humiliations of the Killer Act final. And for being the original #skinnywitch during the auditions. I could point out that she agreed with me, that she could have argued me down and pointed out how crazy I was. She was even the one who told me to talk to Rose. But what's the point?

In the days that follow, the clip of Rose singing 'Breathless' for the first time goes totally viral worldwide, with over 20,000,000 hits.

Twenty *million*.

Workmates are emailing the link to each other. So are school kids. So are mums at home and students at university. They love her in Spain. They love her in South Africa. They love her in China and New Zealand and India. They simply adore her in America.

They love that she's brave. They love that she's only sixteen and she's got one of the best natural singing voices they've ever heard. They love that she can play piano and guitar, and writes her own songs. They love that she's got a normal, relatable body shape and she's not some 'stick-thin twiglet' like every model and celebrity, and her ex-bandmates, of course. Most of all, they love that she stood up to those 'frenemies' who dumped her, and that she found her inner confidence despite what they did to her.

The more they talk about Rose, the more they talk about us. It's on the news. It's in the papers. It's everywhere.

SINGING SENSATION ABANDONED BY
FRIENDS FOR BEING 'FAT'

BLOSSOMING ROSE, AND THE SPIKY
THORNS WHO DUMPED HER

By now 150,000 people have 'liked' our hate page. It features the clip of us dancing together at the auditions, while Rose stands apart, lost and alone. Altogether, that clip has been watched nearly a million times. So this is my new life: I am famous, and it totally sucks.

After that, the holidays pass in a haze. I don't know if I'm sad, or frightened, or just numb. In the mornings I wake up, reach out my arm and grab my phone from the bedside table. I type in my password and check to see what's happening. I check our band page, and our hate page. One video is very popular. After two days, it already has over a thousand views. It shows three cartoon girls with our faces superimposed on their heads, being blown up, shot and killed in various gory ways. Apparently there is an app where you score points by shooting at a picture of my head in some sort of arcade game, but I haven't managed to find it. LOL. I mean, hysterical. Well done whoever spent their evening putting *that* together.

There have been good messages too, supportive ones from good friends and people I hardly know, but it's the bad ones you remember.

. . . freak of nature . . .

. . . selfish bullies . . .

. . .. mean cows . . ..

. . . #totalloser . . .

And another chilling text to my personal number:

I'm still watching you, freak. You can't get away from me now.

Between The Lines

Those texts are the worst. It's like there's someone inside my phone, watching me. I don't feel safe anywhere, but my room feels less unsafe than most places. I don't go shopping; I don't go to work. I just shut myself away until there are less than forty-eight hours till school starts again for the summer term. I know I can't stay hiding at home for ever, but I have no idea how I will face everyone. All I can think of is a sea of faces, all pointing at me, all staring and jeering. With Nina Pearson in the foreground, calling me a witch.

Over breakfast, Mum tries to cheer me up before she

goes to work. She suggests various jobs I could do in the café to help her. I put her off, because I really don't have the energy and besides, I don't think it's a great idea to be seen in public places. Instead I sit in my room and work through my revision for school. I never thought I'd be grateful for exams, but it helps to think about the War Poets, or the Periodic Table, rather than How Sasha Bayley Got Carried Away And Ruined Her Life.

I listen to music. The same songs, over and over: The Killers. The Cure. The Smiths. They sing the pain, so I don't have to. Later, I watch TV.

Mum comes home at half past three. She says the café was quiet, but I can tell she's worried about me. Not long afterwards, I hear her on the phone to Dad. Oh God, I am so famously messed up that *even Dad* is calling to find out how I am.

Mum's trying to keep her voice down, so I sit on the top stair to listen.

'I worry about her. She's not talking. She hardly eats. She spends all her time in her room on her computer, or that bloody phone you gave her. I think she might be checking out all those vile things people are saying on the internet.'

There's a pause while Mum listens to Dad.

'But it wasn't *like* that, Pete. She's been *trying* to apologise from the moment it happened.'

Oh great. So even my Dad thinks I'm the kind of person who just dumps my friend and abandons her.

'Do you want to talk to her?'

I certainly don't want to talk to *him*, I decide, rushing down the stairs and past her. I've been cooped up here too long. It's time to go out. Go anywhere.

It's April: one of those sharp, blue days where the sun tries to remember how to warm the fields. I huddle in the porch of the cottage, shrugging on my jacket and my wellies as fast as I can so I can be out of the house before Dad persuades Mum to try and make me talk to him. I put my phone and my house keys in my pocket and head down the lane. I'm aiming for the track that starts beside the railway, which takes me up into the high fields of Mr O'Connell's farm.

There's one good thing about living in a cottage in the middle of nowhere: the paparazzi don't like being so far away from the city, and they hate it when a passing tractor drives a huge, long dent down the sides of three of their cars. I'm sure it *was* an accident, but Mr O'Connell, the farmer who owns the land opposite, is an old friend of Mum's, so a part of me does wonder slightly.

Anyway, they haven't got any decent pictures of me, and I'm not doing any big interviews to up my profile and give 'my exclusive side of the story' – although goodness knows, they keep asking – so they've gone.

I start down the lane. From the ridge at the top of the hill opposite the cottage, you can see the bowl-shaped area that Mr O'Connell gives over to the Bigelow Festival every summer. In July, it's like a medieval village or a circus, full of tents and flags and colour and noise. Now, it will just be a patchwork of green and brown, spotted only with sheep and their lambs, and the occasional black-and-white cow. Far away from people. Far away from everything. Just where I want to be.

I stick my earbuds in and put on the first track I come to. It's Youssou N'Dour, a musician from Senegal who Rose introduced me to ages ago. He's very different

142

from my recent choices, but still – I let him play. The warm rhythms of his music help distract me from the sharp breeze that whips round my legs, freezing the denim of my jeans.

Far ahead, the lane goes over a little bridge over the railway line, leading towards Castle Bigelow. Just as I'm about to turn off it, onto the track that heads up the hill, my phone vibrates in my pocket with a text. Instinctively, I pull it out to look.

The time is getting closer, freak. And when I see you, you are going to die.

Oh no. Nonononono. Not this. Not more. Not that.

Before I know it, my legs have given way and I sink to my knees. I look around, but there's no one there. My hand starts to shake so much that I can hardly read the words on the screen. Then, gradually, the panic slowly subsides into a sludgy, icy feeling of dread.

They hate me and they want to kill me. Thousands of them. Thousands and thousands. But I don't know who they are and I can't stop them. Nobody has ever taught me how to be hated this much. I don't know how to do it.

Oh, Rose, if I could apologise again, I would. But you won't let me.

I don't know whether to go back or go on. My brain is numb. Someone could be here, hiding anywhere. I move ahead, dragging myself on as much as my jelly legs will let me, pulling my earbuds out as I go. Youssou N'Dour is not the soundtrack to how I'm feeling now. All I can hear is my blood pumping in my ears. I have no idea where I'm going, or what I'm doing. I just want to get away.

143

After a while I find myself on the railway bridge, looking down at the track. My brain feels like jelly too, and I'm tired. So tired. I still seem to be alone, apart from a train far away in the distance, snaking through the countryside. I know the line well. The train must take a big detour behind Crakey Hill before it reaches the stretch of line leading to Castle Bigelow station. It will take about five minutes. Meanwhile, the sky is still cloudless, blue. The air tingles with suspense.

The sound of the engine is strangely hypnotic. I don't want to walk any more, so I pull myself up onto the high stone parapet and look down. The train is out of sight now – gone behind the hill, but I can hear it getting closer, swiftly carrying passengers on their journeys. Strangers, going about their busy lives. Some will be on their phones, texting or talking. Are any of them talking about me?

My mind starts to wander. What is the driver up to, I wonder? It can't be that complicated to drive a train, can it? Stop for the red signals, stop at the stations. Always stay on the lookout for awkward things on the line.

Soon the train will come out from behind Crakey Hill and reach the bit of track that comes straight towards me, sitting on my little bridge. I wonder if he will be surprised to see a teenage girl here. A girl in a country jacket and bright yellow wellies, with her hair in a ponytail and her mind in a mess.

My phone vibrates again. This time I ignore the message, but I can't resist going onto Interface and checking the latest numbers. The habit is too deep-rooted.

15,672 likes for the Manic Pixie Dream Girls.

157,100 'haters' for the hate page.

593,101 hits on the clip that shows us dropping Rose.

It feels as though the whole world has an opinion about me.

This morning, when I Googled my name, I read a report saying that a Member of Parliament mentioned me on TV yesterday, wondering if the government should intervene in schools, to encourage girls to have a more positive body image. I was quoted as an example of the kind of girl they need to do something about.

Sasha Bayley. She's famous. But by now I'm not sure who she is. Even my own father doesn't seem to know me any more.

I'm still looking at the screen when I feel a presence behind me and whip round, terrified. It takes me a while to register the face. I know him. I've seen him on posters round town, and onstage at George's party. What is the guitarist from Call of Duty doing standing three feet away from me, in the middle of the bridge, looking like he's just seen a ghost?

He licks his dry lips. 'What are you doing here?'

I breathe out slowly.

'Sitting.'

He looks at me, and through me, and beyond me to the track, and moves forward two gentle paces. A long way behind me, I can hear the train round the corner of Crakey Hill, beginning its journey down the straight.

Suddenly, I see what he is thinking. I do seem to be perched quite precariously on the edge of the parapet. I wasn't concentrating when I sat down. I wasn't really thinking at all.

'It's OK,' I say, to reassure him. 'I know what I'm doing.'

145

That seems to make it worse. He looks more anxious than ever, flicking his eyes from the train to me, and back again. He takes another step towards me and spots the phone in my hands. He looks at the screen, and I suppose he sees the numbers. Those great big numbers that grow bigger, every day, showing how famous I am.

He catches my eye and says: 'Don't. Please. Just . . . don't.'

'It's OK,' I repeat, holding up my hands to reassure him. But again, it seems to have the opposite effect. The train is nearly here now, braking gradually for the station, but still travelling at high speed, too fast to stop. He grabs me around the waist with his left arm and holds me.

'Get off!'

I manage to yank one of my arms free, my phone still in my hand. He tries to grab me again, pulling at my arm with his right hand. In a smooth, fast swish, the phone flies from my grasp and arcs into the air, over the parapet and down towards the approaching train.

The driver glances up to see the two of us above the parapet, and I watch, in slow motion, as my whole life smashes to pieces on the wooden sleepers between the bright silver lines of the track.

This is Sasha Bayley

For a long time, we just stare at each other. Me and the guitarist from Call of Duty, with his tousled hair hidden under a beanie. His name's Dan, I think. Somebody told me. One of the girls from the band's fan club, probably. They said his eyes were the colour of stormy seas, or something like that. It may be true. They're grey, or blue, and troubled. But that's understandable, because HE'S JUST MADE ME SMASH UP MY FOUR-HUNDRED-POUND PHONE.

It's in smithereens, with endless train carriages still trundling over it. I bet the driver didn't even see it happen.

'I can't believe you just did that! Look what you made me do!' I pant, when I get my breath back enough to talk.

'Are you OK?' he asks, pulling back from me. 'I mean, you said you were OK, but I thought you were going to . . .'

He's wearing an old green jumper under a muddy shooting jacket. Now that I look closely, I realise that he has a rifle bag over his shoulder. He must have been going out shooting. It's always dangerous to attack a boy with a gun, of course, but I am so incandescently angry that I could punch him or slap him or pummel him. I could throw something at him, if I still had anything to throw.

'OK? Of *course* I'm not OK. You made me drop my phone . . . down there.'

I'm so furious I can hardly explain myself. Instead I lean forward and point under the disappearing train. Dan grabs me again and I shake him off.

'How *could* you?'

'I'm sorry!' He looks white and shocked too. 'I just had to do something! It looked like you were going to . . .'

'Well, I wasn't.'

He steps back from me again, still breathing hard.

'Right. OK. But maybe it's for the best. Whatever you were looking at on your phone . . .' He stops and gazes out down the track, taking a deep breath before continuing. 'It looked like it was hurting you.'

There's a pause, while I take in the total *ridiculousness* of what he just said.

'*Hurting me?* That phone's my lifeline. Don't you understand? It's the only thing I have that tells me *anything*. How am I going to tell my mum where I am? How am I going to find out what people are saying about

148

me? How can I tell my dad you've just made me smash up the last thing he ever gave me? He's in *Vegas*, by the way. I can't exactly shout.'

I *am* shouting, though – at Dan. I'm getting hoarse with it, because it feels like I haven't used my voice for so long. He looks as if I've just slapped him.

'Your dad? I'm sorry.'

'It's no good saying you're sorry. You hardly know me and you've just smashed up my life. If people need to call me . . . If someone needs to call me . . .'

If Rose ever decides to call me, how can she do it now?

I turn on my heel and start heading away from the bridge, up the track that leads towards Mr O'Connell's fields. Dan comes after me, still hangdog apologetic, which is good, because I can keep telling him off. It's such a relief to let off steam after so many days of hardly talking. And how could he *do* that? My tone is as scathing as I can make it.

'I hardly ever see my dad and that's the first thing he's given me since a Barbie doll.'

'I'm sorry.'

'It was the latest version. It had HD video and voice commands and everything.'

'I said I'm sorry.'

'You're sorry, but I bet you can just go out and get yourself another phone whenever you want to. I have to *earn* my money.'

He falls into step beside me. He has long legs, like mine. And he's athletic. When he walks fast, his cheeks get a ruddy glow. I have to admit it suits him. For an unprovoked iPhone-smasher, he's not bad looking at all.

'Oh, God, and it wasn't insured,' I remember. 'I bet I

have to keep paying that stupid contract. Look, don't let me keep you.' I stop and turn to him. 'I'm sure you need to go and . . . shoot something.'

'Oh, that.' He looks at the bag on his shoulder, almost as if he's forgotten it's there. 'It's not a gun, actually. It's a telescope. I lent it to a friend. I just use my dad's old gun bag for . . . carrying.'

We've reached the end of the stony track and from now on it's a question of climbing stiles and tramping through muddy fields. Dan clearly doesn't know where I'm going, and has no reason to come with me any further. He sighs.

'I didn't mean to . . . Look, I didn't know about your dad. Or your contract. I didn't really think. Promise me you'll look after yourself?'

I stick my chin out and glare at him again. 'I always do.'

He doesn't seem so sure. Even so, he turns away, with his telescope in its bag knocking gently against his shoulder, and doesn't look back. I watch him go.

Once he is halfway down the hill, I pause and instinctively feel for the smooth lines of my phone case in my pocket. My muscles seem to move faster than my brain, which has to remind them it won't be there. No way of telling Mum where I've got to. No way of finding out what's happening with the numbers, or if the crazy stalker is still watching me. I can't plug my earbuds back in and listen to music, either. I have to put up with the quiet of the landscape: wildlife in the hedgerows, a tractor at work in a far-off field, and another approaching train, travelling in the opposite direction.

In the peace of the countryside, it seems harder to

believe that those messages really happened. Do thousands of people really want me to die?

I mean, really – I made one stupid mistake. I tried to put it right. I can't help it if the TV cameras were there for that one bit and not for all the others.

It was never me who called Rose fat. Never, ever me. I didn't care what size she was. I still don't. I was only uncomfortable with her being in the band because she didn't want to dance and she was . . . different. She was totally different! Surely everyone can see that now: more talented, more dedicated, more unique. I have nice legs, apparently, but she has a voice and a deep, poetic soul, and an extraordinary talent for the piano, and a whole career ahead of her. I always suspected it. I always encouraged it, as much as I could.

Actually, it's good to stride through the fields and think, really think.

There's this Sasha Bayley, and the one everyone else thinks they know. This Sasha Bayley is *not* a freak or a witch, and she will make it through somehow. I don't know how, but somehow. Mum and I survived when Dad left us and our world fell apart. I can survive being hated by strangers. And even, perhaps, by Nina Pearson. As long as I can stay alive, of course.

That last text still haunts me. Being stalked takes things to a whole new level, but I will cope with that too, somehow. I'm angry now, as well as frightened. The anger helps.

The walk home seems strange. I can't remember the last time I wasn't listening to music, or a podcast, or at least checking my mail as I trudged along. This time, in the near silence of farm machinery and birdsong, I can feel a lyric forming in my head. It's about railway lines and battle lines and lines in newspapers. I feel as if I'm fighting a war. The song might be called 'Between the Lines'. Its images shimmer around me and gradually form themselves into words and a tune.

I'm still humming it to myself as I head for home.

You Don't Know Me: Part 1

When I get in, Mum's busy doing accounts at the kitchen table. She smiles with relief when I walk through the door.

'Sasha, darling. I was worried about you. You're all right, aren't you? You'd tell me if you weren't?'

'Of course.'

Of course I wouldn't. What's the point of explaining if there's nothing the other person can do? I mean, she can't exactly find out who's stalking me, or give me twenty-four-hour protection. Knowing she's there is good, though. I kiss her forehead through her frizzy, grey-streaked fringe and make us both a mug of tea.

When mine's ready, I take it up to my room. There's something I need to do. It's funny: when Rose was here, she was the songwriter so I never bothered, apart from 'Sunglasses'. Now, these new lyrics seem to be pouring out of me. They're probably all rubbish, but I still feel the need to get them down. I dig out an old notebook that Rose gave me ages ago and I never used. As soon as I find a pencil sharp enough to write with, the lyrics flow onto the page. And the next page. And the next.

Now I need to see if I can capture the tunes that come with them. I wish I was better at playing guitar.

The 'teach yourself' book is hiding behind two unwashed mugs at the top of my bookcase. I reach up and bring it out. Rose has always had a guitar teacher, but John Lennon learned this way, she told me. So did other guitar greats like Eric Clapton and Jimmy Page. And Rose's spare guitar – she named it Molly – is right there in the corner, asking to be used.

By the time Mum calls me to lay the table for supper, I've just about mastered two chords: A and C. Sort of. Given that the guitar is badly out of tune. I still have a lot to learn. My hands are aching, but it's a good ache. It reminds me of when Dad tried to teach me in Vegas. The pads of my fingers feel numb from holding down the strings and strumming them. I'd forgotten that guitar playing was such hard physical work.

After supper, I add D major to my repertoire. Instantly, it unlocks one of the tunes in my head, and I can start to describe it with my fingers. It's amazing what you can do with three simple chords. Perhaps, looking back, I was giving Rose more credit than she deserved. Or maybe not.

OK, so she knows an awful lot more than three chords. This morning, Ivan Jenks announced that she'll be recording 'Breathless' for release as soon as possible.

Anyway, it's bedtime and I've written half a song. I may have lost my phone because of some IDIOT, but it hasn't been an entirely wasted day.

For the first time in weeks, I sleep straight through, without nightmares, and wake up feeling better. From the amount of sunlight in the room, I'd say it was mid-morning. One day left until I have to face everyone at school again.

I get up and check over the lyrics I wrote last night, before assessing the state of my bedroom. As always, it looks as though there has recently been a minor explosion in the vicinity. It's a constant work in progress, my bedroom: something I mean to tidy, and turn into a 'calm, relaxing sanctuary', but which ends up as a snapshot of my messy life.

I tackle it bit by bit. Slowly it becomes less of a disaster scene: the washing machine is on full-time; my wardrobe re-emerges from under its curtain of tops and dresses, and now contains only clothes that still fit me; the clean, white surface of my desk reappears from under the mass of papers. Eventually my carpet is empty except for a pile of clothes to get rid of, and Rose's two cardigans, which I really must return. I slip the one with the coral bead edging on again.

At school the next morning there are several men with cameras outside the gates, trying to take pictures. They call out my name, but I ignore them, hiding my head under the biggest hat I could find in the porch this morning. It's good to be surrounded by people. I feel safer here, even though I still don't know what to expect from my friends.

Nell gives me a brief smile in the locker rooms, but Jodie hurries her away. The rest of the day is pretty bad, but not quite as horrific as singing to millions of people on live TV when you've just betrayed your best friend, or being told that somebody wants to kill you. About eighty per cent as horrific, I'd say.

One thing I realise: I used to be quite popular. I never really knew. But people used to include me in conversations, and call me over if something interesting was happening. Now they always seem to be whispering, and the whispering stops whenever I come by. The people I thought were my friends seem to be busy whenever I approach, while others that I hardly know grab me to have their picture taken with me, grinning and pointing, so it can be a trophy on their Interface page. Every single teacher looks at me with pity or disgust.

When I get back to my locker at home time, someone has scratched DROPTHEFATGIRL into its surface. The pointed letters, inscribed with something sharp, set my heart racing. All the way home on the bus, I keep checking behind me to see if anyone's following me.

In the evening, after homework, I check on Rose online. If I can't talk to her, this will have to do. Besides, she is everywhere – on every chat show and news clip, with Linus or Roxanne or Sebastian – talking about her win. She has been for weeks; I wonder how much sleep she's had.

'And how does it *feel* to be a total internet phenomenon?' they ask her in a news clip. 'I think your song's got sixty-five million views now. What's that like?'

'Unreal,' Rose says. 'I'd just like to say thank you to everyone who's supported me.'

'I bet you would. It's a beautiful song. And tell me, you've had some people being pretty mean about . . . your figure. But you've shown that it's possible to rise above all that. So, are you comfortable with your body image now?'

There's a long pause, and I watch Rose silently squirming at being asked the question. But she avoids rolling her eyes, takes a deep breath and smiles graciously.

'I don't think anyone is totally comfortable with their image,' she says. 'But I'm OK with myself. All I ever wanted to do was write songs.'

'Isn't she fabulous?' Linus chips in from beside her, beaming. 'Isn't she wonderful? She's a real advert for the non-typical girl. She shows there's hope for us all.'

He laughs and pats his own impressive stomach. But Rose *is* a typical girl, I think angrily. Just not typical of singers and people on TV. It's sad to watch her smile fade slightly while everyone else in the studio laughs along with Linus, but I wonder how many people notice. Soon she's fixed her grin back on and she's busy talking about how amazing it was to meet Jessie J backstage.

I still miss her. I'm wearing her cardigan now. Across the room Molly, her guitar, is propped up against the window, where I left it last night. If people knew that Sasha Bayley, official #skinnycow, was looking after Rose's spare guitar for her, what on earth would they think?

The thought makes me sad, then it makes me giggle. It

gives me the idea for a new song. I grab my notebook and start writing again.

> *'You don't know me*
> *You think that you do*
> *From the pages and the papers, but*
> *I'm a different girl inside . . .'*

Then I try a few experimental chords, to match the tune in my head. From now on, this feels like the closest I will ever get to Rose.

I'm back at my computer a few days later, looking at pictures of her doing a fashion shoot for an entertainment magazine, when an email arrives in my inbox. It has the subject, 'Rose Ireland research'. So many people want stories about her. Is there anything left that they don't know – apart from how I really feel about her, of course? Warily, I open it.

> Hi Sasha. I'm doing a background piece on Rose Ireland and her stunning rise to fame. I noticed Andy Grey talking about the record-breaking votes you got with your band in the early stages of Killer Act. I've looked at these more closely and they intrigue me. Don't they look unusually good to you? Is there something you'd like to talk to me about? I can help you tell your side of the story. It's time to set the record straight. You can contact me using the details below. Fiona Kennedy.

I read it over and over.

What kind of 'background piece'? It doesn't sound very flattering to Rose.

. . . *unusually good* . . .

What does Fiona Kennedy mean by 'unusually good'? Of course those votes were unusually good. We couldn't believe it at the time. It was the weirdest experience, from the first time we saw '24 votes', to when they went into the thousands. We were just lucky, weren't we?

But staring at Fiona's words, I suddenly wonder. For a girl band no one had heard of, those votes were *insane*. Looking back, I can see why the journalist's intrigued. Honestly, can anything *else* horrible come out of this story for me?

Not just for me. For *us*.

Of course, if there was something wrong about the votes, I wouldn't be the only one to suffer. I've given up trying to contact Rose, but Jodie and Nell should know about this too. Whether we like it or not, we're all in this together.

With a sinking heart, I go downstairs to call Jodie's number. I know she doesn't want to talk to me, but I don't think she'd forgive me if I didn't warn her.

To my surprise, when I call, she answers. I'm so used to being ignored by Rose now that I've come to expect it.

'Hi. Yes?'

Cold, clipped Jodie. I hate it, but at least she's listening.

'Look, something's happened. There's this journalist who thinks she's found something to do with our votes. We need to talk.' I tell her about Fiona Kennedy and her suspicions. 'Don't you think something was strange?'

'Not really,' Jodie says. 'The Head had us as her

ringtone, remember?'

'Yes, but . . .'

'Ignore her. That's what I do. Ignore them all. Our lives are ruined anyway. Don't let her make it any worse.'

The accusation in her voice hurts as much as if she'd smacked me with a ruler. Sometimes I wish she wasn't such a drama queen.

'They're not *ruined*,' I say, trying to summon up the weird feeling of hope and courage I felt coming back from Crakey Hill, after that boy *smashed up my phone*. But right now, it's hard to recapture.

'Anyway, see you tomorrow,' she says gruffly, over the increasingly loud noise of heavy metal in the background. 'Got to go now. My brother's being an idiot. *Turn it down*, Sam! Elliot! I can't hear myself think.'

Elliot. Elliot Harrison. The weird computer geek who's best friends with Jodie's brother. The guy who put our video online. What else did he do?

Little White Box

I catch him first thing the next morning, in the corridor outside the sixth-form common room, where I've been waiting. He looks startled when he sees me. I don't blame him.

'Elliot, I know about the votes,' I say.

I don't, of course, not really – but one look at his shifty face, which has gone red to the tips of his ears, and I can see I'm on to something.

'What votes?' he mumbles, trying to move past me.

'The votes we got for Killer Act. *I* know, and there's a journalist who knows too, and she's going to do an article on you, so . . .'

'*What?*'

He stops dead and stares straight at me. Looks like Fiona Kennedy was right.

'Those votes. You made them happen, didn't you? She's on the case, Elliot. You have to tell me, or else I'll just talk to her and she can talk to you direct.'

'Look,' he says nervously, 'not here. Let's go into town after school. I promise I'll tell you there, OK?'

When the final bell rings, I find Elliot waiting for me in the reception area. Outside, the photographers have gone at last, but I wonder who else might be watching me. I try not to think about it.

'There's a gaming shop that's usually quiet,' Elliot says. 'We can go in there, if you like.'

'Sure. Whatever.'

It's a twenty-minute walk into town through the rain, and actually I'm glad of his company. He walks with a sixth-former's confidence, and now, if somebody *is* watching me, they'll see that I'm not alone.

As we get to the edge of town, the rain eases off and the sun pokes through the clouds. Castle Bigelow can look quite pretty, with its old, painted buildings lining the high street, and the grand stone entrance to Castle College crowning the top of the hill. I take off my hat and stuff it in my pocket, enjoying the fresh air on my face.

Inside the gaming shop, Elliot explains everything.

'I wanted things to be nice for you,' he sighs. 'That's all. I watched your videos and they were really funny. But that one – 'Sunglasses' – was special. I thought it was fantastic. I kept humming the song to myself. You looked . . .' he coughs and his voice fades to a nervous grunt, 'gorgeous doing your . . . dancing. I thought people should see.'

'We wanted to keep it secret. It was *our* video.'

He hangs his head and grunts some more. I think it's some form of geek apology.

'OK, so you were trying to be nice,' I say, frustrated that an act of so-called kindness could end up doing so much damage. 'But why did you rig the votes?'

'Because I could,' he says, meeting my eyes again.

So he did it. He really did it.

He perks up a little and looks proud of himself.

'I knew more people would pay attention if you had votes. And Interface have the most pathetic internal security. I mean . . . for an operation their size. It's astounding they're so easy to hack. They were kind of asking for it really.'

'How did you do it?'

I breathe carefully and try to keep the tears out of my voice. The one time I thought the four of us had done something good together – something we could be proud of, before we spoiled it all – it was all a mirage, faked by this boy in front of me. It was just a dream. Elliot doesn't notice. He carries on eagerly.

'Well, Interface voting's all anonymous, so I created some new accounts to vote. I kind of automated the system so it could create multiple accounts to speed things up. It wasn't quite that simple, but that's the basic idea. I did it at school, so they couldn't ever trace it back to me directly. But they could if you tell them, Sasha.' He frowns anxiously.

I close my eyes for a moment, defeated.

'So you're a hacker,' I say.

'Yeah,' he grins. 'And I'm brilliant. Not to blow my own trumpet or anything, but . . . I'm pretty special on computers. I'm thinking of working for NASA one day. Or Interface. There's so much I could teach them.'

'If you don't get jailed first.'

His grin fades slightly.

'Yeah, well, about that . . . please don't tell on me, Sasha. Please?'

'OK,' I sigh. I wasn't going to tell on him anyway. I just wanted to understand.

'Look, if you want to know,' he says, 'I only did it until you did that gig at George's. After that, I didn't need to.'

'So those last votes . . . when it went into the thousands . . . they were real?'

'Yeah, they were. Honestly. People really liked you. Once they knew about you, it went viral. And I owe you, Sasha. If there's ever anything I can do . . . just call me. I mean it. OK?'

I smile wryly.

I would . . . but I don't have a phone.

Next day, Mum offers to meet me in Castle Bigelow after school to replace my iPhone with the cheapest thing we can find. I didn't completely explain how my precious phone got broken. Actually, I said it fell out of my pocket while I was walking and I lost it. Mum didn't have the heart to be totally angry with me, given the whole 'being talked about as a teen bully on the evening news' scenario.

It will be torture to be out in public, watching out all the time to see who's watching me, and waiting. But it went OK yesterday, and this trip has to be done: I *need* a phone.

We go into West Country Mobile and ask for the cheapest pay-as-you-go smartphone they do. I can't believe I'm going to have to pay for my old contract *and* my new calls. The whole thing is so unfair it makes me want to scream. And it all goes back to Elliot. Elliot and Dan Matthews. I mean . . . boys. Honestly, what is the point of them? All they do is make life unnecessarily complicated and mess things up.

The new phone is disgusting and I don't really understand how it works. But I don't really care. It also means I have a new phone number, which is a nightmare, but I still haven't got round to sorting things out with my provider yet about my old phone. Dealing with hate mail can be pretty exhausting, even if all you're doing is trying to ignore it. On top of that, just getting to school and back and keeping on top of my homework is about as much as I can do right now.

I'm busy checking out the new screen and keypad, and thinking about the practicalities, as I trail after Mum down the street towards the car park. Ahead of me, a group of three school kids, not much younger than me, are walking down the pavement, laughing. They've just been to the chip shop and they're sharing a bag of chips and a large Coke. I lift my head. The chips smell delicious – all hot and vinegary. I give the trio a friendly smile.

They look at me and stop dead.

'Oh, my God, it's her!'

'Who?'

'The one from the show. The one who dropped Rose. Look!'

Before I know it, the youngest and smallest of the group has stepped forward, grabbed the Coke from her friends and thrown it all over me.

The shock makes me shriek. For a second, I can't feel anything, and then a cold, wet sensation penetrates through my hair, down my neck, into my clothes. I drop the phone and stand there, gasping. The boy reaches into his pocket and gets his phone out, laughing gleefully.

'Smile for the camera!'

The older girl's already filming me on hers. Then they both take several pictures of me gasping, before casually moving on.

Mum hasn't noticed. She's still walking away down the street. It's only taken a few seconds, but a crowd is starting to form. More people. More phones. I stoop to pick up my new, damaged one from the pavement and get up to find more screens in my face, more flashes. Now Mum turns round. She runs towards me, gathers me up and hurries me along.

'Don't worry, darling. It's over. It's over.'

But it's not over. How can it ever be over? Sitting in Mum's car, driving back home, I have to fight hard to stop myself from breaking down. I am Sasha Bayley. I am not a bad person. I don't deserve this, even though so many people think I do.

When we get home, there's a Land Rover parked on the verge outside the cottage. Instantly, I struggle to fight a new wave of panic. Do paparazzi drive muddy Land Rovers? So far they've all been in low, fast saloons. Oh *no*. I can't bear for them to see me like this.

Mum notices the Land Rover too, and watches it suspiciously while she parks.

As I open the car door, ready to run to the house, the passenger door of the Land Rover opens too. Two legs swing out. I catch my breath. A tall male figure steps out and starts to cross the road.

Dan Matthews.

The second time he's nearly given me a heart attack.

'What the hell are you doing here?' I shout furiously, as my heart rate starts to subside. 'How did you even know where I live?'

He gives me a nervous smile.

'You're quite famous now, you know. I asked a few people and someone knew your address. Oh my goodness. What happened?'

I put my hand to my sodden, dripping hair.

'Coke.'

He peers at me for a second, and works out roughly what must have been. 'I'm so sorry.'

'Don't be.'

He looks uncomfortable. 'Well, anyway . . .' He approaches me, holding out a package. 'I just came to give you this.'

It's a white box. I recognise the packaging instantly. I've seen it before.

'What?' I ask, wonderingly. Not angry now, but very, very confused.

'It's an iPhone. A new one. You said about your contract. You'll need the same thing. I noticed you had the latest version . . .'

Oh my God. The boy has just bought me a new iPhone. A proper one, all wrapped up. And now he's standing there, looking at me like a lost puppy.

'Wow.' I pause to swallow. 'Er, thanks.'

'It's OK.'

'My God!' Mum calls out, skirting round the Nissan to

join us. 'Is that what I think it is? Sasha? Sorry, I'm Sasha's mum. Hello.'

She stands there, waiting for an explanation, while I make awkward introductions and Dan describes briefly what happened on the railway bridge. And Mum glares at me, because I've obviously been lying to her.

'Don't be ridiculous,' she says to Dan. 'Sasha can't possibly keep it.'

'No, honestly,' he insists, 'it's fine.'

'She doesn't need it,' Mum declares, still overwhelmed by the generosity of the gift. 'We've just got her a new one.'

'It's a bit ruined,' I point out with a sigh. I bring it out, dripping, from my pocket.

'I'm sure we can get it fixed,' Mum says, flailing a little, not sure at all.

Dan looks at me. He and I both know that even if we could get it to work, it simply doesn't bear any comparison to my wonderful, wonderful iPhone, with its contract that I'm paying for anyway. Whereas this new one would solve all my problems. All my technical problems, anyway.

'It's OK,' I say to Mum. 'He's, like, a millionaire.'

I mean, he must be, right? He goes to the posh school and plays gigs in a smart jacket. He sounds posh. He *looks* posh, with his quiff of curly hair and his glowing just-played-rugby skin. Embarrassed, yes, but definitely loaded.

'That makes no difference,' Mum says grimly. And I know she's probably right, but the little white box alone is *so lovely* . . .

'I can't take it back,' Dan says, shrugging and backing away towards the Land Rover.

'Why?' she asks.

'Just . . . keep it. Really. Keep it.'

He jerks his head back towards the vehicle, where I can now see his brother Ed poking his head out of the window.

'Come *on!*' he calls. 'You're taking a million years, bro'.'

'Sorry. Got to go.' Dan shrugs again.

He dashes off, before we can do anything else. Wow. Imagine being able to spend that much on a piece of technology and not really have to think about it.

But I'm wrong.

Later, after a long, hot shower to remove any trace of Coke – and humiliation – I'm on Interface on my computer, when I can't help looking up Dan. On his page, there's an open message from Call of Duty's drummer, saying:

> *Hey mate, can't believe you sold your guitar to buy a phone for a girl. What about band practice, dude?*

Oh, OK. Maybe he did have to think about it.

Reluctantly, I re-evaluate a lot of my earlier opinions about boys. Particularly guitar-playing boys . . . or *ex*-guitar-playing boys. It's the most romantic gesture I can think of – for a boy who's not even going out with the girl in question. I can feel the tingle right down to my shoes.

Before I can think about it too much, I risk a message on Dan's page. He probably won't notice. He may think

I'm a sad stalker, but then – seriously – the boy tracked me down to my home address. So far he wins the stalking prize. I type quickly:

> *I heard about the guitar. So sorry – you didn't have to do that.*

Almost instantly, a message pings back.

> *No problem. I'll earn the money back. Meanwhile, there's a spare one I can use.*

I can't help myself. I start typing again.

> *Is it old and crappy? And by the way, sorry I thought you were rich.*

I click 'Send'. His reply is super-fast.

> *Yup. But that will make it sound authentically bluesy. And not rich. All money spent on looking like a toff at Castle School.*

He says 'authentically'. It's such a Rose word.

> *But you like looking like a toff. What about those jackets you play in?*

> *Oh God, those. Ed's idea. Hate them. We look idiotic.*

Well, Call of Duty didn't exactly look idiotic at

George's party. Nu-uh.

Yes, you do, I write back.

It wouldn't do to let him get up himself, like his brother. There's a long pause, while my heart rate speeds up again. It's the first time since #dropthefatgirl started that I've looked forward to a message, instead of dreading them.

If you ever want to hang out, he says we play together on Sundays. At my house. We could pick you up.

For a girl who has just been Coked in public, I suppose I could be feeling a lot worse.

Catch My Breath

Sure enough, I'm all over the internet again the next morning. The picture of me, shocked and dripping, is going all around FaceFeed and several people's Interface pages. Everyone thinks it's *hilarious*.

#manicpixiecokegirl

Rose-hater gets it in the face! #dropthefatgirl

Check out this pic! ROFL

Everyone except Dan, who messages me a smiley face to cheer me up, and Elliot, who's mortified when he sees me in school, and Jodie and Nell, who are waiting outside my locker to give me a big hug and a bar of chocolate.

'You poor thing,' Nell says, squeezing me.

'Yeah. Harsh,' Jodie adds, looking apologetic. 'I know it's been tough.'

They've decorated my locker with stickers of hearts and sunglasses, to cover up the graffiti there. I'm sure the stickers must have been Jodie's idea. That's the thing about Jodie: her life is a drama, but she's good at the good stuff, as well as the bad.

'I'm OK. This is beautiful. Thanks, guys.'

'It's so good to be talking again!' Nell squeaks. 'I hated avoiding you.'

Jodie kicks her, surreptitiously. I wasn't supposed to know they'd been avoiding me, but it was obvious enough. Anyway, it doesn't matter now.

'Has Rose been in touch?' Nell asks, ignoring Jodie's kick.

'No.'

'What? Not even after yesterday?' Jodie says, appalled.

I shrug. 'She's given up on me. I'm not surprised, I suppose. Anyway, she's busy.'

Jodie rolls her eyes. 'You're telling me. Did you know they're doing a Rose Ireland Special in the summer? They're filming it now. A whole TV programme about how wonderful Rose is.'

She doesn't make it sound very wonderful. Right now, it doesn't feel it. It would have been nice if Rose had texted. Or something. Just once. I take out my new phone, just to check. Still nothing.

173

'What happened to your phone?' Nell asks, confused. 'Your last one was white. This one's black.'

So I tell them about Dan – the basic details, anyway. 'Oh. My. God.'

When I get home, I do as much GCSE revision as I can face before getting back to the guitar. Working on my new song, 'You Don't Know Me', is much easier whenever I picture the smug faces on that threesome in town when they laughed at me. They thought they were being so clever. How would they have felt if some stranger suddenly poured cold liquid over them? Anyway, at least that's all they did. It could have been worse.

When my fingertips are sore from the guitar strings, I sit at my desk and idly check for messages from Dan. There's one to ask if the new phone's working OK. I assure him that it mostly is. Then I remember what Jodie said about the 'Rose Ireland Special' and look it up. Sure enough, Rose is having an hour-long programme made about her sudden rise to fame, narrated by Andy Grey. I wonder if it will feature pictures of Coke Girl. It probably will.

On her Interface page, there's more news about the ad. It will be launched in May, and from our school, of all places, because Interface are big on getting schools involved with their projects:

Interface, in partnership with education: where the stars of the future are born.

Which is not strictly accurate, of course. Rose was born in a hospital in Trowbridge. And as soon as Interface got their hands on her, she left school and hasn't been seen there since. But how weird will it be, standing in a crowd of students from St Christopher's, watching Rose cut a ribbon or whatever it is she's going to do?

At least we'll get to see her, though. She still hasn't been home since Killer Act, except for one night, to pick up some clothes. Her gran told Mum sadly that she's just too busy to spare the time. She's recording her first single. She's working on an album, or doing interviews. There are videos of her on Interface News, working with some famous visiting musicians who've asked to meet her. And pictures of her being ushered into the VIP area of some smart restaurant in London, or shopping for designer clothes on Bond Street, or squeezing herself into yet another belted shift dress for the pages of a magazine.

Rose looks OK in belted dresses, and they show off her amazing waist, but they're a bit frumpy and they were never her style. What's happened to the stripes and flowing skirts and boots she used to wear? Maybe I can ask her when she comes to cut that ribbon. Or maybe not. Perhaps they'll explain it on the Rose Ireland Special. Oh God this is hard.

When a new message pings through, despite everything, I wonder if she's decided to get in touch at last. However, when I check it, my heart sinks. It's from the journalist, Fiona Kennedy, again:

Re: Rose Ireland research.
I haven't heard from you. Still intrigued by voting irregularities on Killer Act. I feel your story hasn't been told. This could be your opportunity to put your side of it.

Which translates as: 'Please tell me how you cheated.'

Sorry, no luck, I reply. Meaning: 'No.'

She types fast. The next message pings through quickly.

> *Don't waste this chance. You were utterly
> abused by those programme makers. They
> made you look like the bad guys, but we all
> know how they manipulate the contestants. I
> bet they put you under a lot of pressure to drop
> Rose. Isn't that right?*

I catch my breath. Yes she's right, of course. I'd love nothing more than to get my own back on Linus Oakley, Ivan Jenks, and everyone in that big, rich company who made a news item out of our broken friendship and just left us to deal with the pieces. But something makes me hesitate. I trusted a lot of people in order to get into the mess I got us into. I'm not so quick to trust anyone now.

What is your story, exactly? I ask.

> *You leave the story to me. Just tell me how the
> voting worked and I promise I'll make Interface
> look pretty stupid.*

If there was a problem, wouldn't we all look bad?

> *Only Rose has anything to lose. And you don't
> owe her anything. Not after the way she
> dropped all of you.*

Rose dropped *us?* Nobody's suggested *that* before. It's true, though, and reading it in black and white gives me a shiver. It's not as if I haven't tried to apologise in every way I know how. Rose acts as if we never existed.

Don't you agree? Fiona writes.

I realise I've gone silent for a while. I've been thinking.

I can make it financially worthwhile, if that helps, she adds.

That's what pulls me out of my reverie. I was honestly starting to waver, but now it's clear what sort of journalist Fiona is. My first serious bribe. If it didn't make me feel nauseous, I'd be tempted to have it framed.

Sorry, I can't help you, I type.

She instantly shifts her tone.

Don't you think the public have a right to know what happened? If I have to do this story without your help, I'm afraid it won't reflect very well on you.

Suddenly she's not my new best friend any more. In fact, she's pretty intimidating. She messages me six more times during the evening. The only way to avoid her seems to be to shut down my computer.

At school next day, I share my worries with Nell and Jodie over lunch. It's such a relief to be back together again.

'She won't leave me alone.'

'I wonder why she picked on you,' Nell muses.

'You mean, she didn't contact you too?'

'Not that I know of. Mum doesn't pass on the messages from journalists. She just puts the phone down on them.'

Jodie agrees.

'Mine does too,' I say. 'But this was on Interface. Don't you get messages like that?'

They shrug and share a bemused look. Obviously not. Why me? Why did Fiona have to pick on me?

'Can't you block her?' Nell asks.

'I don't know. Can I?'

Nell sighs.

'I thought you were all techie.'

I did too. But I must admit, I tend to use stuff without worrying too much about all the background details.

'You should get Elliot to check out your account,' Jodie says.

'*Elliot?* You must be joking!'

She shrugs. 'He has his uses. He did mine when he was round with Sam. It took him about five seconds.'

'He does owe me, I suppose.'

I catch Elliot at school and tell him about Fiona. This time, he seems more upbeat.

'If she's getting threatening like that, it means she doesn't have any proof and she's desperate. I think we're OK. Interface won't co-operate and they're the only ones who could work out what I did.'

'OK,' I say, 'but how do I stop her pestering me? She's a nightmare. Jodie said you might be able to help.'

'You do have proper privacy settings on your Interface

account, don't you?'

'Ye-es.'

By which I mean 'no'. Elliot can tell.

'So *that's* how she got hold of you. I did wonder. I've got some time on Saturday. Can I come over then?'

'Sure,' I tell him.

In fact, I've been having problems getting my new phone working properly with my new SIM card, so having a computer genius around will be no bad thing. He may have slightly ruined my life, but I can't help liking Elliot. He is the most motherly geek I've ever encountered. Nobody's ever worried about my privacy settings before.

Practically Perfect

On Saturday morning I spend a happy three hours back in the warm white attic of Living Vintage, sorting out a new delivery of clothes collected by Mr Venning during his travels in Wales.

'There'll be nothing there,' Mrs Venning assures me airily. 'Welsh vintage shop owners are far too canny. They'll have had the best stuff already.'

But she's not entirely right. I find a few pearls to show her: a perfect fifties prom dress, an original eighties jumpsuit (which would have been perfect for the band), and a pair of plastic Vivienne Westwood shoes. With access to music again, I have the soundtrack from *Pretty in Pink* blaring in the background, to suit the vintage vibe. It's safe here, and beautiful. It's the kind of place to skip around with a feather boa round your neck singing 'Please, Please, Please, Let Me Get What I Want'.

Rose would have loved it here today. She'd have done a whole little playlet on the prom dress and re-enacted her fabulous Molly Ringwald impression. The shoes would have been perfect for her and we'd have gone down and pleaded with Mrs V for them.

Or maybe not. She loved it here once, but I suppose it can't compare with going to movie premieres and fashion shows. Old Rose would have loved the clothes. New Rose could probably meet the real Molly Ringwald in Hollywood if she wanted to, and wear real pearls, not cast-off shoes that have been moulded to someone else's feet.

Suddenly I find myself on my knees on the floor, feeling stupid for missing her so much, when it's so one-sided. Mrs V catches me there, ages later, staring into space, and sends me home.

When I get in, I double-lock the door behind me – a new habit, since those scary texts started arriving – and go upstairs to go over my notes on English Literature. Except what I end up doing is trying to learn a new chord, and reminding myself of some of the songs I've been working on. I'm in the middle of trying to work out how to play D minor, so I can get the sad tone I want for the chorus of 'You Don't Know Me' when I notice a new message on my computer screen.

Hi. What are you up to?

It's Dan Matthews, polite as always, checking I'm still OK. I tell him about the whole D minor problem and he tries to explain to me how to turn it into a complicated chord progression involving 7s and 9s that I don't really understand. He seems to assume that I'm way further ahead than I am. We progress to Skype, so he can show me, and then he offers to come round on his bike, because I am really, really bad at copying people doing stuff on a fuzzy computer screen, and it turns out his house is only a ten-minute cycle ride away.

So that's nice.

Ten minutes. It's enough time to do your hair, check your hair, realise you've overdone your hair, undo your hair, put on some lipgloss, try out the D minor chord again and notice you're in your oldest, saddest pair of jeans, but not have time to do anything about it. That guy cycles fast, even with a guitar in its case on his back.

I welcome him in and he comments on the double-locked door thing, but I say nothing. Instead, I offer him a cup of tea and he comments on the your-kitchen-is-full-of-incredible-cake thing. This, I'm happier to talk about. I tell him about Mum and the café. He realises he's been there a few times with friends from school. I tell him about Mrs Venning next door.

'We get our gig gear from that place,' he grins. Like we're two musicians just shooting the breeze about our bands.

OK, I would like my life to just run on a little loop of this moment for a while. Me and Dan in the kitchen, sampling cake and talking music. Until he takes his guitar upstairs and he shows me the chord progression he was talking about, plus how to tune the guitar properly. That's all, but it's so good. If he finds me half as interesting as I find him, he doesn't show it. Boys at school tend to want to tease you in class or get up close and personal at parties, and there isn't much in between. That's been my experience, anyway. A boy who doesn't tease or fumble within seconds of meeting you is a pleasant change. One who can play guitar like an angel is practically perfect.

An hour goes by in a moment, and then he has to go.

'That was fun,' he says, clearly meaning it with his smile. 'You made great progress. D'you want to come round tomorrow?'

He means hanging out with Call of Duty at his house. Not that I've been picturing Dan often, imagining what he's up to, including his rehearsals with the band. OK, so I have. A part of me wants to go, but the rest thinks it's a bad idea. There's his brother, who's nasty, and that girl, who's so perfect. Plus, it's all about playing music in front of people, and my recent experiences of that – today aside – have been . . . not so wonderful.

I look up to tell him no. His storm-cloud eyes look straight in to mine.

'Yeah. Sure. Thanks,' I say

'OK. Great.' He grins and gathers his guitar.

Sasha Bayley, what are you getting yourself into?

Around And
Around And
Around

In the evening, as promised, Elliot comes over to check my privacy settings. He sits at my desk, hunched over my computer, and after a minute or two of flicking around my Interface pages, he puts his head in his hands.

'You don't have any.'

'What?'

'Privacy.'

'*What?*'

He turns to me and sighs.

'Look here. All your contact info. The stuff you want your friends to see? *Everyone* can see it. It must have taken that journalist two seconds to find your Interface address. Click this.' He clicks a button. 'And go here and click this. And this. Don't say that. Never say *that*. God, Sasha!'

I grin.

'Sorry. Thanks.'

He starts staring intently at the screen, scrolling up and down, changing Interface pages, examining my user history, sighing and occasionally groaning with exasperation.

'Look at all these trolls.'

'Where?'

'Here. All these people saying rubbish stuff about you. If you'd clicked this,' he points to a button at the bottom of the screen, 'you could have blocked them. Sasha, this is terrible. All this stuff . . . You haven't been reading it, have you?'

'No,' I say, feeling uncomfortable, because I could pretty much recite every word. 'Not all of it.'

'Well, don't.'

'OK.' I bite my lip. I don't mean the next bit to come out, but somehow I can't help it. 'Except . . . there are some things I have to see. To stay safe.'

'What do you mean?' He frowns at me.

I take a deep breath. I have to tell someone, and it can't be Mum, because she'd worry. Jodie and Nell would freak. There isn't anyone else.

'I've got this . . . stalker,' I say. 'Somebody's watching me.'

He frowns.

'How do you know? What did they say?'

My fingers will hardly work but slowly, stiffly, I scroll around to find the latest message.

Saw you in your big hat today, freak. Don't worry, I'm still waiting.

It arrived yesterday, as soon as I got my old phone number working.

Elliot's voice is tight and clipped as he hunches over the screen.

'Show me the others.'

I show him.

I know where you live, Sasha Bayley. And I'm waiting.

I'm still watching you, freak. You can't get away from me now.

The time is getting closer, freak. And when I see you, you are going to die.

He turns to look at me again.

'They threatened to kill you, Sasha.'

'I know.'

'That's criminal. Even you must know that. They taught it in school in, like, Year 8. You should go to the police.'

I shrug. 'What's the point?'

It all sounded so simple and straightforward when they explained it in school. When it's a message sitting on your screen, it's different. It's just between you and the person who hates you so much they want to kill you. But they're a total stranger. It could be any one of the 327,000 people who've signed the Manic Pixie Dream Girls' hate page up to now. What could anybody do?

'They could find out who did this,' Elliot says.

Oh. Actually that sounds quite useful.

'Mind you,' he adds, 'so could I.'

'Really?'

He nods. 'But don't ask how.'

'Would you?'

'Sure. Give me a couple of days.'

'Thanks, Elliot.'

He pulls back the chair and shakes his head at me.

'Sasha, can I just say something?' he asks.

I nod.

'You are mega hot, just so's you know. But you are really, incredibly stupid about the internet.'

I would mind, except that from what he said just now, he possibly has a point.

'Yeah, maybe,' I grin.

He looks at the time in the corner of my screen.

'Oh. Nine o'clock. Not so late on the weekend.' He turns round to give me a carefully practised, casual smile. 'I don't suppose you feel like, er . . . going anywhere?'

I shake my head. My cheeks are still burning from the 'mega hot' thing.

'Sorry, Elliot. Busy. Revision. You know.'

He smiles regretfully. 'Sure. Yeah, of course.'

'But thank you. For everything.'

'No problem.'

Quickly, without another word, Elliot shoulders his backpack and heads for the door.

*

On Sunday morning I wake up early and work like a mad thing. My exam timetable is stuck to the wall above my desk. Only a few weeks to go. Days with one paper are shaded in purple, and days with two are harshly outlined in red. I wonder how Rose is coping. Is she even doing her GCSEs any more? Will she fit them in between interviews and dress fittings? She was on track to get very good grades, but I suppose she won't really need them now.

I check her fan page again. There's a picture of her in another belted dress, and she's started sharing her diet tips. That's a bit weird. Rose never had any diet tips. She just lost weight when she was miserable and put it on when she was happy. She hated people obsessing about their weight, because that's what she used to do, she said, at her old school, and all it did was stress her out. The new Rose seems to be very concerned about her figure, though.

Perhaps it's because she's a proper celebrity now. Her fan page has half a million members, who call themselves 'Rosebuds'. So many people – girls and boys alike – write on it to say how much she's inspired them. Teenstar247, for example, says she has been bullied for her size since she was ten, and she'd lost all her confidence. Now, thanks to Rose, she knows she can fulfil her ambition to be an artist:

We can do whatever we want to do. You've shown it's what's inside that counts. It's our hearts that matter.
I love you, Rose.

I imagine Rose reading every message. Has she worked out how to use whatever top-of-the-range laptop they've given her? Perhaps not, because she never seems to reply, and she clearly doesn't write the so-called updates herself. Rose would never say something like, 'Back to the studio today. So exited!' She can spell, for a start.

Even so, she must know about these people. What is it like, having them tell you that you've turned their lives around? Some of them write songs and poems for her. Others take pictures of roses and decorate them with glitter, paint and even makeup. They post them on her page and it looks beautiful.

At 2.15 the muddy Land Rover pulls up on the verge opposite the cottage, with Ed Matthews driving. He largely ignores me, but Dan leaps out to help me up the step, into the back. I'm already glad I said yes to the practice session today. Having it there, shimmering like a prize, gave me the incentive to get masses of work done this morning.

Ed steers the Land Rover confidently down the winding lanes, his right elbow resting on the open window beside him. The old radio blares classic rock and both brothers sing along. From my seat in the back, I join in.

'You know Queen?' Ed says, whipping his head round.

'Er, yes.'

I spent my first few years with a dad who played old-fashioned rock, pop and country on every radio in the house, and then there was Rose. If there was a GCSE on twentieth-century lyrics, I'd be heading for an A-star, no problem.

'Cool,' Ed says, nodding his surprised approval. We spend the rest of the journey headbanging to 'Bohemian Rhapsody'.

The boys' house is a tall, square stone building set into the side of a hill. The front drive is full of cars: a smart BMW that I'm guessing belongs to their dad, a zippy little hatchback that must be their mum's, and now the Land Rover. There's a large double garage beside the house, and I'm idly wondering why none of the cars are in it when Ed takes a key from his pocket and opens up the doors. All is explained: the dark interior contains Call of Duty's drum kit, along with a couple of mic stands and several large amps. There's even a pool table at the back.

'A proper rehearsal space!' I whistle.

'Yup,' Ed says proudly. 'Cars can get wet. Drum kits can't. And we annoy the old guys less out here than we did in the house. Dan, go and get us something to eat. The others'll be here in a minute.'

Dan shrugs and walks off. He's obviously used to being told what to do by his older brother. That leaves Ed and me alone together, which is less than ideal. I haven't forgotten 'the Massive Pixie Dreamboats', and the way he laughed at our 'one video'. Nor has he, it seems. The mood is tense while he secures the garage doors open and starts plugging things in and switching them on inside.

'So, er, well done for making the finals,' he offers, eventually.

I nod silently. He knows what happened once we got there.

'You're kind of famous now,' he continues.

I can't help a bit of a shudder. He takes pity on me.

'Dan says you're teaching yourself guitar. See much of that friend of yours?'

'Rose?' I shake my head.

'Oh. Right.'

'She's not my friend any more,' I sigh.

He looks at me with a lot more sympathy than I was expecting.

'You did what they asked. I bet people don't know the whole story.'

'No,' I say, looking at him properly for the first time, amazed at that he, of all people, should understand. I also happen to notice that when he's not sneering – and he isn't any more – he's still got that Abercrombie model thing going on. When he smiles, it's hard not to smile back. By the time Dan returns, armed with crisps, snacks and biscuits for later, the tricky atmosphere has passed.

Soon Cat, the rock-chick bassist, arrives, in skin-tight denim leggings with studs down the edges, tucked into high-heeled ankle boots that make her legs look extra long. Her blonde hair is artfully messy, her denim jacket has been perfectly and expensively graffitied, and her eyes are quickly narrowed in my direction.

'Ed?' she asks with her sweetest smile. 'Are we auditioning or something?'

'No,' Ed says. 'We don't need to. Sasha's a friend of Dan's. Dan said she could join us for a practice session.'

Cat's eyes narrow still further, until they are slits of thick mascara. 'Really?'

Her voice is cold. The brothers ignore her. They set up their instruments and I help where I can with mics, stands and leads. Cat hovers in the garage doorway, making sure her legs are shown off to their best advantage, and watches Dan. Her face clouds to scowl at me whenever his head is turned. It only takes five minutes of studying her to know for certain that she fancies him, that for some reason he's not interested, and that both brothers are fed up with her attitude. They ignore her as much as they can.

Raj, the drummer, arrives on his bike.

'Hiya Pops. Hiya Brian. Oh, hello,' (to me). 'Sorry I'm late.'

It turns out that all the boys have a nickname. Ed is 'Pops' – I assume because he's the oldest. Raj is 'Sticks'. Dan is 'Brian' after Brian May, the guitarist from Queen, and also Brian Cox, the scientist. The boys explain it's because both Brians are interested in the stars (space ones, not celebrities), and of course Dan is too. I remember the telescope. I think the name's funny. Cat rolls her eyes whenever it's used.

'Don't join in with them,' she drawls at me. 'It only encourages them. I don't play their game.'

She says so with a confident smirk, but Ed glances across at her, annoyed.

'You don't need to, when Cat suits you so well,' he says sharply.

She flashes her eyes at him.

'Anyway, Sasha already has a nickname,' he continues. 'Hotlegs, as I remember. That's what the paper said.'

I instantly go pink. Cat examines my legs. So do the boys. My jeans aren't as figure-hugging as her leggings, and I'm wearing old trainers, not high-heeled boots. I doubt I provide much competition, but Cat seems to think so.

'How gross,' she says, rearranging her gorgeous tawny hair with her fingers and leaving the word 'gross' hanging in the air.

A few weeks ago, she would have crushed me. I know I'm not in Cat's league in the glamour stakes. But she so underestimates what I've been through these last few weeks, and her classic mean-girl attempts to cut me out are clearly backfiring with the rest of the band.

I bet Dan hasn't bought *her* a phone, I think to myself, flashing her a friendly smile. She flicks her hair angrily and saunters away from me to set up her bass.

'Right, guys,' Ed announces. 'I think we're ready. I'm in the mood for some Arcade Fire. Raj, can you do the intro to 'Month of May'?

Raj gathers himself for a moment, then launches into a tight, well-rehearsed beat. Cat joins him on bass, sounding as super-cool as she looks. Ed and Dan are soon adding guitar and vocals. I come in where I can. All around me, people are smiling, as they concentrate on the music. Even Cat: she can't stop herself when the tune gets going and she nails a riff. The garage thrums to the rhythm. I spin to the words 'Around and around and around and around', and I find myself laughing. We end that song and Ed announces the next one. If I don't know the words, I look them up on my phone. No worries about harmonies this time – just belting out the lyrics in time to the music.

I have a rock voice. Bert, the musical director at Killer Act, spotted it, but the Manic Pixie Dream Girls sang pop, so I adjusted. Now I don't have to. My gravelly alto perfectly suits the post-punk/indie rock direction Call of Duty are heading in. This is not like singing with the Pixies: it's harsher and louder and, for me, loads more fun. If I could accompany myself on guitar too, it would be perfect.

Dan seems to read my thoughts. When we stop for biscuits, crisps and anything else he could scrounge from the kitchen, he offers to do a quick catch-up on where we got to yesterday.

He hands me his guitar, and I do a run-through of one of the songs I'm working on, 'Between the Lines'. I've been practising every night and having listened to Rose for so long, I know how the thing's supposed to sound. It's starting to feel natural, too. The transitions from major to minor keys send a shiver down my spine.

Cat notices what we're doing, and strops off into a corner to practise some advanced riffs on her bass. She's much better than me, of course, and she really doesn't need to try so hard. Dan ignores her. If anything, he gets closer to me. But he seems to hesitate before putting his hands near mine on the fretboard, to show me what he means.

I am determined not to seem like a groupie, so I pretend not to notice the warmth of his skin, or how well his biceps fit his T-shirt, or the low, sexy hum of his voice as he speaks.

Later I catch him looking at me with the same sort of wonder that George Drury had in his eyes before the disaster kiss at the music festival. This time, I'm not sure the kiss would be such a disaster. But, Dan's such a gentleman that he accompanies me home with nothing more than a smile.

Geeks And Nerds And Freaks

'**B**reathless', recorded in about two days flat, enters the charts at number one. Not surprising, given that the video of Rose playing it for the first time on Killer Act has now reached eighty million hits worldwide. Interface News releases an interview with her to accompany the launch. There she is, in yet another slim, belted dress, sitting on a sofa in what seems to be a posh hotel.

I watch the video on my laptop, sitting in bed and wondering slightly who this famous girl is, the one I hardly seem to recognise. She looks sophisticated in her signature half-up, half-down hairdo and dark, dark eyes to contrast with her pale skin. She seems tired, though, and not as excited as I would expect for a teenager with a song at number one.

Perhaps it's something to do with the interview questions, and the interviewer insisting on trying to find out who 'Breathless' is about. Looking uncomfortable, Rose keeps explaining that it's about no one in particular, just an idea of a boy. I remember how we used to talk about it a lot, listening to music in her room or mine – how great lyrics and poems can be inspired by many things, not just one specific event. Besides, she never had a serious boyfriend while I knew her. Not that serious, anyway, and I bet it's something else, like the 'Sausages' story, that she doesn't need the world to know.

But, when they ask her about recording the song, her face lights up as she describes how incredible it was to work on it in a proper studio, surrounded by some of the greatest session musicians in the business.

'It was one of the best moments of my life,' she says, eyes shining.

Yeah. She doesn't need to sit around in your bedroom, Sasha, talking about lyrics and ideal boys. She's got the best musicians in the world to work with now. No wonder she hasn't been returning your calls.

As I'm thinking this, my phone goes.

'Have you seen it?'

It's Jodie.

'Oh, hi. The interview? Watching it now.'

'Did you see what she was wearing?'

'Not particularly.'

'It's Dolce & Gabbana. I've just checked it out in this week's *Grazia*. It costs over a thousand quid.'

196

'It looks good on her,' I sigh. Although I'm not sure Mrs Venning would approve.

Jodie snorts. 'I thought it made her look old.'

'You're just jealous, Jodie.'

'Who? Me? Yeah. *Totally.*'

'I'm not so sure. D'you think she looks happy?'

'Yes. Of course I do. What are you on about?' Jodie says, as if I'm mad.

Watching the screen, Rose looks blissful *now* – now she's talking about the music. Maybe I was wrong about before. Do I just *want* things to be difficult for her, because she chose singing over staying with us? Am I that mean?

Once I put the phone down, I feel a new song forming in my head. Something hurt and confused, called 'Broken', maybe, or 'No Way Back'.

With 'Breathless' at the top of the charts, you'd think half the girls at school had been in Rose's closest circle, and they still haven't forgiven the rest of us for what we did. I'm getting used to being deliberately knocked in corridors every day, and Nina Pearson having the sound of me shrieking when I was Coked as the message alert on her phone. It's normal now to see photos online from parties I wasn't invited to. I used to feel sorry for the geeks and nerds and freaks and loners keeping their heads down in corridors, avoiding the looks and comments. Now I know how they feel, because that's me too.

Except that I'm *special*. Still famous. Still sucks.

That Coke video has gone viral. People are talking about it in Japan. Rose Ireland fans send me hate mail every day. And worst of all, somebody, somewhere is watching me so closely they know what hat I'm wearing. They're thinking about me and I'm thinking about them, all the time.

I'm talking to Jodie and Nell near the vending machines as Elliot careers down the corridor towards us, practically knocking us over. A friendly geek. I see him in a new light now. And he certainly seems happy to see me, despite the awkwardness in my room the last time we met.

'I've found her,' he says to me, out of breath and excited.

'Her? Who?' I ask.

He looks uncertainly at Jodie and Nell, who stare at me, confused.

'It's OK,' I say to him. 'Whatever it is, you can tell all of us.'

He pauses for a moment and lowers his voice. 'Your stalker. She's here,' he says. 'She's in this school.'

'No!'

My smile vanishes. I suddenly feel ice cold. I'm being stalked by someone in this *building*?

'WHAT?' Jodie shrieks. 'You have a *stalker*?'

I nod dumbly.

'Why didn't you tell us, you idiot?'

'Because . . . I knew you'd freak.'

'I'm freaking NOW. You have a STALKER?'

'You don't have to tell the whole school,' I whisper nervously.

Jodie lowers her voice and turns to Elliot. 'So, who is it? Someone we've heard of?'

He nods.

'It's Michelle Lee,' he says. 'The number traces back to her phone.'

Oh my God. Michelle Lee. She's one of the most popular girls in school. The last time I saw her properly, she was giving me a hug at George Drury's party. She's his girlfriend, the Cheryl Cole lookalike. I need to sit down. Nell takes me by the elbow, clearly worried about me.

'Do you want to go to the Head?' Elliot asks, with what sounds like a little reluctance. 'We should report her.'

'You bet,' Jodie says, hands on hips, eyes blazing.

But I shake my head. I need to think about this first. They take me into the nearest empty classroom and find me a chair. I breathe deeply. I don't know whether to laugh or cry. *Michelle Lee?* I would never in a million years have expected it to be her.

'Why on earth would Michelle stalk you?' Nell asks.

I shake my head. 'No idea.'

'What did she do, exactly?'

I tell them about the texts.

'She threatened to *kill* you, and you didn't tell us?' Jodie bellows, raising her voice again.

'I . . . I didn't think you could help.'

In fact, I assumed Jodie would stomp around, just like she's doing, and panic, when all I wanted to do was forget it. I don't want to forget it now, though. Not since Elliot's news. I can feel my anger slowly rising to the surface, to match Jodie's tone. It was different when I thought it was some scary stranger sending me those messages. But a girl at my school? Someone who sees me every day? Making me so frightened I could hardly go out on my own?

How dare she?

'If you do report her to Mrs Richards,' Elliot says, 'and you should – can you just not mention how you found

199

out about her? I kind of used certain databases I'm not supposed to know about, and . . .'

I sigh. 'Mrs Richards will guess, you know. She'll work it out. She's not that stupid.'

He hangs his head.

'Yeah. Whatever.'

'Mrs Richards is too good for her,' Jodie grumbles. 'Way too good for her. God, if I could get my hands on her . . .'

Jodie has a point. Maybe it's possible to deal with this without bringing in the Head. I thought this person could be some crazy armed stalker, hiding in bushes with God-knows-what weapon. Now that I know she's just a girl in Year 12 with excessive hair extensions, I want answers.

'I want to meet her,' I say. 'I want her to look me in the eye and tell me why she did this.'

Nell looks nervous. 'Are you *crazy*?'

'Probably,' I admit. Being stalked by a Cheryl Cole lookalike can have that effect. But I realise I don't really want to do it on my own.

Meanwhile, Jodie is still blazing with fury on my behalf.

'Let's do it,' she says. 'The drama studio. Tomorrow, after school. It'll be empty then. We'll come with you, won't we, Nell?'

Nell gulps and nods. 'Of course.'

I grin at them gratefully, get out my new phone and send Michelle a message on Interface, while Jodie dictates.

We need to talk. Drama studio. Tomorrow, four o'clock.

'D'you think she'll come?'
'When she sees it's from you, she will,' Jodie says.
Two minutes later, the message comes back.

OK.

I'm terrified and excited. I know it's probably the wrong thing, but it feels so good to be doing *something* finally.

You Don't Know Me: Part 2

As soon as I get home I pull out the guitar, to help me understand how I'm feeling. It's becoming second nature these days.

Before, making music was just a game – something we did to have fun and relax. Now, it's what I do when I need to find the real me again. It's how I explore my happiness and sadness. I'm starting to understand those days when Rose was composing songs and she didn't need to see me. I used to feel a bit hurt, though I never told her, but if she was making things out of words and sounds the way I am now, I get why she needed to be alone for a while.

I've already filled up my first notebook with lyrics, and now I write them on an app I've downloaded onto my new phone. Some are hopeless – in fact, many of them are. Others are pages long and contain only two lines that I might seriously use. Others are brief and perfect – to me, anyway. They seem to capture moments of pure emotion. Some already have their tunes attached, in my head, or recorded on my phone, using Molly the guitar.

The very worst is probably 'Nina? Be seein' ya': a funny, angry verse I wrote one day when I got in from school. I sing it often, because belting out those words as I strum the guitar is as good for the soul as one of Mum's chocolate gateaux. The best, I think, is 'You Don't Know Me'. I thought that song would turn out angry too, but it didn't. It twisted away from me as I wrote, and ended up hopeful.

I do love that little song. Tonight, I sing it over and over, thinking of Michelle.

'You don't know me
You think you do but
You have never felt the fire I feel inside . . .
If you knew me, you would want to understand me
Don't judge me; don't hurt me; don't wound me
Get to know me'

Somehow, capturing all my fear and anger and frustration, and fragmenting it, then recombining it into the words of a song, makes it easier to bear.

Afterwards, I Google Rose on my computer again. It's become second nature by now. According to the E!

channel, she's lining up a tour of America. She'll finally get to see all those places we dreamed about. She recently sang at a birthday party for a visiting Hollywood star. She supports two animal charities. She's working on an album.

The news on FaceFeed is that she has hired a tutor to help her with her GCSEs. His name is Jamie and he is tall, blond and fit. They go out on dinners together a lot. There are endless pictures of her arriving with him at expensive restaurants in a black, fur-trimmed coat and dramatic makeup, looking ten years older than she really is. Jodie was right about that. It's partly due to the makeup and partly because she looks tired. Very tired. I'm sure it's not just my imagination. But then, she's a busy girl.

Her Interface page states that she's finally recording the advert that was her prize for winning Killer Act. Rose's face will be projected onto several large buildings in major cities in England, the US, Japan and China when the ad launches in May. Our school will be bursting with cameras and news crews for the big moment. The song is expected to become her second number one.

Oh yes, and she's not only coming back for the launch. She's going to be moving back to Castle Bigelow for a little while, so she can work on the new album. According to her Interface page, she:

cant' wait to get home to the green fields of home, wear it all started. Castle B, here I come!

Who *writes* this stuff for her? Why does she let them? And, more to the point, why on earth didn't she tell us she was coming home?

Finally, according to the celeb-watching sites, she has

lost weight, but is still 'attractively curvy'. She is planning on buying a flat in London, and she has already bought her granny a car.

I don't know how much of the news is accurate, but it's true about the car: it's a little red Fiat, parked in the lane leading to the farm. Aurora Ireland admitted to Mum that she doesn't dare drive it in case it gets scratched or dented. She likes to admire it from her bedroom window, though. It reminds her of Rose.

'She's beyond up herself now,' Jodie grumbles at lunch next day. 'She's gone through herself and out the other side.'

'I must say, I'm surprised,' Nell admits. 'Did you see that bit about her fainting at a fashion show? They thought she might've been drinking.'

I shake my head. 'Don't be silly. That doesn't sound like her. They'll say anything.'

Nell picks at her unappetising pizza topping. 'I suppose so . . .'

'But you know these pop stars and their crazy lifestyles,' Jodie shrugs.

'Was she really not going to tell us she was coming home?' I ask. This is the thing that's been bothering me most.

'What d'you mean, not tell us?' Jodie says. 'Didn't you get the invitation?'

'What invitation?'

'Haven't you checked your email today?'

Actually, I haven't. For about the first time in my life, I was so busy thinking about meeting up with Michelle Lee later on, and wondering if she'll really show up, and if she'll bring half of Year 12 with her, that I totally forgot to turn my phone on this morning. I haven't checked it since last night.

Nell sees my blank look. 'We've been asked to have a special meeting with Rose when she comes. Next week. For that Rose Ireland Special thing she's recording. They want us to get together and confront our issues. They say it will be a good way to get closure.'

It's quite funny to hear Ivan Jenks's vocabulary coming out of Nell's mouth. You can almost see the quotation marks in the air.

'Did they mention preserving the drama, by any chance?'

'No,' Nell sighs. 'Not this time.'

'Well, I'm not doing it,' Jodie says firmly. 'Why should we? You were right, Sash. They're just going to make us look stupid again. Mum says we should keep our heads down until this whole things blows over.'

'I suppose that's true,' I agree, reluctantly. 'But—'

'Anyway,' Jodie goes on, 'can't you just picture it? Us all huddled round one of these tables in our school uniforms and Rose wafting in in some designer number and fifteen layers of control pants? She used to be so cool, but I swear they make her look more like Roxanne Wills every day . . .'

'Oh, it wouldn't be here,' Nell says. 'It's wherever Rose is staying. Wait.'

She gets out her phone and scrolls around to find the email from the TV people. While she does so, I mouth, 'Wherever Rose is staying?' to Jodie. She rolls her eyes.

'I know. I mean, it's not as if she can stay with her own grandparents, right? Not when she's got a whole entourage of people with her. God, I never believed she could turn into such a monster. She's like Queen bleeding Elizabeth the First now, doing her progress round the country. She needs a mansion.'

'Here we go,' Nell says. 'It's a place called Lockwood House. Isn't that the posh hotel on the road to Bath? I'll check it out. Hey, you're right!'

'Right how?' Jodie asks.

'It's Elizabethan. Look at it. All Tudor beams and stuff. It's really, really posh. They do four-poster beds and horse riding in the grounds and there's a spa and English teas with champagne. I wonder if we'd get one of those . . .' She goes all dreamy for a moment.

'We're not going, remember?' Jodie says.

'Oh, right.'

Nell puts her phone down on the table in front of her, looking dutiful but slightly disappointed. I lean over to get a look at Lockwood House. It is a gorgeous, ancient, stately-home affair, with a sweeping drive lined with vast oak trees and what look like Rolls-Royces and Aston Martins parked outside.

I have to say, if I was offered the chance of staying there for a few days, instead of my room at home, I'd certainly have to think about it. Actually, I wouldn't: it would be Lockwood House every time. I turn the screen towards Jodie and say nothing.

'Blimey!' she splutters.

'And we wouldn't be in school uniform,' Nell adds. 'We could wear nice stuff.'

'And it would give us a chance to find out how she is,' I muse aloud.

'Oh yeah,' Jodie scoffs. 'And it would give *her* a chance to find out how *we* are.'

I nod. 'Well yes, that too.'

The mood shifts. We all sit around, brooding, while Jodie scrolls through more pictures of the hotel. Whereas five minutes ago it seemed obvious that this meeting was a stupid, crazy, rude idea, now it seems like an interesting, crazy, rude idea. We get to see Rose, finally – and goodness knows, I need to. We get to see Lockwood House close up. We possibly get to sneak some champagne, if we're lucky.

True, we remind the public who we are, which is the last thing we need, but perhaps we really will get some sort of 'closure'. Closure: coming to terms with a bad experience. It's a horrible, horrible word – not a Rose word at all – but I actually need some. What's going on between us now still hurts.

'So?' Jodie says eventually. 'I take it we're going?'

Nell and I nod.

'We're going to regret this,' she continues.

She's probably right. We've done a lot of stuff we've regretted. We're good at it.

'Do you think Mrs Venning will lend us some stuff?' she asks. 'You're right, Nell: we need to look the part.'

'I'm sure she will,' I say, with a little sigh.

It's not a happy sigh. Not an 'I'm going to be an English lady at a posh country house hotel' sigh. Not even Jodie's 'I'm going to give Queen Rose a piece of my mind' sigh. It's not jealous or angry, it's melancholy.

Melancholy – which *is* a Rose word. I don't know what's happened to her, exactly, but I still miss her.

Back Into The Light

f irst, though, we have something else to do that we may quite possibly live to regret: Michelle Lee at four o'clock. I spend the afternoon in a semi-panic, just thinking about it. I could never go through with it if it wasn't for Jodie and Nell.

After school, we meet again to go to the drama studio. As Jodie predicted, the place is deserted. We leave the door ajar and head inside to wait. The time ticks by: 4.10. 4.15. Just as we're starting to wonder if Michelle has simply decided to ignore me, Jodie puts a finger to her lips. We hear the sound of high heels on the tarmac outside. Michelle is not known for her sensible footwear. She is also, thank goodness, alone. I have no idea what we'd have done if she'd shown up in company.

She pokes her head round the door, searching us out in the dim light. She's all glossy locks and big eyelashes and total innocent surprise.

'Hello? Sasha Bayley? Can I help you?'

I step forward, into the shaft of light from the open door. Jodie and Nell step out behind me, like henchmen. This could totally be a scene from an action movie. But with heels and hair extensions, in Michelle's case.

'Yes. I think you can,' I say. 'The texts. I know it was you, Michelle.'

I'm getting good at this, after challenging Elliot about the votes. I don't think I sound nearly as nervous as I feel. Michelle steps gingerly into the room, but maintains her innocent expression.

'Sorry? Me what?'

I pause for effect. I do believe Jodie and Nell have got their hands on their hips behind me. I hope we look like Charlie's Angels.

'You sent me death threats. I've got them all. And they come from your number.'

Michelle stops dead and her breathing quickens, but she regains her composure.

'I don't know what you're talking about. *Death threats? That's crazy. I* never sent any death threats.'

There's a wild, panicked look in her eyes now. Nell and Jodie step forward to stand beside me. I take my phone out of my pocket and show her the screen. Its dim light glows eerily in the gloom of the darkened studio. Elliot has organised it so all Michelle's messages show up, one after the other.

For a moment, she can't speak. I can see little beads of sweat on her forehead, silhouetted by the light from the open door. When she does talk, the words struggle to come out.

'I . . . I don't know what you mean. Those aren't from me. I didn't do that. I . . . I don't even know you.'

'That's true,' I say with a sigh. 'You don't. But you still sent these. We can prove it.'

Please don't ask me how. Please don't ask me how. I don't want Elliot to go to jail for hacking the database.

More sweat beads appear on Michelle's forehead. I keep talking while I have the advantage.

'See that third message?' I ask. 'It's a criminal offence to send death threats. I'm going to have to go to the police.'

'No!'

Her sudden shout echoes through the drama studio. She holds her hand out to face me, palm up, in a gesture of horror. Her mouth is a big, round 'O'.

Mine is a thin, straight line. Beside me, Jodie looks very menacing, and even Nell looks slightly less babe-ish than usual, and more than slightly annoyed.

'Why did you do it?' I ask.

Michelle crumples. Straight down onto the floor of the studio, crying.

'Because of George. Because of you kissing him at the festival. He told me all about it when you were on TV. He didn't realise what he was saying, he was just boasting to his friends. You evil . . .'

Through her tears, she looks up at me angrily. I glare back at her.

'I did not kiss him. He kissed *me*,' I point out in a rage. And then it hits me. 'So this isn't about Killer Act at all? Apart from me being on TV.'

Her mouth forms an ugly, self-pitying pout.

'Who cares about a stupid talent show? I only care about George!'

I wait for a moment while she cries some more. Wow. She really has it bad for the boy. I would feel some sympathy – given his tendency to kiss other girls behind speaker stacks – if it wasn't for the fact that SHE RECENTLY THREATENED TO KILL ME.

Jodie looks at me, raising an eyebrow. Oh yeah – the whole kiss thing. Haven't mentioned it till now. I'll have some explaining to do shortly. But for now I just shrug and turn back to Michelle.

After a while, the sobbing dies down.

'But I didn't mean it, any of it. Please, Sasha.'

'You know what they said in those cyber safety classes,' I say, echoing Elliot's little talk. 'It's a criminal offence. Look – the evidence is here. I *have* to call the police.'

I flash the phone screen at her again, with the messages still on it, backlit against the semi-darkness, and she flinches away from it.

'Please! No! Anything! No! I didn't mean to say those things. They were just a joke. I . . .'

She sobs harder. Jodie lowers over her, eyes flashing. She knows how it must have felt for me. When 370,000 people already officially hate you . . . that's no joke.

'Police now?' Jodie asks, pulling out her BlackBerry. 'I can call them from here if you like, Sash.'

I simply stare at Michelle. Her whole body is shaking with the effort of her frightened crying. She's not a

212

hulking stalker in the bushes; she's just a stupid, selfish girl. She's a stupid, selfish girl and I am free of her.

After a couple more sobs, she tries to get up from the floor, but it's not easy in high heels. Eventually, I hold out a hand to help her. She takes it without looking at me.

'Are you calling them, then?' she asks, sulkily, rising to her feet.

'I haven't decided,' I say. Although I have. I don't need them now, and Elliot doesn't need the trouble. 'If I *ever* get a message like that from you again . . .'

'You won't! You won't! I promise. And those other ones . . . you'll delete them, right?'

'No.' I eye her coldly. 'Even if I did, they'd still be out there somewhere. Once it's on the web, it stays there, remember?'

'Oh!'

She looks so upset that a tiny part of me wants to comfort her, but I'm not going to. Things were bad enough before, but she put me through hell. What she did was horrific and now that I come to think of it, she still hasn't apologised to me. She just cried. She's still crying as she runs back out of the studio.

Jodie and Nell put their arms around me.

'You were fantastic!' Nell says. 'Pure Powerpuff Girl.'

'I was thinking Charlie's Angels actually.'

Jodie laughs. 'OK. That works.'

We make our way slowly, arm in arm, back into the light.

It occurs to me that not sharing things with Nell and Jodie was possibly not my best idea. Sure, I used to share most things with Rose, but SHE'S NOT HERE NOW. And sure, Jodie freaked about the whole stalker thing to start with, but once she calmed down she was actually very helpful. More than that, she was brilliant. I couldn't have done all that stuff in the studio without her. OK, so I was stupid for not telling her before.

Slowly, gradually, I start talking. I accept Nell's offer of a revision night together, and while I'm over at her house, I tell her and Jodie about George Drury. They're sympathetic. It feels so much better now it's not a guilty secret any more. And I tell them about my songs. They don't laugh at me, they want to hear them. When I play the recordings on my phone, they really like them. They have suggestions for improvements – good suggestions, which I take on board.

Next time, we meet at my place and I play them on my guitar. When we get to 'You Don't Know Me', Nell says, 'Ooh! This one's good!' and she and Jodie sing along. Their harmonies take the song to new places. It's almost like the old times. Almost.

Why did I spend so much time being jealous of what Rose could do, rather than trying it myself? I suppose she was the serious musician, the sophisticated girl from London, and I was just the dancer, the party girl . . . But nobody can go through what happened to Jodie, Nell and me and be 'just' anything. We are Charlie's Angels and we are amazing. OK, so we don't have two million fans and a hot record deal, but we're still here. I think we can be pretty proud of that.

Like It's Going To Be That Easy

We don't do catsuits this time, or sequin shorts, for the 'closure' meeting at the posh hotel. For a start, we are so not in a sequin shorts mood. And also, Lockwood House is not a sequin shorts place. Yes, if you're Kylie, filming a video. No, if you're anybody else, doing anything else at all.

Jodie forsakes her normal lumberjack shirts and combat boots for a pale blue dress with a pleated skirt, a tie-on pearl collar and high-heeled Mary Janes. I have never, ever seen her look like this. She sighs at herself in the mirror, adding a dash of orangey-red lipstick and brushing her hair into dark, obedient waves.

'If you're going to do these things, you might as well do them properly. Do I look ladylike enough, d'you think?'

'You look . . .'

'Weird, right?'

She sighs again. Nell and I stare at her reflection.

'If you're sure . . .' Nell says, uncertainly.

'It's not Dolce & Gabbana, but it'll do,' Jodie pronounces.

Nell chooses a red dress with a high neckline and a short, dainty skirt that makes her look uncannily like she's channelling Taylor Swift. I'm not sure who *I'm* channelling. I just know that the simple navy shift dress I'm wearing suits my mood.

'Wow! Grown up!' Nell says.

'Perfect funeral attire,' Jodie observes.

She's right. That's how it feels: the funeral of a friendship. Conducted under the lights and boom mics of reality TV. Personally, I wouldn't want to watch it, but maybe somebody will.

They send a car for us, and a producer with another sackful of release forms for us to sign, giving them the right to use the film how they like, and us the right to do nothing at all.

I sit in the back with Jodie and Nell. The car whisks us round the dusky lanes in near silence. When we arrive at the gates to Lockwood House, we turn off the country road with its untidy hedges, and into a new world of landscaped avenues, crunchy gravel and soft, hidden lighting under the trees. As we round a corner, the trees seem to part like a magic curtain, and there is the house ahead of us: long and low, built in mellow gold stone that seems to glow in the evening light, with tall, mullioned windows and a steep, sloping roof. White peacocks, strutting on the lawn outside, turn to look at us. They look a lot more at home here than we do. Outclassed by a flightless bird on arrival. Fabulous.

A man in a smart green jacket miraculously appears at the front door as we draw up to it, and shows us in. Inside, the hallway is large and dark, lined with old oak panelling, lit by a dim chandelier. We wait in our vintage finery, admiring portraits of grand Elizabethans in big gilt frames, while the receptionist sends someone off 'to see if they're ready for us'.

'I wish they'd brought us here when we were studying the Tudors,' Jodie grumbles under her breath. 'It would have saved a lot of trouble Googling Elizabethan architecture.'

'I doubt they do school visits,' I whisper, as a woman in an immaculate silk dress and heavy jewellery descends the stairs.

'To think Rose is actually staying here for weeks,' Nell breathes.

'Hi girls! She's ready for you now,' announces a voice from behind us. It's Janet, the floor manager from our audition, with her trusty clipboard under her arm and her trusty harassed expression on her face. 'We thought we'd meet in the parlour. My . . . don't you look different?'

It's impossible to tell whether she means different, good or different, bad. She's already bustling us off down panelled corridors, past more portrait-lined rooms, to a roped-off area at the back of the house, with a temporary sign on a post saying 'Quiet – Filming'.

So this is Rose's new world. The room we enter is not large, but it's elegant and comfortable, scattered with sofas and armchairs in rich, jewel colours, set off by the vivid blue of the portrait-lined walls. It would be more comfortable if it wasn't currently crammed with camera equipment, lights, sound equipment, a cameraman, a producer and a worried-looking hotel manager, anxious that everyone has everything they need. As it is, we hover in the doorway, searching for Rose, uncertain what to do.

'If you'll just sit over here,' Janet says, bustling us towards an arrangement of sofas near the window, 'we can get on. Rose will be joining us in a minute. Now, when she comes, I want you all to be totally natural. You're just catching up and explaining what you've been up to since the show. Obviously there's been some . . . awkwardness . . . so you might want to talk about that. I can give you some suggestions if you need them. Does anyone want a drink of water?'

We shake our heads. So no tea, then. And no champagne. Just a rising feeling of nausea and the certainty that, yet again, we're making a mistake.

We all take the same sofa, squeezing up together, with Nell in the middle. No need to wonder what Jodie's thinking – what is Queen Rose up to? Is she in her state room, arranging peacock feathers in her hair, like some sort of star from *Downton Abbey*? Meanwhile, a makeup lady dashes in to powder our faces, in keeping with the 'totally natural' look.

After a few minutes, we hear footsteps in the corridor. A young man in a black T-shirt appears and nods to Janet: 'She's here.' The lights are given a final adjustment. The cameras roll. A new wave of nerves and nausea hits me.

Behind the producer, Rose emerges slowly, peering past the crew to find our faces, pausing when she does.

Rose! Here at last. I want to get up. My instinct is to hug her, but I quickly remind myself – this is the new Rose, the one I hardly know. Instead, I stay close to Jodie and Nell.

She's not what we expected at all. She's dressed in black leggings and a grey hoodie, with no visible makeup, and her hair in a messy bun. Instead of rushing over to say hi, she waits in the doorway, clutching a bottle of water, staring and saying nothing. Without makeup, she looks even more tired than usual. And now, in our finery, we look like idiots.

Janet goes over to her and mutters something in her ear.

'Sorry,' she mouths, and goes out again. When she comes back, she takes a breath at the doorway and comes over to meet us, with a big fake smile on her face.

'Hi! Sasha! Nell! Jodie! How great to see you again.'

She sits down opposite us. Her voice is forced and her eyes look desperate. We smile our own rictus smiles. In the silence, you can almost hear the tumbleweed rolling across the room. This has to be the worst TV ever.

I glance across at Janet, who nods at us and makes a rolling motion with her hands for SOMEBODY to say SOMETHING.

'So, er, Rose, how do you like the hotel?' I ask.

Really? Did I just say that? Like she's a stranger, visiting from Japan.

'It's very nice.'

Nice. Not exactly a Rose word. Not for an Elizabethan mansion. She looks down at her hands, which are twisting nervously in her lap. I notice that the hoodie is cashmere. So she's not totally slumming it, outfit-wise.

'You three look . . . nice,' she says, staring at us.

Her hands are going like socks in a washing machine now. She doesn't want to be here. We don't want to be here. She still hasn't forgiven us. She seems to be regretting the whole trip. When she looks up, her eyes are deep pools of misery.

Tears form and threaten to spill over. 'I'm sorry.' She turns away and wipes at her face with a cashmere sleeve. Then she turns to Janet. 'Can we do that again?'

'Don't worry,' Janet says. 'We'll edit it out. Keep going. Perhaps you could talk about how you all feel now, about what happened on the show?'

'What, like when a million people all sent us hate messages?' Jodie asks.

Rose gasps, but it's hardly news any more. Everybody avoids everybody else's eye. I want to say something to break the silence, but all I can think of is the railway bridge, and how I felt before Dan came and found me. Charlie's Angels are nowhere to be found. This was such a bad idea. One of our worst.

More tumbleweed. Janet checks her notes.

'So why don't you talk about what you've been up to?'

Jodie nods. 'Sure. Why not?' She purses her lips for a moment, then leans forward with a dangerously innocent, quizzical expression.

'So, Rose . . . what have you been up to recently? Apart from the fashion shows, and the number one?'

Rose blinks and takes a breath. She knows when Jodie's playing with people.

'Erm, I'm doing the ad for Interface. You know we're

launching it at St Christopher's? And we're, er, trying out some songs for the album,' she adds with false brightness. 'There's such a great recording studio at Jim's house, and I'm going there every day. And then there's the tour.' Now her words tumble out in a rush. 'It's been very busy. I had no idea it would be like this since I won. It's lovely, of course. I've had such a great time. I've met lots of my heroes. I get to stay in beautiful places.' She flaps her hands around, indicating the room. 'It feels like I'm always on the move.'

She laughs a high, nervous laugh.

'Wow,' Jodie says, in the flattest voice in the universe. It comes out remarkably like 'Oh yeah?'

'So I haven't had much time to keep in touch,' Rose goes on with a brittle smile. 'I'm sorry. But how are you all?'

I've been thinking about the recording studio at 'Jim's house'. It's well-known around school that Jim Fisher, who's one of the biggest guitarists from the Eighties, has a stately home a bit like this one not far from here, with its own studio in the grounds. So Rose is on first name terms with Jim Fisher. His last house guest, according to school rumour, was Elton John.

'We're fine,' I say, dully, remembering the moment I was Coked. She could have texted. It would have helped. It would have helped a lot.

'Well, that's good,' she says, brittle as a pane of glass. 'I'm glad you came today. It seems a long time since we were the Manic Pixie Dream Girls.'

The name makes all of us flinch. It doesn't conjure up happy memories.

Then I realise how it must look: the three thin girls on

one sofa, radiating hostility, and the 'attractively curvy' one opposite them, looking upset. Oh my God. Just like it was before.

Why is this happening? What about the hate campaign we went through, when all her fans turned on us, and all the apologies I sent her, and the fact that a part of me still wants to go over to her and give her a hug? Why is all the real stuff so impossible to say on 'reality' TV?

After another long tumbleweed moment, Janet takes pity on us and says with a sigh, 'Well, that was very . . . er . . . Thanks for coming, anyway.'

They turn the cameras off, at last, and kill the lights. Some of the tension seeps out of the room.

'How's the new song going?' I ask Rose as we're getting up to go. 'The one for the ad?'

She looks startled that I'm still talking to her. 'Oh, it's fine.'

'Is Jim helping with it?'

She glances at me, to see if I'm being serious or teasing her about her famous friends. To be honest, I don't know myself.

'Yes. He is, actually. As much as anyone can.'

She sighs. She seems even more exhausted close to, and the smile she gives me is one of the saddest I've ever seen. Especially from someone in a cashmere jumper.

Janet announces that our driver is ready.

'Well, that was *nice*, wasn't it?' Jodie spits, as we're led quickly down the corridor.

It's still early evening. Jodie's mum invites us back to her place for a cup of tea and some much-needed food to recover. Homework will have to wait tonight. None of us

222

can concentrate after that disaster.

We take our drinks and pizza slices up to Jodie's room. Her brother Sam pops his head round the door with an excited grin. Next to him is Elliot, in a World of Warcraft T-shirt. He gives me a quick, shy smile. I smile back. I've already texted him about the Michelle Lee thing, so he knows that went OK.

'How was your meeting?' Sam asks. 'Did you see any other famous people? Are you seriously going to be on TV again?'

'It was an epic fail,' Jodie sighs. 'I hope we're *not* going to be on TV again. I don't even know why she wanted to see us.'

'Oh.' The boys look disappointed and leave us to it.

'We are, though, aren't we?' I say dejectedly, once they've gone.

'What?'

'Going to be on TV again. Looking like the three Wicked Witches of the West.'

'Oh God,' Jodie adds. 'Wait till Ivan Jenks has finished editing us. Did you see how they set us up? With us three on one sofa and Rose all alone on the other?'

'Well we did kind of choose our own places . . .' Nell interrupts, but Jodie ignores her.

'It's going to be worse than last time.'

'Oh, no,' Nell objects. 'It can't possibly be worse than last time.'

'She looked so unhappy,' I say, still puzzling over it. 'Like she didn't even want to be there. And if she didn't want to talk to us . . . why did she ask us to come?'

That's the biggest mystery of all. We sit around for ages, going over and over the weirdness of the meeting, but the only thing we can all agree on is that it really can't go out on the Rose Ireland Special. We're going to have to do something to get them to edit us out. We know we have no control over the TV company, because of those release forms we signed, letting them do whatever they wanted with the recording. We'll have to appeal to Rose.

'I'll call her,' I offer.

Like it's going to be that easy. Like she answers my calls any more.

When I try, it goes to voicemail. Next day I message her on Interface and, as expected these days, we get no reply. I call her gran, and ask her to pass a message on. She promises she will. Nothing.

After school, we call the hotel, to leave a message for Rose to get in touch, and we're told that they have no record of a Rose Ireland staying there. We know that's a ruse to protect celebrities' privacy, so we explain that we're old friends. (Not that you'd think so, if you'd seen the TV footage they just shot, but anyway.) Still nothing. So we call the TV company after all. They keep putting us on hold, or not getting back to us. Besides, we know they won't help us. By now we're beyond frustrated. We just can't let #dropthefatgirl happen to us again.

Stargazer

fed up, I'm surfing the web at home as usual. According to Rose's Interface page she's

Livin' the high life in the country!

And there's a picture of a pile of clothes strewn across a four-poster bed.

Ew. Whoever Rose is now, she is not that girl. Why even have a fan page if it doesn't say the truth about you? She's turning out as fake as all the stars she used to hate, and I can't bear it. I message Jodie, to share my disgust, but she's busy revising. So is Nell. I should be too, of course, but I'm too upset to work. Too upset, even, to grab

Molly and work on a song. Instead, I find myself messaging other people. Messaging Dan.

> *How are you doing? Not feeling too musical tonight.*

He replies instantly.

> *Got a problem? Need to talk? It must be bad if the music's not working.*

Yeah, it's bad. We chat online for a while, but he soon points out that he's only ten minutes away by bike. He could pop over, if that would help. And yes, it would. I'm not sure what I dare to hope for, or what might happen, but I know that I really need his company.

While he bikes over, I explain to Mum about him being a friend. She gives me her *Oh yeah?* look to let me know that she'll be popping up to my room every five minutes to 'check we're all right', but she can see that I need someone to talk to. She knows things didn't go well with Rose. So all she says is, 'He can't stay late.'

But when Dan arrives, he doesn't even come through the door. He stands in the porch, his face glowing from the ride.

'It's beautiful out here this evening. Check out the sunset.'

I look out at the last pink and orange streaks in the sky. The air is cool and fresh. Dan holds out his hand to me.

'We could go for a walk,' he suggests.

'It's getting dark,' I point out.

'I love it when it gets dark round here. The skies are best then.'

'Good idea,' Mum says, clearly preferring it to the idea of me and Dan in my room, unsupervised for up to four minutes at a time. Under the circumstances, so do I.

'I'll get my jacket.'

We walk for miles. Down the track and up the path that leads to the ridge at the top of Crakey Hill. The sky turns from purple to inky blue, and then black, streaked with thin grey clouds that occasionally block out the silvery sliver of the new moon.

I start to tell Dan a bit about the whole Rose fiasco, but it's such a lovely evening that I give up. I'd rather enjoy just being out together. Dan quickly catches my mood. He sticks his hands in his pockets and glances round at the hills and valleys. We can see the lights from about three houses and a dim orange glow over Castle Bigelow, but mostly it's just black. It could be scary, especially with the occasional bat swooping overhead, but actually – when you know practically every tree and bush, and you're not on the lookout for a mad stalker lurking behind them – it's peaceful.

'I hated it when I first came here,' he says. 'We were in Cheltenham before. I thought that was a small town, but compared with here it was like New York. But Dad's a stargazer. He wanted us to be somewhere they're not hidden by the light. I was bored witless when he first showed me, but it gets you. See there? That's the north star. That's where you start. Underneath it – that shape like a saucepan – that's the Plough. And over there, that V shape, that's Taurus. I just think it's amazing that we've been looking up at the same stars, in the same places, since before there were officially humans.'

He leans in close so I can see exactly where he's

pointing. I lean in close back, because I can. I feel better already.

'It's a shame about the moon being so new tonight,' I say, watching the silvery crescent slip behind another wisp of cloud.

'No, that's good,' Dan counters. 'You want it to be really dark so the stars show up more. Even moonlight can be a distraction. Tonight's ideal, almost.'

He sells his guitar to buy phones for girls he hardly knows. He talks about moonlight. He has those beautiful, curving biceps under his T-shirt, from all his rugby and guitar playing. I remember them from when we practised together.

'Uh huh. Right. Ideal,' I murmur.

He takes my hand to guide me along the path past a brambly patch of hedgerow. The starlight casts a faint silvery silhouette around his profile as he looks up to the sky again.

'Out there somewhere is the perfect planet for us.'

'What, us two?' I ask, dreamily.

'No!' he laughs. 'Everyone. When this one dies and we need a new one, I mean. I want to help find it.'

Oh right. The end of the world: not quite what I was imagining. I try to focus more on what he's actually saying.

'So you want to look for planets? As a job, or a hobby?'

'Both,' he grins. 'As a job, if they'll let me. There are some great physics jobs working with telescopes. And they put them in places like South Africa and the Arizona desert.'

'So you'd get to be a guitar-playing, travelling astronomer?' I check, trying to keep my tone playful.

Don't let it sound as though you think this is perfect, perfect, perfect, Sasha Bayley.

He laughs. 'I s'pose so. You make it sound more romantic than it would be.'

He stops and gazes at me again. We do one of those endless stares we seem to do. I am thinking about the word 'romantic', and I'm pretty sure he is too. If the boy doesn't kiss me now there must be something seriously wrong with him.

But he doesn't kiss me.

Then the other alternative occurs to me: perhaps there is something seriously wrong with me.

The moment's gone. We're both embarrassed, trying to pretend it didn't happen. As another cloud is blown past the moon, I briefly catch sight of the thin, bright ribbon of railway track far below us.

Dan frowns and looks down the valley, following my gaze. He shudders briefly.

'Are you OK?' I ask.

'Yes. Sure. It's just . . . thinking of you sitting on the parapet like that . . . thinking you were going to . . .' he sighs. 'Anyway, I get it now. I was way off.'

'You were right behind me!'

'I mean . . . my fears were way off. You're such a strong person, Sasha.'

I laugh, surprised. 'Me?'

'Look what you've been through. Look at you now. You're so . . . together.'

'You should have seen me recently. You're the strong one,' I say. Because he's so positive and optimistic, despite his silences and his unexpected awkwardness. 'You're not even too worried about the world ending!'

He laughs. 'Oh, for me it's simple. Astronomy taught me that. Hey – lie down.'

'What?'

'Seriously. It's not so cold. There's a soft spot here.'

He chooses a flattish bit of grass and lies on it, patting the ground beside him. He looks at me innocently.

'OK,' I laugh, slipping down beside him.

'Now look up.'

I do, at the inky blackness of the night, speckled with tiny spots of light.

'See those stars? This is what I think about. You could fit the Earth more than a million times into the Sun. And the Sun's a pretty small star, in the scheme of things. Smaller than lots that you can see up there right now. It's just a tiny part of the Milky Way, which is bigger than we can comprehend, and even *that* is just an outlier. I mean, we're on, like, the third rock from the Sun in a totally non-impressive galaxy. With all of that going on, we're tiny specks of dust, really. We're only here for, like, a millisecond compared with the thirteen billion years it took to create all of this. So my concerns – anyone's concerns – they don't really matter in the general scheme of things. Don't you think so?'

I look up at the twinkling stars (they really twinkle – I'd never noticed) and nod. Dan sounds so reassuring. Thirteen billion years of history, and now here we are, two specks of dust, lying side by side, floating through space on our not-so-special planet.

Except, no. Now that I consider it, that's not what I think at all. I so want to agree with him, but I can't.

'I've never thought of myself as a speck of dust,' I admit, staring back up at the sky. 'I mean, you see the stars and I see the space between them. There's this vast, empty universe and most of it is just . . . nothing. And yet, in the middle of all the nothing, here we are. Doesn't it feel like a miracle to you? We may be specks, but we're so complicated and amazing. It just makes me treasure each person more. I'm sorry, I—'

Oh wow. I didn't know I thought all that stuff until it came out of my mouth, but it's true. I guess I think we're miracles. I didn't want to contradict him, but he cuts me off with a grin.

'You're cool,' he says, sitting up now, and putting his arms around his knees. 'I love the way you think.' He turns to face me again and stares at me for a long time. I sit up too, so our faces are close in the cool night air, and I stare right back. Our breath forms little steamy clouds between us. His head dips a little towards mine. And then it stops. Again.

'You're shivering,' he says, concerned. 'It's got a lot colder. Shall we head back?'

He gets up and holds out his hand to guide me down the path, and it feels as though the crisp night air is sparkling with starlight. Was I cold? Was I really shivering? I'm not sure. As we tramp down the muddy path home, the warmth of his hand on mine gives me an inner glow. Still, I'm more confused than anything. Why didn't he kiss me? What's wrong? Is it to do with Cat? It doesn't seem to be. She just annoys him. So what's the problem? I really don't want the George Drury fiasco to be my main experience of lip contact until I hit my twenties. Why did Dan take me up here at all, if not to kiss me under the stars? I mean, I love astronomy and everything but . . . I just don't get it.

Even so, I still have the tingle from being close to him. He keeps hold of my hand along the track, until we get back to the cottage door.

'See you next Saturday?' he asks. 'For another session?'

His eyes look into mine searchingly and he pulls my jacket more tightly round me.

'Oh – music!' I say. 'A music session. Yes. Right. Of course.'

Thank God I worked that out quickly.

'Great. And don't worry about the internet stuff,' he says. 'It will pass.'

I grin at him. 'Yup. Got it. Speck of dust.'

He senses I'm teasing, and gives me an ironic salute. I watch him get on his bike and head for home, under his canopy of stars.

Just Do It

When I get in, I sit on my bed with the guitar on my lap, and a notebook beside me. Three scraps of songs come pouring out in quick succession. One about the expanding universe, one about the new moon over the valley, and one called 'Out of Reach', which has a minor chord change in the middle that I'm quite proud of. When I've written as much of them as I can, I set my phone to 'record' and put the finishing touches to 'Get To Know Me'. It's nearly ready now.

By the time I turn my computer on, there's a message waiting for me from Jodie. Apparently her brother Sam has an idea about how we can get to Rose.

Sam, it turns out, has a friend who is a Directioner. In

fact, he has several. They have what they call the 'patented, approved method' for reaching your 'targeted celebrity' in the hotel of your choice – in their case, One Direction members, wherever they happen to be. All it requires is transport, clothing, ingenuity, a little bit of acting ability, the absence of security guards, and the ability to get up very early in the morning. Apart from the last part, it sounds relatively easy to do.

Over Interface, we talk through the details, deep into the night. Nell joins in. We don't know about the security guards, but we didn't see any. They seem unlikely. Rose is popular, but she doesn't have a hundred screaming fans outside her window, like One Direction. Clothes will be easy and acting ability should be fine. Getting up early will be painful, but worth it. Sam has agreed to provide transport, in return for a blow-by-blow account of whatever happens, which Jodie has made him swear not to reveal to a living soul afterwards.

We set the date for Saturday, when we'll tell each of our parents that we're visiting each other that day to do a homework project, and I'll tell Mrs Venning I may have to miss Living Vintage again. I'll have to miss Call of Duty too, but there will be other Saturdays. I realise that in the course of all the planning, I haven't actually updated the girls on Dan, but that's no bad thing. For now, the focus is on Operation Fix the Rose Ireland Special, and I don't mind dreaming about him privately for a while.

On Saturday morning, my alarm goes off at six-thirty. Fifteen minutes later, I'm creeping down the stairs, dressed and ready, careful not to wake Mum. Jodie and Sam are waiting outside in Sam's old Subaru, with the engine running quietly. Next, we pick up Nell. Her house is on a modern estate, built on the edge of Castle Bigelow with views across the fields to the vast local Tesco. Like us, she's wearing a black shirt and skirt under her jacket. She hops in enthusiastically, full of nervous excitement about the day. Jodie demands music and Sam finds a hip-hop station. We all rap along to Dizzee Rascal and Sebastian Rules.

The countryside is at its best in the early morning light. The fields look almost blue under the uncertain sky. A pink glow is shifting to pale gold on the horizon. It's funny, I think, how so many people who live here want to grow up and be celebrities and move away from here, whereas the ones who make it, like Jim Fisher, spend a fortune on coming back.

Soon the road is winding its way towards the gates of Lockwood House.

Sam pulls up a short distance from the front door. We get out and Jodie eyes the battered Subaru nervously. It looks very out-of-place in these grand surroundings.

'Don't worry,' Sam says. 'I'll shove it round the back somewhere quiet.' He taps his pocket. 'Call me when you're ready.'

We give him one last nervous wave and he drives away across the gravel.

Nell stops and stretches her arm out in front of her, palm down.

'What?' Jodie asks.

'Just do it,' Nell says.

We put our hands on hers, and then I remember.

'Seminal leotards,' Nell and I say in unison.

Jodie shrugs and joins us. 'Seminal leotards.'

Nell leads the way because she's studied the lay-out. There's an archway beside the main building, and we pass through it into a cobbled courtyard, where various people are unloading crates of food and flowers from vans, and taking them inside through a side entrance. This is where the staff come and go, out of sight of the guests.

'Look as if you know what you're doing,' Jodie mutters.

We march past the busy people and in through the door. Nobody pays us much attention in our dark clothes, boring jackets and sensible shoes. We're in a service corridor, grubby and beige, with old, dirty carpet. Nell hovers for a moment, uncertain, then leads us right, down another corridor, until we pass a door with a small window in it at head height. Peeping through, Nell squeals with delight.

'Yes!'

She opens the door and we're at the back of the main house, not far from the Blue Room of the Rose Ireland Special fiasco. In fact, we can see the door to it a few metres further along.

'I'm sure we passed a loo on the way here on Tuesday,' Nell says.

We walk quickly, in single file, hoping not to be spotted. Nell squeals again. At the end of the passage is a door marked 'Ladies'. Inside, we commence part two of the plan. We stash our jackets inside the towel cupboard under the basins. Nell gets her makeup bag out from her tote and we all put on lashings of lipstick and mascara, to make ourselves look old enough to work here. I get three little white frilly aprons, borrowed from the café, out of my bag and pass them round. We put our hair in the neatest ponytails we can manage, stash the bags with the coats, and we're ready.

'At the end of this passage there's a staircase to the main floor of bedrooms,' Nell whispers. She doesn't need to whisper: there's no one else here, but it feels right, somehow. 'We take that and go to the middle of the corridor. That's where the best rooms are. If she's not there, she'll be on the floor above. I think.' She gulps. She also studied the hotel website to look for the rooms where Rose is most likely to be staying. We're in her hands now.

'Talk in some kind of accent,' Jodie advises before we set off. 'It'll make us seem more realistic.'

'What kind?' I ask. 'French?'

'No. Russian or Italian or something. Just la-di-da-di-da-di. It'll help. And look out for a tray.'

'Oh my God,' Nell says, hyperventilating slightly. She's really not cut out for this stuff, but we agreed we had to do it together. Taking a deep breath, she leads the way and Jodie and I, doing our best chambermaid impressions, follow.

We start with the first floor. It's tricky, because whenever we see real hotel staff approaching, we have to nip out of sight so they won't get suspicious of our slightly dodgy uniforms. We also have to find an abandoned breakfast tray outside someone's bedroom – which I do – and dress it up by putting fresh white napkins (brought with us for the purpose) over all the empty plates and bowls. Armed with the tray, we follow Nell to the door halfway down the corridor. This will, apparently, take us to a suite with big windows overlooking the gardens. I knock, while Jodie calls out 'Room service!'

After two minutes of anxious waiting, a stubbly man in a towelling robe comes to the door.

'I didn't order any food,' he says, confused and grumpy, looking at the napkin-laden tray.

'Oh, I'm so-a sorree-a,' Jodie says, in the WORST Italo-Russian accent I have ever heard. Didn't she practise? 'I thought you-a ask-a for eet.'

God, Jodie. Shut up.

'Well I didn't.' He looks at us crossly, then hesitates. 'Although, now I'm awake . . .'

'No no no! It's-a fine,' I say in a bit of a panic. Damn – my accent's as bad as Jodie's. 'This ees-a cold now. We get you a better one.'

We bow and scrape and scuttle away as fast as we can, stifling our giggles until we're at the far end of the corridor. What on earth will real Room Service think when he calls down to complain?

'We'd better get moving,' Nell whispers. 'They might start looking for us soon.'

'Corr-a ect-a,' I agree.

We try a couple more doors, getting no reply, or an unfriendly glare from someone who's unhappy to see us.

'Let's try upstairs,' Jodie says.

We take the nearest staircase and tiptoe up it, listening out for sounds of danger – which is basically anything.

I hear it first, and stop dead. Jodie crashes into me and swears under her breath.

'What?'

'Listen.'

It's a noise I thought I never wanted to hear again: Linus Oakley, on his phone, talking loudly.

Jodie looks at me and grins. We're close. He's on the floor above us, but heading away down the corridor to the far staircase. We stand just out of sight, listening.

'What? What? I can't hear you. Reception's terrible in this place. What's that? No, she's fine. Just a bit of stress. Nothing the girl can't handle. She'll be in New York when you need her. Yes, she can do that show. And that one. It'll be a pleasure. What? Seventeen, I think. Sixteen? Can't remember. No, it's not a problem she's below the drinking age, Al. She doesn't drink. That's just something the papers said. She really doesn't. It's stress, I'm telling you. Look, Al, *I'm* the one who needs a drink. I'll call you back.'

He disappears down the stairs.

We creep along the corridor.

'I think it's this one,' Nell whispers, as we reach the door in the middle.

I hold the tray and Jodie knocks.

'Room service!'

As we're standing there, a rattling trolley rounds the corner, piled high with sheets and towels. It's being pushed by a girl dressed in a similar outfit to ours, except she's got the official one, which is smarter and more expensive. Even from the other end of the corridor, she stares at us.

'Room service!' Jodie calls more loudly, bashing on the door now, as if she's trying to knock it down.

The girl with the trolley heads in our direction, suspicious, peering at all our faces in turn. Nell is lipstick-pink with embarrassment. I look down at the tray, trying to hide my face with my fringe. Jodie has a glint of desperation in her eye.

239

Just as she's about to knock for the third time, the door opens.

'I didn't order any . . . Oh.'

Rose is standing there, in leggings and a sweatshirt, with her earbuds in.

'Quick!' Jodie hisses. 'Let us in.'

Just as Trolley Girl reaches us, we nip into Rose's room and out of sight.

'Phew.' Jodie closes the door behind us with her bottom and leans against it. 'That was exciting.'

I glance around the room. Big windows, thick curtains, huge four-poster, which I recognise from the photo on Interface, and a general sense of wow. It's also very messy, with clothes and papers scattered all over the place. Rose has obviously made herself at home.

Rose, meanwhile, is giving us the same sort of stare that the chambermaid did.

'What are you doing here? Oh my God, is that food?'

She moves in on my tray. I whip off the napkins to reveal the empty plates underneath.

'It was part of our cunning plan,' I explain. 'To see you.'

'Oh.'

'Sorry.'

'It's OK.' She sighs, standing stiffly in the middle of the room. It's just like before: us three on one side and her on the other. And like before, this is not the Rose of all the glamorous photographs on Interface. Her cheeks are hollow, her hair is a tangled mess, and there are dark purple smudges of tiredness under her eyes.

'We didn't think you'd be up,' Nell says into the awkward silence, echoing my thoughts. We'd expected to find her in bed this early in the morning, not dressed for a run.

Rose looks down at her leggings and customised Nike trainers as if even she can't believe she's wearing them.

'I go running every day. But I can skip it, seeing as you're here. Why *are* you here?'

'We're here because we really need to talk to you,' I say, marvelling that we've actually done it.

Jodie waltzes over to the big four-poster and sits back on the crisp white duvet, covered with a thick wool blanket.

'Mmm. This is lovely. The thing is, Rose, we need to ask you a favour.'

'Oh yes?'

'That TV thing we did . . .'

'It was terrible,' Nell chips in.

'We hate it,' I finish off. 'Can you persuade them not to show it?'

'Oh.'

Rose's face crumbles. It wasn't far from crumbling before. She looks as fragile as an eggshell.

'So?' Jodie challenges her.

There's a slight pause, while Rose looks from one of us to the other.

'Of course,' she says. 'If that's what you want. I'll ask them.'

She sighs as if all the air is leaving her body.

OK. So that was easier than we were expecting. Jodie, certainly, had been prepared for fireworks, stamping, shouting and regal-style sulking. But there's none of that at all.

'Was it me?' Rose asks tremulously. 'I didn't know

what to say. I thought it would be so good to see you, but . . .'

She falters and stops.

'But it was a nightmare,' I finish off for her, gently. 'We've been trying to get in touch with you ever since. Why've you been ignoring us?'

'Have you? I didn't know.'

'What d'you mean, you didn't know?'

She dips her head.

'I . . . I don't check my phone. I get so many messages these days, Elsa checks it for me.'

'Who's Elsa?'

'My assistant. Sort of. I suppose. She works for Linus, really. She helps me out. She writes stuff for me on the internet. I'm not sure what she does.'

'Well, she does it with hideous grammar,' I mutter.

'Wait,' Jodie says, getting up from the bed and coming back over. 'You *have an assistant to answer your phone?*'

'Yes,' Rose says in a tiny squeak. 'I suppose so. When I got fam— I mean, after the show, I got so many messages they filled up my message box. I don't have time to answer them all, so Elsa does it for me. She passes on the ones I need to see. I don't know why she didn't pass yours on. Perhaps she didn't want to disturb me.'

Oh God, I suddenly wonder: did she even get any of my apologies all those weeks ago?

'Disturb you from what?'

'The studio,' she says, not looking very happy about it. 'Trying to get new songs ready to show Linus.'

She's still looking down. Her lips tremble when she talks. I could swear a teardrop lands on the Nike trainers. Then, to all our astonishment, she sinks into a little

242

puddle on the ground and buries her head in her hands.

'I'm sorry, I'm so sorry,' she mumbles. 'I just wanted to see you again and . . . I've made a mess of it all.'

Living The Dream

Jodie's face says it all. This is not the monster she came to see. This is not a monster at all.

She comes over from the bed. I'm already next to Rose, taking her hands in mine. We all sit cross-legged on the floor. Nell stretches out a hand and strokes Rose's hair.

'Hey, you didn't make a mess of it,' she says. 'We did.' Rose shakes her head.

'No. When you came, you looked so beautiful, the three of you. You were so cool, sitting there together. And I'd just come in from a rubbish day at the studio and I was hopeless.'

'But we couldn't think of anything to say,' Nell interjects.

'Nor could I. I just sat there like an idiot. I shouldn't have agreed to see you on TV. I shouldn't have agreed to any of it.'

'Then why did you?' I ask.

Her blue eyes stare up at us from her pale, soulful face.

'It was the only way to see you. I had to talk to you before going back to St Christopher's for the launch thing. I didn't want that to be the first time we . . .

So she'd pictured that moment too. The awfulness of it.

'You could always have called,' Jodie says, pointedly, unable to resist.

Rose looks down again, contrite.

'I know. I should have called you a long time ago. But I didn't, because I was angry. Then I didn't because I was embarrassed. And now there's never any time. I can't explain it. If it's not in the schedule, it doesn't happen. And anyway, I wasn't sure you'd want to see me after . . . everything.'

'We wouldn't want to see *you*?' I ask. 'What about you wanting to see *us*?'

'Oh, I've wanted to,' she says eagerly. 'So much. But I've been in this bubble. It's constant meetings and interviews and singing. I don't seem to have time for anything of my own, But all this time, people have sold so many stories about me and none of you ever have and you've been great, like you always are, and I know you didn't mean what happened . . . I just got lost in my bubble. I'm so, so sorry.'

There's a long silence in the plush, untidy room while we all adjust.

'We're sorry too,' I say.

'I know.'

This is the moment, perhaps, that the TV cameras would want to capture. The 'closure'. Except it's very still and undramatic, and nobody cries, and nobody says anything for a while. Everybody's sorry. That's all there is.

Nell is the first to go over and give Rose a proper hug. 'We've missed you.'

'Awhmmooooo.'

Rose mumbles it into Nell's shoulder, but I take it she's missed us too. When I approach her, she reaches out an arm and folds me in. The cashmere of her hoodie is soft against my cheek.

'Although technically,' Jodie says, 'you can't get lost in a bubble. I mean . . . just saying.'

Rose reaches over and throws a cushion at her. So do I. So does Nell. But Rose, despite all this, still looks fragile and close to tears.

'What's happened?' I ask. 'I look you up all the time, you know – on the web. I hardly recognise you now.'

She hangs her head.

'I know. I hardly recognise myself sometimes. I try to do what they tell me, but it's hard. Answering all those questions . . . trying to look like a pop star . . .'

'Why would you even want to?'

'Because . . .' She struggles to explain it. 'Because of the music. Because if I don't, they might not let me sing. And I *so* want to sing, but even that's gone wrong now—'

I'm about to ask her about that when Jodie interrupts her.

'And of course, there's all of this.'

She indicates the room, with its plump armchairs and ancient fireplace, the hangings on the bed, the designer shoes arranged in neat rows beside it, the Hermès handbag open on the coffee table.

'Yeah, I suppose,' Rose sighs, although I can tell that's not the big thing for her. 'I mean, it's beautiful. And I get to record in Jim Fisher's studio, and he's like a legend. And I sang at this party and I got to meet Paul McCartney. I mean, I'm really lucky, right?'

She looks from me to Jodie. What can we say? Paul McCartney? Of *course* she's lucky.

'But you said about the music . . . ?' I prompt her. 'Going wrong? It hasn't, surely?'

Rose sighs.

'Can you pass me my handbag?' she asks Jodie, who's closest.

'Sure. Is this the one Victoria Beckham has loads of?'

Rose nods, embarrassed again.

'I think so. Ivan gave it to me. Ivan Jenks, from Interface. Do you remember him?'

We shudder slightly. Of course we do: Mr Preserve-the-Drama. Jodie passes the bag over, pausing to admire the soft orange leather. Rose extracts a matching leather case from it, and from the case a shiny black tablet, like an iPad. She turns it on.

'Linus came over this morning to show me a rough cut of the new ad. We're still working on it, but it's terrible. *I'm* terrible. I don't think I can do it.'

'You can't be terrible,' Nell assures her. 'You were at number one last week.'

Rose shakes her head, unconvinced.

'Come on,' Jodie says. 'Show us. We'll give you an honest opinion.'

'Will you really?'

Jodie laughs. 'You know me.'

Rose grins. She fiddles around on the screen for a moment – she clearly hasn't mastered the technology yet. But eventually she finds what she's looking for. She traces her hand across the tablet screen and a video appears. It opens on her, sitting at a white grand piano in what looks like an abandoned warehouse, wearing a tight white dress with gold sparkles, which looks difficult to breathe in. Her hair is caught up in a gold headdress. She plays an introduction and accompanies herself as she sings.

'This is my moment
It's when the stars come out for me
I have finally made it
It's all I ever wanted it to be . . .'

Real-time Rose watches us, waiting for our reactions. I'm not quite sure what to do. I had my this-is-great face all ready, but the Rose at the piano has the same sort of pained expression as the one who was forced to 'jiggle' at our audition. The sound is good, but it's clear to me that her heart isn't in it. However, maybe a stranger watching would mistake her awkwardness for sincerity. I'm not sure. I hope so. Meanwhile, Nell is already smiling, although I hope Rose hasn't noticed it's her be-nice-to-Rose-in-case-she-cries-again smile. Jodie's eyebrows are practically in her hairline. And not in a good way.

On the video, the shot changes to show Roxanne Wills, standing on a mountaintop against an azure sky dotted with puffy clouds, also wearing a white dress – but one so short it could pass for a swimsuit – holding her arms out wide.

'Who does she think she is? Jesus?' Jodie mutters.

Rose bites her lip.

Roxanne sings more stuff about moments and pre-
ciousness and specialness and making it. Then she and
Rose appear together, in what seems to be a marble-lined
villa somewhere hot. It is possibly supposed to be like a
judge's house from *The X Factor*, or possibly like heaven,
or maybe both. Rose is still at the piano, while Roxanne
stands beside it. Their voices rise for the chorus:

> *I've found my moment*
> *Living the dream.'*

Eventually, mercifully, the video comes to an end. Nell
and I both plaster on our encouraging smiles for Rose.
She ignores us and looks straight at Jodie, who doesn't
even try to hide her reaction.

'You've got to be kidding me.'

Rose hangs her head. 'I keep trying to put genuine
emotion into it, but it just comes out cheesy.'

'It's not cheesy,' Jodie says. 'Believe me, it's beyond
cheesy. It's not even fun cheesy, like we used to do. It's just
. . . cheesy-cheesy.'

Rose looks panicked. 'But it's an easy tune. I don't
know why I can't do it.'

'It's not you,' I say. 'It's the song.'

I feel as if I'm pointing out the obvious here. Rose
would never have wanted to touch a song like that when
we were together, but she shakes her head.

'It can't be the song. Everyone loves it. Roxanne makes
it sound so real.'

'That's because Roxanne has no sense of integrity,'
Jodie says. 'She could sing a shampoo ad like her life

depended on it. Oh wait – she did, last week. You should be glad you can't do that.'

Rose gives her the ghost of a smile, slipping the tablet back in its case. 'I suppose I used to think like that. But everyone loves her. And they've got this whole stack of numbers like that for me to sing on the new album and I can't do half of them. That's why it's taking so long in the studio. I try to love them, but I can't . . .'

'I don't get it,' I say, interrupting.

'Get what?'

'This stack of numbers like that one. What about *your* songs?'

'Oh!' Rose shakes her head. 'I can't sing those. They wouldn't sell, apparently. What?'

We're all staring at her. She's being incredibly weird.

'The number one?' Jodie reminds her. 'That song you wrote? Over a hundred million views?'

'Oh, that. That was a fluke. And because of the competition. And good will because of . . . well, you know . . .'

My God. She actually thinks she's no good. After everything that's happened, she genuinely believes that. She thinks people just feel sorry for her.

'Who told you this?' I ask. 'Linus?'

'Well, yes,' she agrees. 'And Ivan. Everyone on the management team. They want me to be commercial. They want me to sell a lot of records. Nobody will believe a girl like me singing love songs, which is what I write. That's why I go on the runs. And do the diet. To lose some weight so—'

A girl like me. What have they been saying to her? Oh yeah. I can imagine. *Not just large but **large**.*

'But people love you the way you are!' Nell yelps, horrified. 'That's the whole point!'

'No, they don't,' Rose assures her. 'Not like this. They don't, because . . .'

We're all staring at her again. Flustered, she loses her train of thought.

'Because what?' Jodie asks.

'Because . . . because . . .'

'Give me that!' I instruct, holding out my hand for the tablet in its fancy orange case.

Rose hands it over. It takes me a few goes, because I don't know the software, but I finally get Interface on there, and Rose's fan page. Her official one. The one with over a million fans, and all the messages I read every day. I hold it out to her.

'Do you ever look at this?'

She looks surprised.

'Sometimes. Well, Elsa reads things out to me.'

I can feel my jaw clenching. Those fans aren't writing to Elsa, they're writing to Rose. Jodie catches my eye and even Jodie looks a bit scared of me.

'Well, read it,' I say, handing the tablet over. 'Read the first message, and the second, and . . . the fifth.' I haven't looked at them yet today, but I know what they'll say.

Rose scans down, reading quietly to herself. Her face clouds. She goes over to the nearest chair and sits down, still reading.

There will be a message from someone who's been bullied at school, saying she's given them hope and saved their life. There will be another from someone with a broken heart, saying she's the soundtrack to their pain, and they listen to her every day. There will be several telling her she's an inspiration, and there will be pictures: the pictures of roses, in glitter and fabric and arty photographs. There will be a few horrible ones too, saying she's fat and ugly, because some people think it's OK to say hateful things to strangers they can't see, but they'll be drowned out by angry defence of Rose by her fans. There won't be a single one, I guarantee, that wishes she'd be more commercial, or that she'd stop singing from her heart.

By now the tears are pouring down her cheeks, but it just makes me frustrated.

'I can't believe you don't read this stuff. I mean, I know you don't because you never reply. Not in your own words. Elsa does it for you sometimes – spelling it wrong. But why? When all these people love you, Rose? Why?'

She looks up at me, her face taut with wonder and pain.

'I had no idea . . . I don't know why.'

And then, for a while, she ignores us, scrolling down and down, through just some of the thousands of messages, stroking her finger over them, pausing to smile at a compliment, or grimace at some sad story.

While she reads, Jodie wanders around the room, stroking *her* fingers over the soft silk of the curtains, admiring Rose's new set of matching luggage, trying on some of her jewellery collection at the dressing table, waddling around in a pair of her new high-heeled Jimmy Choos. Rose only looks up when Jodie topples over on one of the heels and snaps it.

'Oops. Sorry.'

Rose ignores the broken heel.

'I didn't know. I mean, I knew I had fans. Elsa tells me

252

the numbers every day. But they just felt like numbers.'

'They're not just numbers,' I whisper.

To me every person, every message, seems very real. It's *so* not fair that I'm the one who's addicted to Interface and I had to be the one to get all the haters, while Rose gets all the love.

She puts the tablet down with a sigh.

'They're so lovely. I want to reply to all of them. They're going to hate the new song, aren't they?'

'"Living the Dream"?' Jodie asks, idly slipping into an embroidered coat from the wardrobe and checking herself out in the mirror. 'I look good, don't I? No, sadly my dear, they're not going to hate your new song, because they'll love everything you do. But they *should* hate it. It's smug, and forgettable, and it sucks.'

'It's just hard to do it justice when every line feels like a cliché.'

'Every line *is* a cliché,' I sigh.

'Nell?' Rose asks, keen to get everyone's opinion.

Nell's caught between her desire to make Rose happy and her natural honesty.

'It sucks,' she says at last. 'It really sucks. But it's not you, Rose. Like Sasha said, it's the song.'

Rose comes over and squeezes each one of us in turn.

'You have no idea,' she says, 'how much I've missed you. I can't believe I didn't call you.'

We gather around her, Jodie still in the embroidered coat, and hug each other tight. I feel us knitting back together. I could stay here, like this, all day.

As if she's reading my mind, Nell asks, 'So when have you got to go back to the studio?'

Rose checks the time on her watch. She's one of the

few girls I know who still wears a watch. The rest of us use our phones, but Rose probably doesn't know where her phone even *is*. I'm starting to realise that while I've been obsessed by the internet, and everything that's happened, Rose probably doesn't have much of a clue. Sometimes it would be relaxing to live in her world, even if you do miss the important stuff.

'I'm supposed to be there in half an hour,' she says, interrupting my train of thought. 'Jim said he'd be around today, and he might help me out with some tracks. He's a brilliant producer now, as well as playing. Normally, I'd just not go for a few hours, so I could be with you. But I don't want to miss him.'

She bites her lip, uncertain.

'So you're passing us up for some ancient rock god?' Jodie challenges.

Rose looks miserable.

'Pop god, actually,' I correct Jodie. 'But I see your point, Rose.'

And I do. Jim Fisher has played practically every stadium in the world. He's played with David Bowie and Michael Jackson. He's sold gazillions of records. Now he helps produce them. If I got the chance to spend even five minutes with him, I would. And besides, it's clear to see that even though Rose is miserable about many things right now, she's still passionate about the music.

'I know!' Nell bounces with excitement at her own idea. 'Why don't we take you there? Then we've got a few more minutes together, at least?'

'Would you really?' Rose asks.

I grin. 'We wouldn't miss it for anything.'

Still Want To Be You

When we explain to Sam where we're going, his tongue practically hangs out.

'Jim Fisher's actual house? No problem. Hold tight, ladies.' He swings the Subaru back down the drive like it was a Maserati.

On the way, Rose explains the most extraordinary thing: these last few weeks, since she recorded 'Breathless', she's been wishing she were us. Correct: *she's* been envying *our* lifestyle.

'I know it sounds mad,' she says, 'but you've still got each other. It's my fault. You tried to apologise right from

255

the start, Sash, but I was still so angry with you, because you were my best friend. Then I was too ashamed of myself to call. Then it all got crazy. But after this birthday party I performed at, when Paul McCartney came over to say hello, all I wanted to do was tell you about it. It didn't seem real unless I'd told you.'

I shake my head at the wonder of this. Paul McCartney. If I'd been there, we'd have been squealing together about it all night.

'Kerlanggg,' Jodie says, swivelling round from her place in the passenger seat, next to Sam. 'Any other megastars you'd like to name drop, while we're here?'

Rose grins. 'See? What's the point of meeting a Beatle if you can't call me a name dropper?'

'Weren't there loads of people you could talk to about it, though?' Nell asks. 'I mean, weren't you at a party?'

'I was. But it's not the same. Linus has met him lots of times, so he wasn't that interested. Elsa doesn't really like the Beatles. She doesn't really like anything except grime and hip-hop. I didn't really know anyone else. I had two glasses of champagne and I felt very dizzy. When I got back to my hotel room, I was all by myself. It was so bizarre – three hours before, there had been hundreds of people all singing along to "Breathless", and it was the most amazing night of my life. Then . . . there was no one.'

'That's what groupies are for,' says Jodie, sagely.

'I don't have groupies!'

'Well, there's your problem,' Jodie explains. But the half-smile on her lips shows that she isn't seriously recommending screaming fans at the bedroom door as a solution.

'What about your tutor?' Nell asks. 'We thought you were going out with him. Aren't you?'

'Jamie?' Rose boggles her eyes. 'Really? He's gorgeous, but . . .'

'But what?'

'He's twenty-five. He's got a girlfriend. She's twenty-five too. He only goes out to keep me company sometimes. I keep telling Elsa to tell the press we're not dating, but they don't care. Oh my God. I can't believe I can finally explain all this.'

She glances round at us all again, giddy with relief.

'I know what you mean,' Sam says cheerfully from the front. 'I often find that when I've just been singing to *a roomful of rock stars*, it's a real downer afterwards.'

'Shut up, Sam,' I tell him.

Rose grins shyly.

'I know it sounds crazy, but . . .'

'You don't need to explain,' I reassure her. 'We get it now.'

We reach a pair of grand wrought-iron gates, set in a gap in the wall. Sam leans out to an intercom stuck on a gatepost and explains that we're delivering Rose. The gates swing open automatically and we drive past elegant stables to one side, with a neat orchard of apple trees on the other. The breeze whips the pretty white apple blossom around, depositing petals on the car like confetti. At the end of the orchard we approach a wide circular drive leading to a grey stone Georgian house, with a red Ferrari parked outside the front door.

Jodie turns round to Rose.

'So this is where you work?' she drawls, eyebrow raised,

as we crunch along the gravel.

Rose blushes. 'Yup. This is the office. At the moment, anyway.'

Jodie takes in the picture-perfect view.

'I still want to be you. Just so's you know.'

Sam parks a respectful distance from the Ferrari and Rose leads us round the side of the house to a series of outbuildings at the back. One looks like a party barn – a bit like George's. Another houses an indoor pool. The third – a long, low, modern building made of wood, steel and glass – is the studio.

Rose knocks and enters. We all troop in behind her. The place is a rabbit warren of little rooms. One, the largest, is littered with instruments, speakers and mics. Next to it is a booth with a huge mixing console and a sofa. Then there's a glass-fronted cupboard with a microphone, another room containing nothing but a drum kit, and at the back a kitchen area with a view across miles of farmland, where we can see chestnut horses being exercised in one of the fields behind the house.

'Do you know what?' Jodie says, looking around, 'I think I just might be living the dream.'

'Oh, don't,' Rose says, stifling a laugh.

An elderly-looking man approaches the studio door, knocking the mud off his boots. He's dressed for farming or gardening, in a sleeveless green jacket covered with sensible pockets, old trousers and a frayed checked shirt that shows off his healthy tan. I assume he works on the estate. He certainly doesn't look like a sound engineer. Not that I'd know what a sound engineer's supposed to look like, but I imagine black jeans and an AC/DC T-shirt.

'I thought I heard you,' he says, coming in. 'Oh!'

He looks surprised to see five of us in the corridor, but not unduly bothered.

Rose steps forward.

'I hope you don't mind. I brought my band today. My old band. And—'

Before she can finish, Sam steps up to join her, holds his hand out for a handshake and almost bows.

'It's an honour to meet you, Mr Fisher.'

Oh my God, he's right.

Up close, I realise that the 'elderly' appearance came from the wavy grey hair, but the face is not *so* old. It's iconic. I've just only ever seen it on posters and album covers before, wearing eyeliner, above a silk shirt slashed to the waist, and lit by a bank of spotlights. Even meeting him in his old gardening clothes, the temptation to curtsey is embarrassingly strong.

'Hi kids,' he says, smiling a slow, laid-back, Taylor Lautner smile that must have had the groupies going weak at the knees thirty years ago. 'Fancy a coffee? Put the cafetière on, will you, Rose?'

What do you do when you meet a music legend? Well, I'll tell you. You sit down for toast and coffee (God, we're starving), and call your mum, at his insistence, to tell her where you are. It's clear that Jim's wild touring days are over. His latest wife and kids are on holiday with their grandparents in America and he shows us photos of them on his phone. There is something bizarrely normal about Jim.

Normal, that is, until we get into the studio proper, the place they call the 'live room', which is crammed with his collection of guitars, lutes, banjos, ukuleles and practically anything else with strings. It's worthy of a museum, but it's all right here, for him to pick up and play every day. It also has loads of keyboards and computer equipment, but nothing like the equipment in the control booth beyond, which has one whole wall of computers and monitors. It's pure geek heaven. Sam groans with pleasure.

'Oh God. Elliot would kill to see this stuff.'

'Dave rang to say he'll be over in an hour or so,' Jim tells Rose. 'He's the sound engineer,' he explains to us. 'Lives nearby but his life revolves around Formula 1. He'll come by when they've finished the interviews. I thought you were sounding better yesterday, Rosie. Shall we carry on with that Mariah Carey cover?'

Rose shakes her head.

'It's never going to work,' she says. 'I wondered . . . I wondered if you'd mind if I tried out one of my own songs today?'

'Sure,' Jim smiles. 'Whatever you like.'

Rose puts on some headphones and sits at one of the keyboards. We go out into the control room to give her room to concentrate, then stare at her through the window, so she can't. After grinning at us self-consciously, she turns away and I watch her tuning us out, and thinking about the music. For now, there's just her and a piano and a song.

She pauses for a long time before putting her hands on the keys to play, scanning her memory for lyrics she hasn't sung for a long time, and summoning up the emotion of the song. When it comes, it is slow and sad, almost desolate, called 'The Mistake I Had to Make'. It's Rose at her most vulnerable and raw, and it has all the intensity she couldn't bring to 'Living the Dream'.

Like 'Breathless,' this song oozes her jazz and blues influences, but standing here, watching her so close, I recognise the emotion in them in a new way now. It's real. I'd always assumed up to now that 'Breathless' was just Rose's idea of a breakup song – like we used to say, something based on the films we've seen and books we've read. I thought she'd perfectly copied other people's feelings. Now I'm not so sure.

When she's finished, there's a universal 'wow'. We wave at her through the window and pour into the live room to 'wow' in person.

'Where did that come from?' Jim asks.

'I wrote it a long time ago.'

'Well, why didn't you sing it, girl? *That's* what we've been looking for. That's got the chill factor. Why have you been messing with all this rubbish when you can do that?'

Rose smiles shyly.

'Because I'm an idiot,' she says. 'I didn't listen to . . . the people that know me.'

She gives us a wonky smile.

Jim looks confused for a moment, staring from face to face.

'Hey! I remember you guys. You're the ones from Killer Act. My daughter showed me on her laptop. What was that all about, then?'

'Long story,' I say with a sigh.

'Sorted now, thank goodness,' Nell adds.

'Don't believe everything you see on TV,' Jodie concludes.

He smiles. 'Ain't that the truth?'

'Sasha wrote a song about it, actually,' Nell says. 'It's really good. She's been learning guitar. Go on, Sash! Why don't you play it?'

Rose turns to me, surprised, 'You wrote a song? You play guitar?'

'Not really,' I say hastily, going pink. 'I mean, I've started to write a few songs. I don't really play guitar yet. I—'

'Yes, you do,' Nell says, smiling proudly. 'Don't be so shy, Sash.' She turns to Rose. 'You should hear the song, it's wonderful.'

Jim grins at me. 'You're a songwriter too?'

'No! God – I wish.'

I really wish. Suddenly, I *really* wish. Despite all the weirdness Rose described, I'd so love to be able to come to a place like this, and work with people like Jim.

'Well, come on, play it, then.'

Jim carefully considers his instrument collection for a moment, before handing me a battered acoustic guitar.

'No. Really.'

He's a legend. I only know about six chords. This is silly.

'No. *Really*,' Jim says. He says it with a smile, but it's the kind of smile an adult gives you when there's actually no choice. 'I'd like to hear your song.'

Everyone stands back to give me space. Luckily they don't disappear into the control room to watch through the window. I couldn't bear that. I put the guitar on my lap and strum a few chords. It doesn't look like much, but it makes the most beautiful sound. Jim sees my look of surprise at the sweetness of the noise I'm making and grins.

'Yeah. I played that with Eric Clapton a few times. It's a good little guitar. OK, we're listening.'

And so, on an instrument that has played alongside one of the greatest blues players of all time, I play 'You Don't Know Me' – slowly, carefully and as well as I can. Goodness knows I'm not perfect, but I've kept the chord sequence simple so I can play it properly. I find it easier to sing when I'm playing, too. More than that, I'm singing my own tune, my own words. The emotion comes naturally, just like it did for Rose.

'If you knew me,
You would want to understand me.
Don't judge me, don't hurt me, don't wound me
Get to know me.'

Rose watches me intently. Of course, she's never seen me play guitar seriously before. She's never heard me sing my own lyrics, either, apart from a couple of verses of 'Sunglasses'. It's hard to tell what she's thinking.

When I finish, she looks at me with tears in her eyes. Rose always took things harder and felt things more deeply than the rest of us. From that point of view, nothing's changed.

'Oh my God, Sash,' she says. 'I'm so sorry.'

'What for?'

She looks bewildered. 'I knew that people were mean to you . . . when I won. But . . . I had no idea, not really. It was bad for you, wasn't it? For all of you.'

'Yes, it was,' I say.

There's silence for a while.

'You don't know me . . .' she murmurs, rolling the lyrics round her tongue. 'Do you know – that's exactly what I'm thinking when I'm singing that stupid song for the ad? Everyone assumes you're happy but if the music's not working you're scared, and you're so lonely sometimes you could curl up and die. Hey – do you mind if . . . ?'

'What?'

'May I play it?'

'Of course.'

Nell gives a whoop of approval.

'I mean, it's your song,' Rose goes on. 'If you don't want me to . . .'

'No. Play it. Here.'

I hand her the guitar. While she works out the chord sequence, I get my phone out of my bag and find the app where I finalised the lyrics. Jim makes a few suggestions for how to pull it together in the middle eight. He hands us all headphones, so we can hear the sound as it progresses, track by track. Using one of the keyboards as a drum kit (which blows Jodie's mind slightly), he helps us lay the tracks down. Slowly, gradually, over the next forty-five minutes, I hear my song truly come to life.

I think Rose expects me to mind that she's singing my lyrics and playing my tune. I don't mind at all. She plays so beautifully and sings it better than I ever could. Eventually, she moves from the guitar to the piano, transposing the tune for the keyboard, developing a left-hand bass part to give it a new dimension.

The guitar is sitting there. I pick it up again. The sweetness of playing along to Rose's lead is something I've never experienced before. It's making music; it's what Rose has naturally done all her life. Now I can do it too.

Jim's busy in the control booth, talking to the sound engineer, who's just arrived. Meanwhile, Nell and Jodie start harmonising over the chorus while we play. Nell films some of the action on my iPhone, but when Rose needs it back for the lyrics, she points at her orange bag and Nell pulls out the smart new tablet. It takes beautiful video. Nell experiments with close-ups and long shots while we each do our part, making the song better with each new version.

Finally, we hit on a mix that we're all happy with. The creative tension that's been building up in the room bubbles and fizzes, like lemonade when you've shaken the bottle. That was, I realise, the most fun I have ever, *ever* had. Including talking to Dan under the stars. Which probably means there's something wrong with me, but whatever. I have to do this again one day. I don't know how, but somehow I must.

'Sounding good,' Jim calls through to us from the mixing booth. 'Do you want to do the vocals together?'

'Why not?' Rose says. 'Is that OK with you, Sash?'

Like I'd have a problem with recording my song with a number one artist.

We squeeze into the special booth for vocals, standing round the mic to perfect the sound, while the others make faces at us through the glass. In the end, we get it in two takes.

About A Boy

It's not until the early afternoon that I get the chance to talk to Rose alone. Jim, Nell and Jodie are examining the contents of the fridge in Jim's enormous kitchen, and Sam's talking techno-geek stuff back in the studio with Dave.

Rose and I sit on the kitchen doorstep, where nearby pots of thyme and rosemary fill the air with the scent of herbs, and strolling chickens cluck contentedly in the yard ahead. She seems happy enough to be here, but she definitely looks thinner, close to, and still very pale and drawn.

'Is there anyone actually looking after you?' I ask.

She yawns, stretching in the sunshine. 'My aunt pops

by to make sure I'm OK. Gran calls. But the team looks after me, I s'pose. I'm doing those runs. I'm on this special diet . . .'

'That's exactly what I mean!'

She yawns again. 'I want to get healthy. But I might be overdoing it,' she admits.

'And . . .' I hesitate. 'All that sharing you have to do. In interviews. Talking about personal stuff. I can see you hate it.'

'Oh God. You watch my interviews?'

'Every one.'

She shivers ruefully. 'I hated talking about my parents,' she confesses, pulling at a stray stalk of rosemary and playing with it. 'But Linus said I had to. It was good that people were interested in me. It's easier now: people talk about the music, mostly. But of course once that new song is out . . .'

'Yeah.'

She looks at me and smiles. 'I'll have to lie and say how much I love it. But at least you'll know the truth. I miss times like this, Sash. Times when I can really talk.'

She sniffs at the sprig of rosemary and tickles my nose with it. It smells like Mum's herb bread. But I'm already thinking back to the studio, when Rose played her new song. If we're really talking, there's some more stuff I need to know.

'Is there something you never told me?' I ask.

'About what?'

'About a boy. "Breathless" didn't come from nowhere.'

She avoids my eye. 'Well, you know, it came from various places. Books and . . . stuff.'

I just don't believe her. Not any more. Songs can come

267

from many places, but she didn't get those emotions from books – I know it. This was something she lived through, I'm sure.

'Uh huh. Books. And stuff. And that other song? "The Mistake I Had To Make", wasn't it?'

She scratches at the gravel with the toe of her shoe and coughs a couple of times to clear her throat. 'Er . . . '

I try to think through when she could possibly have had such an intense experience of love that I wouldn't have known about. After all, I saw her practically every day until the fateful Killer Act audition, apart from . . .

Yes! When I was away. With Dad.

'Last summer,' I say. 'Did something happen then?'

She winces, as if in pain. 'It was a long time ago. It was nothing.'

'I thought we were talking.'

She gives a long sigh and waves a hand about, as if to wave the memory away.

'OK. It was just . . . a mistake. A bad mistake. I was stupid. He had a girlfriend. It lasted six weeks, that's all. It was a mess. Like I said, it was nothing.'

It was *so* not 'nothing'. As she fiddles with the poor stalk of rosemary, the misery of that memory is etched in every line of her face. It's still there, still raw.

'Oh, Rose. I'm sorry.'

'Don't be sorry. I don't want people being sorry for me. Not even you, Sash.'

'Who was he? Someone I know?'

She shakes her head. 'No one you know. Look, it was a stupid holiday romance and I took it too seriously. First love. I'm an idiot. But I got a bunch of songs out of it, so . . . hey!' She gives me a weak smile. 'Can we talk about something else?'

'OK.'

I'm still thinking of what that might be when a loud, shrill voice fills the kitchen.

'Rose! Rose! Rose Ireland?'

Rose flinches, guiltily. We turn round to see a small, thin blonde girl in a shorts and a T-shirt storm into the room. She stops briefly to say a polite hello to Jim, who's casually making a salad for lunch, then homes in on the pair of us in the doorway.

'Rose! There you are! I've been looking for you all day. Are you OK?'

Rose smiles. 'Absolutely fine.'

'Why didn't you tell anyone you were here?'

'Because I was supposed to be here,' Rose stammers. 'It was on the schedule.'

The girl flaps her hand in front of her face, as if to calm herself down from a panic. 'Well, you didn't tell your driver, so we didn't know you'd come. We've been searching the grounds for you for, like, *hours*. I thought you'd had some accident or something. Then the costume designer's assistant arrived to talk about the tour, and she's been waiting, like, forever. I brought the car. If we shift, we can catch her before she goes, like, home.'

She whips a BlackBerry out of her handbag and starts typing rapidly on the screen.

'These are my friends,' Rose says, although the girl hasn't shown the slightest interest in us. 'Sasha, this is Elsa.'

'Hi,' Elsa says, not looking up from her phone screen until she's finished tapping.

Elsa – the manager of Rose's Interface page, her

269

FaceFeed and her phone. No doubt whatever she's typing in now is an insult to spelling and grammar. So this is the girl who 'is' Rose online. The thought of it makes me feel ill.

'There. I've told them I've found you,' she announces. 'Sorry, Mr Fisher. I can bring her back later, but this meeting is, like, don't miss. You know what I mean?'

'What about her friends?' Jim asks.

'Who? Oh, them. They'll have to see her another time,' Elsa says, casting a rapid glance over Nell, Jodie and me. 'If they call me I can fix something.'

'We already did,' Jodie says, not missing a beat. 'Or at least, we called Rose. Did you forget to pass the message on?'

Elsa ignores the dangerous edge to Jodie's voice.

'But it can't be this week, because we're back to London in two days, and then we've got more costumes and tour dates to sort out, and the ad to finish, and a slimming magazine. Everyone wants to know how Rose lost those pesky pounds! C'mon, Rose. I brought some water for you to drink in the car.'

Elsa holds her hand out. Rose glances wistfully at the salad, bread and cheeses being assembled on the kitchen counters. It's not surprising her 'attractively curvy' figure is rapidly disappearing. Rose hugs us all briefly goodbye, and heads off towards the waiting limo.

'Living the dream,' Jodie calls after her with a sardonic wave.

The car disappears down the driveway in a spray of gravel.

Living the dream.

270

So Not Over Her

The thing is, the rest of us *are* living one – or at least, we just did for one morning and part of the afternoon. It still feels dream-like as Sam drives us home through the lazy late spring sunshine, and we remember how Jim had to leave us for ten minutes over lunch so he could talk to David Bowie about something on the phone.

We make a pact not to talk about it with anyone else. Only Sam has a problem with this.

'How can I not tell my mates I actually played guitar with Jim Fisher?'

'It was only the first two bars of "Smoke on the Water" and one of them was wrong,' Jodie snorts. 'And besides, what happened was . . . special. Just for us.'

'Yes,' Nell agrees. 'The whole idea was to keep our heads down, remember?'

With a grumble, Sam gives in. He drops Nell and Jodie off at my place, because Mum was experimenting with pistachio cake recipes for the café yesterday, and I happen to know there are a lot of samples that need eating up. Poor Rose; she loves pistachios. We're in the middle of thirds when my phone goes. It's Dan.

'Sorry not to see you today. Look, Ed got some tickets for a gig in Bristol tonight. It's a band from the uni who're supposed to be pretty good. Do you want to come?'

Oh my God. What is happening to me? I was thinking – on my second slice of pistachio cake – that my perfect day couldn't get more perfect, and now it just did. Dan is totally inviting me out. This is a real date. What else could you call it? I try and play it cool.

'Right. Sure. I'll just see if I'm doing anything.'

While he's listening, I tell Nell and Jodie about the gig and 'check I'm free', to make myself sound to Dan like a girl with a massive social life who needs to juggle. Major mistake. Nell and Jodie's expressions mirror each other exactly. They go from 'Oh wow you got a date!' to 'Ooh – a gig, that sounds cool,' to 'Aw – can we come?' with accompanying puppy eyes, all in the space of about three seconds.

'No, you can't,' I mouth to them crossly.

'Is there a problem?' Dan asks, sensing one.

'No, it's just my friends being difficult.'

'They can come too. Are they the ones from the band?

272

Ed and Raj have been dying to meet them.'

'Yes, they are,' I sigh, glaring at Nell and Jodie, who are still doing their puppy eyes.

'No problem. The boys'll be pleased. We can give you a lift. Pick you up at eight?'

'Sure. Thanks.'

'Yes!' Jodie shouts as soon as I've ended the call. 'A gig! Just what I feel like. Now, what are we going to wear?'

A couple of hours later they're back at my place, armed with major wardrobe ideas, so we can all get ready together. It's almost like the old days: the iPod jammed into the speakers at full volume, a playlist of Abba and Girls Aloud, jostling at the mirror to perfect our makeup and strutting around in various outfits. In the end, Jodie goes for her usual lumberjack shirt, but matched tonight with black shorts and fishnets disappearing into ankle boots, and we agree Nell looks fantastic in psychedelic flowery skinnies and a grey sequinned top that matches her eyes. I go for a simple, short lace dress. Very short, actually, but very demure at the top. With Nell's help, I hold some of my hair off my face with clips decorated with little stars.

All the time, Rose's absence hovers around us like a hole in the air. It's not the same without her perfecting her cat's-eye eyeliner flicks, doing something unfortunate to her hair, then regretting it and changing it. Still, we've had more time together today than I ever thought we would. The buzz of that memory gives the evening a special, secret glow.

The Call of Duty lot turn up in convoy to pick us up: Ed

in the Land Rover, as usual, with Dan beside him and Cat in the back; Raj leaping out of his battered old Polo, eagerly holding the door open for Nell and Jodie, his eyes practically popping out of his head at the sight of Nell in her skinnies. In the back of the Land Rover, Cat eyes me with wary contempt. She's in a short dress too – black leather and sleeveless, with a cut-out design, far more expensive than mine.

'You look tired,' she says.

I probably do, under my makeup. At six-thirty this morning I was dressing as a chambermaid, ready to ambush a major new recording artist. Was that really only this morning?

'Yeah, it's been a busy day,' I grin.

'Oh, what happened?' Dan asks.

'Sorry. Can't talk about it.'

I have his full attention after that. Maybe it's being a woman of mystery (because I stick to the pact and don't say anything), or maybe it's just the left-over buzz from being in the studio . . . Maybe it's just that the time is right. Something is brewing between Dan and me. Something exciting and unspoken, following on – belatedly, perhaps – from our talk under the stars. Dan knows it, and so do I.

The gig is hot, sweaty, overcrowded, chaotic and fabulous. They run out of beer and soft drinks early on and we're reduced to drinking water from the taps in the ladies' loos. It doesn't matter. The band is brilliant: better than Call of Duty, better than us, better than loads of acts in the charts. They deserve a recording contract. Dan says the rumour is that there's a couple of record company scouts in the audience tonight, which may be why they're putting on such an inspired performance. The style is sort of indie-folk-punk, with a tiny girl at the front roaring out the words and holding it all together with her magnetic stage presence.

When she lingers on the high notes, her voice has the same honey warmth as Ella Fitzgerald. Yet again, I wish Rose was here, because she's the only person I could explain this to. However, Dan's right behind me, moving to the music. That feels pretty good too.

Cat watches us all the time. The closer Dan gets to me, the more she tries to get his attention, asking for drinks, asking what time it is, reminding him of songs they've played together. Dan simply ignores her most of the time. In the end, she grabs his elbow and says she's not feeling well. She needs to get home but she doesn't have enough money for the taxi.

I sigh to myself. As a ploy, this is brilliant. Gentleman Dan – it's the perfect way to grab his attention. Presumably we'll have to end the evening now. But, when he looks at her his jaw is set, his eyes are angry. He's not stupid and she's finally exhausted his patience.

'Really?'

Surprised by the strength of his reaction, Cat wavers, hesitates.

'It's OK,' she says. 'Don't worry.'

'No, you're obviously not well,' he snaps. He pulls his wallet out of his pocket and gives her all his spare money. 'Here. This'll cover the taxi. I'll help you get one.'

He goes out, and Cat can't help but follow. When he comes back, he's alone.

'She'll be fine,' he says. 'They use that cab firm all the

time. I told her to call us to let us know she got home safely.'

Poor Cat. Stuck in a taxi, in her tight leather dress, far away from Dan and me. The exact opposite of the effect she wanted. Without her, Dan is visibly more relaxed. He puts his hands on my hips as we dance to the music. I wish all nights could be like this.

The band plays its final number and it's time to go home. Nell offers to go with Raj in his beaten-up Polo. Ed offers to drive the rest of us in the Land Rover, and makes a point of asking Jodie if she'd like to travel beside him, so she can show him the way to her house. Which leaves Dan and me to climb in the back together. I don't say anything, but I light up like a beacon inside.

As soon as we're moving, Jodie starts fiddling with the radio, searching for a station she likes. Soon we're all singing along to Bruno Mars. Dan casually puts his arm over the back of the seat, so his hand is resting near my shoulder. The fact that we're both pretending that nothing's happening makes it better still.

Now it's Girls Aloud on the radio.

'God!' Ed groans, 'Radio South West will play anything.'

'We love this one!' Jodie protests. 'We were singing it this evening. Turn it up, Ed.'

He does. We sing along raucously, except for Ed, who's laughing, and Dan, who isn't concentrating on the music. I can feel his warm breath against my neck, and the heat of his body next to mine. Even though the strongest thing I've had all day was Jim's coffee, I feel as if I've been injected with powerful happy-making drugs, and they make me want to hug the world.

'Something kinda OOOOH!' I sing, keeping up with Jodie in the front, and trying to keep the grin off my face. When Ed takes a corner too quickly, Dan's thrown against me. Somehow, when he straightens up, he's still just as close. When I turn slightly to look at him, his eyes are half closed. I stop singing, and stay with my face turned towards him. He moves his lips towards me, slowly, slowly.

'And now for something a bit different,' the radio DJ says. 'You know the one. You've heard it a million times already.'

There are four chords, and a small sigh. Then Rose starts to sing the famous opening lines of 'Breathless'.

Oh no no no. Not Rose now. Not that song. Every time I hear it, I picture #dropthefatgirl trending on FaceFeed. I freeze.

Dan freezes too. He leans away from me, with pain in his eyes. Then he rescues his arm from behind me and looks out of the window, breathing fast.

'God! Not again!' Ed shouts. 'Not bloody "Breathless". That has to be the biggest breakup song in the world. We were having fun here!' He starts punching buttons to change the station.

The radio burbles classical music, then the news, then a talk show about whether or not to vaccinate badgers.

Badgers? I don't care about badgers. Dan and I are still frozen in the back. Was it me? Did I just ruin the moment?

Whatever it was, it's over. When Ed eventually manages to find some smooth late-night music, it's far too late. Dan's staring at the passing countryside, pretending I don't exist. I'm wishing I didn't. I notice Ed flick his eyes at me in the driving mirror, and they crinkle with concern at the corners when he sees me sitting ramrod straight, a foot away from this brother, clutching my knees.

Jodie remains oblivious to it all, humming to herself in the front seat until Ed finally pulls up outside her house. She waves us all a cheerful goodbye. The next seven minutes, as Ed negotiates the country lanes from her place to mine, are pure purgatory.

'Thanks for a great evening,' I say dutifully, as Dan leaps out of the Land Rover like a scalded cat so I can get past him without having to touch him in any way.

'Yeah . . . great,' Ed mutters, without much enthusiasm, watching us both.

Dan, Gentleman Dan, gives me a short nod, which will have to do as goodbye.

This time, Ed chooses to walk me across the silent, still road to my house. Standing in the porchlight, he says, 'Sorry about that.'

'You saw?'

'Yeah. He, er, he had a bad breakup last summer. I thought he was OK now. Maybe not.'

Yes. I nod but I can't bring myself to speak. It all makes sense now: the nearness without touching, the kisses that never quite happened, the feeling that he was holding something back . . .

But there was something I missed.

At four in the morning the final piece of the puzzle slots into place. I must have been asleep, because I wake up in bed with a start, cold but sweating, and suddenly it's clear.

It wasn't just the words of 'Breathless' that reminded Dan of his breakup: it was the voice that sang them. Because of course, I've just been talking to a girl who went through a breakup last summer. A breakup so bad she wrote a number one song about it. And she comes from the same part of the middle of nowhere as he does. It can't be a coincidence.

Dan's secret ex-girlfriend is my ex-best friend. And he is So. Not. Over. Her.

Falling

Rose. She got everything. The talent. The music. The boy.

I don't really sleep after that. When morning comes, I feel as though my body is filled with lead.

Jodie calls me at ten. She's still buzzing from last night.

'Woo! Sasha and Dan, sitting in a tree . . . So what happened, then?'

So she'd noticed.

'Nothing,' I mutter dully into the phone. 'Nothing happened.'

'What? Wait. *What?* That guy was all over you. What d'you mean, *nothing happened?*'

'He didn't touch me. They played "Breathless".'

'So?'

'I think he used to go out with Rose. Look, I don't want to talk about it, OK?'

'WHAT? HE USED TO GO OUT WITH ROSE? God, Sasha, how can you say that and not talk about it?'

'There's nothing to say.'

'Shut *up*, Sash! There's everything to say. I'm coming over.'

'Please don—' But she's already put the phone down. She's on her way.

She arrives twenty minutes later, bearing chocolate. 'I would've bought croissants, but your mum makes the best breakfasts anyway.' Mum has in fact made me a stack of pancakes, sensing something was seriously wrong. She leaves us to it while Jodie helps me eat them. Or rather, while Jodie eats them. I've lost my appetite.

'So tell me everything,' she says, reaching over for the Nutella. 'Oh blimey. *He's* not Breathless Boy, is he?'

It took me months to work it out, and Jodie about thirty minutes. I cry silent tears. Jodie abandons the Nutella for a moment, and enfolds me in a tender hug.

'Are you sure?' she asks eventually.

'I don't know. I mean, I *am* sure, but I can't prove it.'

'So how did she meet him?'

I think it through.

'The jackets! Those damned military jackets. Dan said they got their gig gear from Mrs Venning. Rose did my summer job for me for the extra cash, remember? She could have met him then.'

'I s'pose so,' Jodie agrees, going back to her pancake. 'Or maybe in the music shop on the high street. They could've been looking at sheet music, and their eyes met.

Or checking out guitars . . .'

'Look – can you not keep picturing their eyes meeting?'

'Yeah, sure. Sorry.'

Jodie eats in silence for a while as I take it all in. Impossible to imagine now that I felt so fabulously good last night, and it felt like it would last forever. It was as if I was speeding towards the edge of a cliff without knowing it, and now I'm falling.

'But why didn't she tell anyone?' Jodie muses. 'Oh, wait: nobody to tell. I was on holiday. So was Nell. You were in America. Still, she could've emailed.'

I find my voice, or what's left of it. 'Rose doesn't do email.'

'She could've called.'

She could have, but maybe she didn't want to. I think of myself as a girl with secrets, but Rose has far more. And I can't help thinking back – painfully – to how I felt about Dan, until last night. Dan's the kind of boy you want to hug all to yourself. If you can.

'Anyway,' I say, 'it was over by the time we all got back. She told me about it yesterday. She didn't say it was him, though.'

'What happened, d'you think?' Jodie muses. 'I mean, if "Breathless" is anything to go by, it was bad.'

'Uh huh.'

'Are you going to talk to her about it?'

I shake my head. 'She obviously doesn't want to.'

'Yes, but if it's stopping him from—'

'Nothing's stopping him,' I sigh. 'Only himself.'

Jodie offers to tell Nell about it for me, but I beg her not to. If she does, Nell will spend her whole time fussing over me. I'd rather she just stayed her usual, cheerful self.

But that doesn't happen. By the time we get to school next day, Nell is not her cheerful self at all. The news has leaked out that we were with Rose on Saturday. A blurry picture of the four of us sneaking out of Lockwood House is already plastered over Interface, and half the gossip websites too.

You'd think people might be pleased that the band got back together. It doesn't work that way, though.

Looking thin and drawn, Rose Ireland has been seen secretly getting back together with the girls who originally dumped her for being overweight.

ROSE BACK WITH BULLYING BANDMATES – SEE PIC

RT @RoseIrelandSinger Stay away from the #manicpixienightmares #dropthefatgirl

Suddenly our band page is filled with hate-filled comments again. Almost every FaceFeed message is an angry rant. It's like having a bucket of cold water thrown over you repeatedly, by people who've never met you. They think they're protecting her. We just feel tired and sick.

In school everybody, it seems, is staring. We take refuge in the practice rooms, but when the lesson bell goes, we have to head back to class. There's a blockage caused by maintenance men with stepladders, dust sheets and paint pots. The Head is having all the corridors repainted in honour of the visiting TV crews for the ad launch. While we wait, several people start crowding round us, asking about Rose. Some even take pictures. They're not threatening, like the FaceFeeds, but I sense Nell starting to get claustrophobic.

Somebody muscles through, all elbows and aggro. It's Nina Pearson, the self-confessed chief 'Rosebud', who seems to have forgotten she always ignored Rose in class because she was 'weird'.

'Can't you just leave her alone?' she spits at us. 'Don't you think she's had enough of you? She's coming to school for that launch soon and I don't want to see you anywhere near her.'

She stands in front of us, shaking with righteous fury.

The crowd around us loves it: the drama, the passion, the serious possibility – they hope – of a fight. They watch us all to see if anyone's ready to start brawling. Instead, Nell crumples in tears, and I catch her. Nina storms off, satisfied, and the others slowly start to melt away.

'This is all your fault!' Jodie shouts out across the heads of the parting crowd.

I look up from Nell to see who she's shouting at. At the far end of the corridor, Elliot Harrison is staring at us, pale and horrified.

'You did this! You made this happen!'

'Shut up, Jodie,' I whisper under my breath. 'If people know what he really did, he's in more trouble than you think.'

'I don't care,' she fumes. 'He stole your phone, he stole that video. He had no right . . .'

There are tears in her eyes too.

'It's never going to end,' Nell whispers. 'Is it? Whatever we do, they'll always hate us.'

I try and hold the moment of us all being back together in my head – how much fun it was, the buzz it gave us – but under the weight of the glares and hatred, the memory shrinks and fades, until it hardly seems real any more.

Beautiful Girl

On the bus on the way home, I'm not exactly in the best of moods. And then a text arrives. Two words:

Sorry. Dan xxx

Gentleman Dan is back, politely apologising for breaking my heart.

Because, you know, it's not as if I needed cheering up or anything. If trending on FaceFeed again feels like being hit by cold water, getting a 'sorry' from Dan feels like being hit by a truck.

Unfortunately, the memory of Dan feels real, very real. Wherever I look, he's there. Up in the hills, where we walked. At home, where he helped me tune my guitar. Up in the sky. I can't even look at the sky without imagining it darkening, and him showing me the constellations, and us disagreeing about philosophy.

Where do you find another boy like that? When will that happen? What if he was the one, and he was never even mine?

Mum gets back from the café to find me at the kitchen table, with a pile of home-made brownies and a cup of tea. I tried baking. It didn't work. She can see from my face that something's wrong.

'Oh God, it's not the internet again, is it? Is it that picture of Rose and all of you?'

'Wha—? How did you know about that?'

She looks guilty. 'Someone at the café said something had happened. I thought I'd better look it up.'

Oh great. Even my own mother has been Googling me.

She leans over, hugging my head into the front of her dress, promising me everything will be OK. That's Mum: she cooks, she bakes, she hugs, she's reassuring. It usually works, but not today. Today, I'm beyond reassurance, because each time something's gone wrong I've tried and tried to recover, and I thought I was a survivor, but each time something new happened and it got worse.

Mum puts cheerful music on the radio and sets about making chicken soup. She has this theory that nothing can ever be so bad that chicken soup can't make it better. Today, even the sound of her chopping celery makes me depressed. The internet hates me and I've just been dumped by a boy I didn't even go out with. Soup is not going to solve this. Seriously.

I go up to my room and do what homework I can face, which isn't much, before going through my playlists and listening to every sad song I can find. Downstairs, I can hear the kitchen radio and smell the stock starting to simmer. Outside, it's a beautiful spring evening. The darkening sky is flecked with pink clouds. A bird in the bushy verge beside the road is chirping happily. Lambs are gambolling in the fields next to their mothers. Actual lambs. Irritatingly fluffy ones, bleating away.

Why do I have to live in the heart of Somerset? Why can't I be in Florida, where the news says there's a threatening hurricane? If this was a movie, there would be thunder and lightning for me to go out into, so I could rage against it and get soaking wet. The best I can do is Crakey Hill at sunset. It's pathetic.

I grab my phone. There's only one person I can think of right now who might get the mess I'm in because frankly, from what I've heard, he's been in worse. As I head up the hill, away from the house, I call his number. To my relief, he answers on the fourth ring.

'Dad?'

There's a long pause at the other end. I can hear the sound of clinking glasses and bar-room chatter in the background.

'Sasha?'

He sounds astonished that it's me. I suppose he would be: I haven't spoken to him since I got back from Vegas, except when he called at Christmas. To apologise for forgetting to send a card.

'Dad? How are you?' I wish my voice wasn't so thin

and reedy, but keeping tears at bay is harder than I'd like.

'Er, I'm fine, honey. How are you?'

He sounds a little bit drunk and very miserable. Exactly how I would be sounding, in fact, if I'd had a few beers or whiskies to soften the blow.

'Has anything happened, Dad?'

That's not what I meant to say, but it turns out that stuff has happened to Dad too, and he wants to talk. When I visited him in Vegas, he was living with a showgirl called Crystal and her little daughter Liberty, but they've gone. It was his fault, he says. He chooses the wrong women. When he finds a good one, like Mum or Crystal, he lets her go. He lets everyone go, or they let him go. How many beers has he had?

I'm up high above the cottage now, looking down towards the railway track and along to the orange glow of Castle Bigelow itself.

'But why're you calling, sweet thing?' he asks. 'Is your mum OK?'

'She's fine. It's just . . . I'm in trouble on the internet, and there was a boy.'

'Yes? What boy? What internet?'

My turn now. I sit on a stile at the edge of a field and tell him everything: every last miserable detail. The thing about Dad is that when you've slept rough in bus stations and on park benches while following your Elvis dream, and when you've split up with more girlfriends than you can remember, and lost some stepchildren too that you were fond of, and drunk *way* too much beer and a few too many whiskies, there isn't much that can shock you, or even surprise you. He listens to the whole story and he doesn't try and tell me it's OK. In fact, he tells me it stinks.

Which is exactly what I need to hear.

'I'm sorry, little one. I wish I could be there. I guess I'm part of the problem, huh?'

'It's OK,' I say to reassure him. I did a lot of that when I was little – reassuring Dad, when he should possibly have been reassuring me.

'All I can say is, you did the right thing.'

'What thing?'

'Opening your heart up to that guy. It's how you know you're alive. I know it got broken, but that's what happens, honey. You just get up and get ready to have it broken all over again.'

'Oh great. Thanks, Dad.'

'That's what it's all about, baby girl.'

'He said . . . he said we're like specks of dust.'

'Who are?'

'All of us. He said we're so tiny, compared to the universe, our problems don't matter.'

'Hey! Are you sure you were in love with this boy?'

I laugh a little. 'Yeah, Dad.'

'Well, he sure talked some baloney. Of course our problems matter. You know that. You know, you make me feel so old.'

Dad is *so* not in reassurance mode. 'Why?'

'Because you're all grown up. Look at you – in love with a boy. Calling me long distance. It's good to hear your voice, baby girl.'

'That's OK, Dad.' There I am, doing the reassuring thing again.

There's a long silence and I think he's forgotten me, but maybe he was just having a longer drink.

'There's just one thing,' he says, quietly, as if he's

talking to his glass. 'You won't get this right now but one day, when you're old and in a bar and thinking about all the stupid stuff you've done . . . maybe, if you're lucky, your beautiful girl will call you and just knowing that she's there, and you made her, that will kind of make it all worthwhile.' He pauses. 'I'm just saying. Ignore me. It's nice to talk to you.'

'OK, Dad. Well, . . . you did give me the phone.'

'I gave you a *phone*?'

'Yes. Not this exact one, but the last one.'

'I did, huh? Must've been Crystal's idea. She had some great ideas, that girl. It takes pictures, right?' he asks.

'Yes.'

'Well, send me a picture of yourself sometime. Shoot a video. Show me what you're up to. Give your mother my love. Don't tell her about Crystal going, OK? She doesn't need to know. Love you, little one.'

'OK. Bye, Dad. Love you.'

I won't tell him that Mum assumed Crystal had left him ages ago. She'd actually be quite impressed to know they lasted so long. It makes me smile to think of shooting a video for Dad. I remember the first time we had the great idea of shooting a video. Look where it got us.

I stay for a while, watching the sky grow truly dark, and the first stars start to appear. The North Star. Ursa Minor.

Dad was pretty drunk when he got to the bit about it 'all being worthwhile' because of me. Trust Dad to bring it all back to how *he's* feeling.

I wonder what stars you can see from Vegas. None, probably, with the bright lights from the Strip blotting out the night sky. Dad won't be looking anyway. He'll still be in his bar, turning to the guy next to him, saying his daughter just called. His 'beautiful girl'.

I never knew he thought of me that way. I didn't think I cared that much, but maybe I do. He's lousy at reassurance, but strangely, I do feel better.

When I get home, the cottage smells irresistibly of chicken soup.

The Mistake I Had To Make

Early next morning, I'm woken by the sound of my phone ringing. It's Rose.

'Sasha! I'm so, so sorry!'

Wow, that word – just like Dan's text. She even sounds like her ex-boyfriend. Come to think of it, he said things like 'authentically bluesy'. They were made for each other.

'What for?' I ask, still feeling groggy from sleep.

'All that stuff about us. It's everywhere. I've been in the studio and Elsa didn't tell me. She doesn't tell me anything. I've just looked it up.'

'It's OK,' I say. 'We're coping.'

'Well, you shouldn't have to. I wanted to explain about us, but Linus says I'll only make it worse if I get involved. I really *am* sorry. But I've got something to send you, at least. It'll be ready soon. Look out for it.'

'It's not a handbag, is it?' I ask, worried that she's suddenly flashing her money around. Jodie's seriously hoping for a Hermès for her birthday.

'No!' she laughs. 'But you'll like it, I promise. It was *so* good to see you, Sash.'

'Yes, you too.'

On FaceFeed, #manicpixienightmares is still trending. #dropthefatgirl is back. Two national newspapers have articles about victims of abuse who can't break away from their bullies, but at least I know I didn't dream what happened at the studio.

The 'something' from Rose arrives a few days later and turns out to be an even stronger reminder. It's the recording of us all singing 'You Don't Know Me'. The soundtrack has been professionally mixed by Dave, so it sounds fantastic, and it comes with a video, which Rose has obviously worked on with someone who's an expert in editing. It uses the stills and video Nell and Sam took using her tablet while we were recording, mixing clips of us working things out and making mistakes and laughing with other clips of the eventual recording, where we're all deadly serious and getting it right.

'It's gorgeous!' Nell says, when I show it to her and Jodie.

'Shall we put it on the band page?' Jodie asks. 'We might as well. It shows we weren't actually torturing Rose at any point.'

I agree we should. The Manic Pixie Dream Girls page has 20,000 fans by now, despite all the haters. I'm not sure how many of them still look there, but if they do at least they'll see a glimpse of what we're really like. I can show Dad. And I'm not in my pyjamas this time, either.

For the next two weeks, I watch as Rose's Interface page gradually changes. Some of the messages from fans have answers now, perfectly spelled, thanking them for their support. The dieting tips disappear. In their place is a list of her favourite songwriters and why she loves them. The moody publicity photo is replaced by a snapshot of her in a makeup chair, boot-clad feet on the seat in front of her, caught off-guard, laughing. The fake pop star is gone; my friend is back. It's hard not to feel a little shiver of pride that I helped make this happen. Also, the page is ten times more interesting now that it's by the real Rose.

At school, meanwhile, the only topics of conversation at school are exams and Interface. And nobody wants to talk about exams, so it's mostly Interface. The launch of the new ad will be on the last Friday before half term. It will appear on every computer and phone with the site installed, which as they keep telling us, is over a billion of the things. They make it sound like the moon landings. And in a way, I suppose it is. They told us in IT that when NASA put men on the moon in 1969, they did it with much less computing power than the average smartphone uses today. So with the power of a *billion* computers, what could we do?

Most excitingly, the button they use to launch it will be pressed from our very own assembly hall, followed by a live, exclusive performance from the stage by Rose Ireland herself.

Except it won't.

A week before they're due to arrive, the Head announces in assembly (with actual tears in her eyes) that instead of using our hall, the big event will take place at Castle College instead.

'It seems,' Mrs Richards says, with a distinct wobble in her voice, 'that our facilities aren't grand enough – I mean *big* enough – for Interface. When they came to do their inspection, they decided that we can't accommodate enough people, and of course Castle College has just opened its new Performing Arts Centre, which I gather is magnificent.'

She pauses to take a breath and master her voice. We all know how hard she's been fighting for funding so that we can have a new, upgraded centre, but St Christopher's hasn't had a new building for twenty years. It's the same as always: Castle College has all the money and facilities, and they beat us at everything.

'But,' she continues, forcing a brave smile onto her face, 'all is not lost. At least *we* will be going. Or rather, *you* will be, and you are the heart of St Christopher's after all. Everyone in Year 11 and above can attend, as well as some of the pupils from Castle College. I will want you all, of course, to be on your best behaviour. *You* are the advert for our school.'

We are furious. Little groups gather in the playground afterwards to complain.

'Evil, stupid, lying corporate toe rags,' Elliot Harrison mutters, to nobody in particular.

'The whole point,' Jodie growls angrily, 'was that the

school who produced the winner was supposed to get the launch.'

'Poor Mrs Richards,' says Nell. 'She was nearly crying.'

'Look at the announcement,' adds a boy standing nearby. 'It's on the Killer Act homepage. Here: "The ad will be launched on 24th May from Rose Ireland's home town of Castle Bigelow, Somerset." See? *Home town.* That's how they got away with it.'

'They don't care what they say,' sighs the girl next to him.

'You can't trust anything on the internet.'

'Well, I bet Rose Ireland'll be happy, anyway. She's got so la-di-da these days.'

'Good point.'

I watch them head back towards their classes, not trusting the internet, but still believing everything it says. They should read her page, I think. But then, who would trust the word of a #manicpixienightmare?

The night before the launch, she calls me. I'm in the middle of trying to work out what to do with my hair, just in case one of the cameras happens to catch me.

'Hi! Are you busy?' she asks. 'Can you come over? I'm sorry, I should have called before but . . .'

Yeah. She's busy. I know. It's wonderful to hear her voice, but her timing isn't perfect.

'Are you at Lockwood House again?' I sigh. 'It's just that Mum only got in a few minutes ago and I'd have to ask if she can face driving.'

'No,' she explains. 'I'm back at home. I kind of put my foot down. Gran's so happy to have me back. Poor thing. She never said anything, but I feel awful for staying away so long.'

Oh wow. She's five minutes away. I check the time. Seven o'clock. Not too late. I'd still have time to finish sorting out my hair and get a couple of maths questions done. There's something in her voice that worries me.

'Sure. I'm coming over.'

Spring is gently turning into summer, and the evening air is cool, but not cold. I've done this walk so many times I could do it with my eyes closed. It feels as though every blade of grass is familiar, every tree in leaf, every rut on the road. Ten minutes later, her gran has welcomed me back to the farmhouse and I'm in Rose's old, familiar bedroom, with its red walls covered in posters of her singing heroes.

Rose gives me a hug and envelops me in the smell of lavender soap. She puts on some jazz and sits on the bed with her feet curled under her, wearing a shabby old dressing gown she's had for years, her hair in curlers, ready to be styled in the morning. I notice there's a new dress hanging on her wardrobe door. It's not a boring shift, thank goodness. It's Rose's old style – bold and flamboyant – an amazing, floor-length multi-coloured rainbow dress. Mrs Venning would approve.

I sit on my usual window seat. The curtains are still open and it's a beautiful starry night outside.

'I just wanted to say thank you,' she says. 'I might not get the chance tomorrow.'

'For what?'

'For my songs. For what I'm going to play. You changed everything.'

'Me? How?'

'Well, you and the others. You told me to play *my* songs. As soon as I got back to my music, it just came flowing out. Linus wasn't happy, but Jim kept telling him how good it was. It sounds like *me*, Sash.'

'Oh. Great!'

This is good. The album's sorted. She listened to sense. So why does she seem so brittle and nervous?

'Are you OK?'

'Yeah. Fine.' She flashes me a smile, forgetting that I'm not fooled so easily. Not this close up, anyway.

'No you're not. What's the problem? Are you worried about tomorrow?'

She's about to deny it, but I catch her eye. Suddenly, I can see the full level of fear she's coping with, and it's a lot.

'It's not "Living the Dream", is it?' I ask. 'It's not *that* bad, you know.'

'No, not exactly. It's about my new songs. It's nothing. I . . .'

'But they're beautiful! "The Mistake I Had to Make" – is that one of them?'

'Yes.' She hangs her head.

I picture her singing the song at the studio, and how delicate and melancholy it was. It will sound fabulous tomorrow, I'm sure, in the new Castle College theatre, with all its great acoustics that our school hall couldn't provide.

Castle College. All the students in the audience. 'Breathless'. 'The Mistake I Had to Make.' Suddenly, Rose's nerves make perfect sense. Those songs, in that place, to that audience. To one boy in particular in that audience. A boy who freezes whenever he hears her voice. It'll be hard for me, but how much harder for her?

There's been too much silence between us for too long, and too many secrets. It's time we stopped keeping them.

'I know about Dan,' I say.

There's a long, long pause. For a while, I think she's going to deny it, but she doesn't. Eventually, she looks back at me. 'How?'

'Because I'm your friend,' I tell her. 'I was going to get there eventually.'

'Did he tell you?' She looks mortified.

'No. But I saw his face when they played "Breathless".'

I don't say any more than that. I might as well spare her the gory details. Yeah, so I'm still keeping a *few* secrets.

She closes her eyes, wincing at the idea of Dan listening to her song.

'He was bound to hear it, Rose. It made number one.'

'I know,' she says in a small voice. Her eyes are still closed. 'But . . . I wasn't sure . . . if he'd know . . . it was about him.'

'Oh yeah. Believe me, he knows. He's not over you, Rose.'

Her eyes snap open. 'Oh no. He is.'

I meet her wary gaze. 'He so isn't. Look, what happened? You guys went out last summer, while I was in Vegas, didn't you? What went wrong? You clearly love him. He loves you.'

Every word of this is hurting. Why am I doing it? Do I want her to deny it all? Because she's not denying it. Not one single word. Not until I get to the end: the 'he loves you' part.

'You're wrong, Sash. He had a girlfriend. She was away for the summer and he . . . Maybe he got bored. Maybe he was lonely, I don't know. Anyway, he went out with me while she wasn't around. He made me think I was the first girl he'd ever felt that way about. I believed everything.'

She shakes her head again, angry with herself. Keen to avoid the conversation, she goes to her dressing table and starts carefully removing the rollers from her hair. She looks at herself in the mirror now, not me. But I'm not finished yet.

'Are you sure he had a girlfriend? Dan?'

My gentleman Dan?

Rose groans. She keeps working on her face – rubbing, brushing, checking. The movements are smooth and fluid from years of practice. I've seen her do it a thousand times.

'Yes, I'm sure,' she sighs. 'You were coming back from your dad's and I couldn't wait to tell you all about him. But the week before you got home, the girlfriend came back from her holiday. She explained everything. They'd been going out for a year.' Rose shuts her eyes again at the memory. 'And I'd bared my soul to him, Sash. It was . . . I couldn't talk about it. I couldn't bear to, it was just so . . . crushing. And tomorrow he'll be there, and so will she, and I'll be . . .'

Onstage, pouring out the memories. No wonder she's nervous. But still it doesn't sound right. Something doesn't fit.

'But what girlfriend?' I ask.

Rose pauses, eyeliner brush in hand. 'That girl from the band. You saw her. I mean – it's obvious, right?'

She shrugs, as if the conversation's over. It's obvious, right? *A girl like me*. The fat girl against the skinny model type with tawny hair and tight leather dresses.

I thought she was over this at last, but she's not. Not even now. I go over to kneel beside her.

'Listen to me.'

301

She looks down. A teardrop splashes onto her dressing gown.

'I know that girl and she's not his girlfriend. Not now, and never was. She's a sad, sad wannabe who tries too hard.'

She shakes her head. Another teardrop. 'You don't understand.'

'I *do* understand Rose. I really, really do. Trust me. He doesn't love her. He never did. But she tries to put off any girl who gets close to him. *Especially* a girl like you.'

She looks at me, uncertain.

'Like me, how?'

'Super-talented. Beautiful. *That's* what she saw. And there's music in your soul, Rose. That's hard to compete with.'

She doesn't dare believe me, but I can see her wanting to try.

'I'd say you were everything to him.'

She shakes her head again, but slowly this time, her doubts fighting with new possibilities.

'How can you be so sure?' she whispers.

Now it's my turn to look down.

'Just take it from me. I am.'

There's a silence, punctuated only by a plaintive trumpet on the record player, playing the blues. Miles Davis, probably. Rose loves his music. It suits the mood, because I realise that those last few words came out more sadly than I meant them to.

'Oh,' she says, suddenly understanding. 'You . . . ? I . . . Oh, Sash. I'm sorry.'

'Yeah. Me too.'

So no more secrets, then. No more.

Miles Davis finally stops playing. The needle comes to the end of the record and bumps its way around the surface of the vinyl, missing its cue to go back to its stand. Hiss, bump, hiss, bump. Rose rises slowly to stop it, while I think about what a combined hopeless mess we are. Rose more than me, though.

'How could you possibly not realise Cat was lying?' I ask her. 'Didn't Dan explain?'

'I didn't give him the chance.' She stands by the record player, looking horrified as the truth sinks in. 'I thought he'd been toying with me all that time. I thought he'd be telling his friends about me. Laughing.'

'I don't think he told a soul,' I tell her. 'For what it's worth.'

Although now I think about it, I wonder about Ed. He mentioned the breakup, so he knew about that. It would explain why he was so hostile to us at first, when Rose was still part of the band. Maybe he just wanted to defend his brother.

She groans again. 'He tried to call me. He emailed loads of times. I ignored him. I tried to pretend it had never happened. I *wish* I'd told you, Sash. I thought I was being all noble.'

I think back to how she was in the autumn term, listening to sad jazz like this, moody, writing 'Breathless'. And I bet the reason she felt ill about singing at George's party was because Dan was there. I kept putting things down to shyness, when in fact it was heartbreak.

Yes. I wish I'd known. I'd never have dropped her from the band if I'd realised what she was going through. I wouldn't have let myself fall for him too. And then the last four months of our lives wouldn't have happened. Well, not like this, anyway. Although, mind you, nor would we be talking about her number one single.

'You should say something to him,' I say. 'You owe him an explanation, you know.'

'I suppose I do,' she agrees, slowly. 'God, I've been hideous, and all this time I thought it was him. He must hate me.'

'Like I said, he doesn't.'

Knowing how much this is costing me – or at least, a little of what it's costing me – she comes over to hug me, for a long time.

'Thanks, Sash.'

'Any time.'

Yup. Any time I can hand over the perfect boy, so you can get back together with him, just ask me. That's what friends are for.

A Definite Disaster

After school next day, they bus us to Castle College in six large coaches, which bring the whole town centre to an impressive halt. The coaches chug slowly up the hill and through the large stone gateway to the school, past several impressive old buildings and slick green playing fields, to a modern steel-and-glass building at the back. A plaque in the hallway announces that it was opened last year by a member of the Royal Family.

'Typical,' Jodie says, glaring at it.

The theatre is huge and modern – not so different from the one at Interface – with a massive box at the back for a bank of technicians to manage computer effects and lights. The comfortable auditorium easily seats twice as many people as our old, stuffy, paint-peeling assembly hall, and we hate everything about it. Stupid seats. Stupid, smug Castle College prefects in their blazers and gowns (they have actual blue university-type gowns), showing us where to go. Stupid lectern on the stage, with a massive screen suspended above it. Stupid Interface TV people, going on and on about 'what a great performance space it is'.

Several rows of seats have been taken out near the stage so at least two TV news crews can set up with their cameras. The launch of a worldwide ad is a big event. Interface News will be doing a live webcast, so we'll be able to watch what's happening onstage in front of us and simultaneously on our phones, via the internet, which is cool but *totally weird*.

Later on, the highlights will appear on the evening news. It was going to be the Head's big chance to show what students from St Christopher's can do. Instead, everyone will have the impression that Rose went to a posh school with amazing music facilities, and that's how she got famous. The truth is, all she needed was dedication, an old vinyl record collection, deep feelings and a second-hand guitar.

I look around for Dan among the Castle College students at the back, but no sign of him yet. When everyone's settled, the Head of Castle College comes on and gives a very long speech about musical achievement and forward-looking technology at his school, while Mrs Richards sits behind him, trying to master her emotions. Ivan Jenks comes in and gives another speech about social networks and community involvement and 'inspiring future generations'. We sit and stare at him impassively, in our alien surroundings. This particular generation doesn't feel too inspired. He doesn't seem to care.

It's 5.50. The news cameras start rolling.

'This is the first year we've reached the big nine zeroes,' Ivan grins, drawing to the end of his speech. 'That's one billion devices. It's a proud moment for Interface. Now, I'd like to introduce you to someone just a little bit special. I think you've all heard of her by now. With a hundred-thousand-pound contract, two hundred million views online and a lasting career ahead of her, she's the new face of Interface. Here she is at last. Rose Ireland!'

A ripple of excitement goes around the room. Dozens of people hold up their phones to take a picture. We were told not to use them this afternoon. But – yeah, right.

Rose steps onto the stage, looking shy in her rainbow dress, accompanied by Linus Oakley. He's grinning happily. She peers nervously into the crowd, looking out for us, I think. But we're just three faces in the darkness. She's never going to spot us here.

When she reaches the lectern, the big screen lights up and Ivan announces satellite link-up with Shanghai. Which is kind of impressive, admittedly, and when they get it working, there at the other end is Roxanne Wills – in China, on tour – wearing yet another shiny mini-dress and cooing about how honoured she is to be a part of this Wonderful. Moment.

Jodie flashes her phone screen at me. She's found a little animation of cartoon eyes rolling. It saves her the effort of doing it herself.

The clock ticks down. Ivan invites Rose forward to

press a large, shining blue button sitting on the lectern. Jodie leans in to me and whispers.

'D'you think it's connected to anything? I can't see any wires. Bet there's a guy at the back who just presses a key on his laptop.'

I shrug. It was Jodie, of course, who told me the sad truth about Father Christmas and the tooth fairy in primary school. Sometimes the illusion is good.

Rose hovers her hand above the button as the seconds approach 6 p.m.

Five. Four. Three. Two. One.

She presses down. The screen above our heads flickers and switches from Roxanne in Shanghai to the Interface homepage. It zooms in on the box with the advert until that fills the screen entirely. The black background with yellow numbers that have been counting down for days shows 00:00:00, then goes black completely. There's a collective shiver in the audience. Then it switches to the opening image of Rose at the white piano. She's there in the white and gold dress. Beneath her, the real Rose closes her eyes for a moment and bites her lip.

Two seconds later, though, the image disappears. The screen goes black. There's the loud sound of recorded laughter. When the picture returns, it's a shot of Rose in the studio, messy-haired and relaxed, trying something out and laughing. This time, she's on electric keyboards. Her outfit is casual. The music that's playing is no longer the introduction to 'Living the Dream'.

But I know it well.

It's 'You Don't Know Me'. This is our video. Somehow, they're playing *my* song.

'It's us!' Nell gasps aloud.

It's clearly not intentional. Ivan Jenks watches the screen, aghast. At first he's paralysed with shock, but soon he starts making grand, panicked gestures to the technicians at the back. This obviously wasn't supposed to happen.

Real-Rose, onstage, looks astonished. Linus Oakley and the Head of Castle College seem positively scared. Another ripple goes round the audience. It's a definite disaster of some description. All the students of St Christopher's are delighted.

I'm watching and listening, confused and mesmerised like everybody else. It's only when the boy beside me waves his phone in my face that I realise the full truth: whatever's gone wrong hasn't just gone wrong on the big screen here: it's happening everywhere. My song, and the video of us making it, is being played on a billion devices.

Well, up to a billion, anyway. They won't *all* be switched to Interface right now. But probably millions will be. Almost certainly millions. And there I am, in front, dressed as a chambermaid in a black skirt and black tights, and playing Jim's fabulous guitar. Rose and Nell are next to me, singing happily, while Rose does her amazing thing on keyboards.

I like it. I think we look good.

Ivan looks in danger of exploding.

Jodie nudges me, thrilled. 'D'you think she knew?' she whispers, indicating Rose.

I must say, now her astonishment has faded, Rose seems to be enjoying the moment too. She did put the video together, after all. She doesn't seem the least bit upset that the world didn't get to see more of her in the tube dress, with a wind-machine blowing her hair, singing about deserving her success. But I can't imagine her thinking of this. Rose was never a rule-breaker. Oh yeah – and she's TOTALLY RUBBISH WITH TECHNOLOGY. This must have been some complicated hacking job, and it wouldn't even have occurred to her. But, I realise, I know someone who *might* think of it.

I look round the auditorium, searching for a particular head of sandy hair. The video finishes and the house lights come up. Everyone starts talking excitedly to each other and heads are bobbing around all over the place, but I just catch a glimpse of him near the back, sitting next to Jodie's brother Sam. He's watching the chaos with quiet satisfaction.

'Who are you looking at?' Jodie asks.

'Oh, nobody,' I say.

Elliot dips his head slightly and puts a finger to his lips. I've never seen a boy look so pleased with himself.

Reaching for The Stars

for five minutes the adults rush around, panicking. Meanwhile the students get busy sharing the news with as many people as they can think of. I'd love to get to Rose, but Linus hurries her offstage and anyway, we're surrounded.

'Aw,' someone says, 'the ad box has gone black again. Look.'

He's checking Interface on his phone. I do the same. It's true: they've finally found a way of stopping our video from playing. If you click the 'Replay' button, nothing happens. But on FaceFeed #adfail is already the top trend. And many of those feeds include a link to the original video on our band page. The number of views is going up by hundreds every minute.

'I didn't know you guys were back together,' another voice says.

'So, like, are you a band again?'

'Did you do this in a real studio?'

'Was that actually you guys?'

'I didn't know you played guitar, Sasha.'

'Was that a Taylor Swift song? I really liked it.'

'Does that mean you get the hundred grand?'

We answer as best we can, but they never seem to run out of questions. When Ivan calls everyone to sit down and finally plays the proper video, nobody seems to care. I take the opportunity of the relative dark and quiet to send Elliot a smiley face. It's all I dare type. He sends one back, winking.

If I were Interface, I'd hire him. He seems to know a lot more about their systems than they do.

Finally, it's time for part two of the show: Rose's concert. The auditorium is already filling up with a new set of Castle College students. I deliberately avoid looking at them closely, but Nell peers avidly into the crowd.

'Ooh, I wonder if Call of Duty are here. D'you think they are, Sash? They must be. You haven't seen Dan for a while, have you? Oh, look, there's that mean girl.'

She points, and I can't help following where she's looking. There, sure enough, is Cat, her shock of hair standing out even among the other big-haired girls in her group of friends. And three rows behind her is Dan. I wish I hadn't seen him. I was trying not to. Worse, he happens to look in our direction, sees me twisting round and catches me staring at him, before quickly glancing away.

Oh great. So he thinks I'm obsessed. Which I'm trying very hard not to be. I look away too, my cheeks burning, and luckily the lights go down.

Onstage a gleaming black grand piano sits, spotlit, waiting. Nell grabs my hand.

'I hope she's all right. Seminal leotards.'

'She'll be fine,' Jodie says. 'She's done this before.'

Not exactly, I think to myself. I hope what I said to her last night was enough. This may only be a school performance, but it will be one of the hardest concerts she's done.

Linus Oakley comes onstage and gives another long, excited introduction. Then he brings on a small band of professional musicians and three backing singers. They get into position and Rose finally comes onstage. She looks more nervous than she did when they were about to play 'Living the Dream' to a billion devices. Her face is white, but composed. I silently wish her strength.

She sits at the piano and leans in to the microphone above the keyboard. She turns to the audience, takes a small breath for courage, and says,

'When we put this show together, I didn't know we'd be in this place tonight.'

She pauses for a long time, and I know she must be sending a message to Dan. I glance round at him, but his face is emotionless, hiding his own hurt. She obviously hasn't had the chance to talk to him yet. He's still pretending they've never met.

'Anyway,' she continues, a little faster, 'I'm very lucky to be here with the band.' She introduces them, proudly, one by one. 'We're going to play a couple of familiar songs, and some new ones that I'm working on for my album. I hope you like them.'

'Hit it,' Jodie whispers, like a funk bandleader. But Rose is not a 'hit it' sort of person. She's a 'sit at the piano, close your eyes, breathe and wait' sort of person. She lets the room settle, nods to the band, and starts to play the intro to 'Breathless'.

Unable to help myself, I twist round slightly to look again. Dan's looking down at his knees. All I can see is the top of his head, but I would say his shoulders were hunched and he was extremely tense. Jodie reaches out for my hand, meanwhile, and squeezes it sympathetically. Nell nods along to the song, still oblivious to the pain it's caused me. I count down slowly in my head until it's over.

Rose waits for the applause to die down. 'The next two songs get their premiere tonight,' she says. 'I wrote them a while ago, but I didn't have the courage to sing them. I'd like to thank my friends for changing that.'

She closes her eyes again briefly. This time, it's the guitar that plays the introduction. It's a slow, delicate tune, a bit like 'Breathless', but not quite as melancholy. After several bars, the rest of the band join in. Rose starts to sing, and her voice is warm and tender.

It's another song about a boy, and the pain of being in love. It's beautiful. But when she gets to the lines,

'I'm reaching out for you and you are
Reaching for the stars'

314

I know what it's costing her to sing them here and now, with the boy in question looking right at her. I glance around again and this time, Dan is staring at the stage, transfixed. He looks thoroughly lost and miserable. I can't take my eyes off him, and I keep worrying that he'll look over and see me, but he doesn't. I'm looking at him, he's looking at Rose, she's looking at her piano keys and pouring out her broken heart.

'What? Why are you staring over there?' Nell whispers, nudging and distracting me. 'Is it Dan? What? Oh! Is he Breathless Boy?'

She goggles at me. Wow – even Nell gets it within seconds of thinking about it.

'Shut up, Nell,' I whisper harshly. There are tears in my eyes. She sees them and pulls away from me, hurt and confused.

There is too much emotion in this room and I want to get out of here, but I can't. I'm stuck.

The next song, 'The Mistake I Had To Make,' is just as good, and just as hard to listen to. It's a massive relief when, after that, Rose announces 'Living the Dream'.

I wipe my eyes surreptitiously. When I glance round, yet again, at Dan, he's studiously chatting to his friends as if he's fine. Onstage, Rose seems better too. Her nerves are gone, and she's almost relaxed. She launches into the opening bars and the song is just as smug and meaningless as ever. Thank goodness, because meaningless is just what I need right now. Jodie turns her phone screen on and plays me the animated rolling eyes all the way through.

When it's over, Linus Oakley steps forward as if to thank Rose and the band, but she puts her hand up to stop him.

'Actually,' she says, 'there's one more number I'd like to play for you this evening. Some of you heard a bit of it earlier, but it was cut off. I'd love it if you could hear the whole thing.'

Linus stands there, frozen. His mouth actually gapes open. Finally, he gets enough movement in his neck to shake his head.

'I, er, don't think so,' he says. 'That was all a bit of a mistake. A technical glitch. We, er—' He turns to Rose, panicking again.

'Backstage just now, I've had so many messages about it already,' she says, interrupting, looking him straight in the eye. 'It's something I recorded with my friends a few weeks ago. It means a lot to me.'

'Yes,' Linus stutters, 'but we haven't rehearsed it. I'm sorry, everyone. We couldn't—'

'Sasha's here in the audience,' Rose says, getting up from the piano stool and coming to the front of the stage.

There's a ripple around us. People look round to try and spot the girl Rose is talking about. I'm shocked and shrinking in my seat, but Jodie stands up beside me with a wide grin and points.

'She's here! She's right here!'

Rose looks across at us, delighted.

'Please, Sash? I'm sorry, I didn't get the chance to ask you before. We ought to do it together, because it's your song.'

'No,' I shake my head. I mean, I'm flattered, of course. Super-flattered. But there's 'nice gesture' and 'COM-PLETELY STUPID IDEA', and this definitely falls in the latter category.

'It has to be you,' Rose says. 'Don't make me sing it on my own, please?'

There is nothing I would love more. That would be absolutely perfect. Rose singing the song on her own, making it famous, doing it beautifully. Exactly what I want. But she's still staring out at me, pleading, and the audience are rustling and calling out encouraging comments, and Nell and Jodie are physically pushing me out of my chair.

'Go!' Jodie says. 'Do it for us.'

'But I haven't rehearsed.'

'You know it off by heart.'

'Yes. But I haven't got a—'

Guitar. I glance at the stage and Rose is already talking to the guitarist from her band, who's holding out his instrument to me. It looks gorgeous – battered and worn and much-loved. And I know for a fact it makes a glorious sound, because he's just proved it over the last four songs.

A sinking feeling tells me I'm going to do this. Somehow, I haven't got a choice. It will be horrific, because Rose is, like, a *genius* and I'm, like, a *beginner*, but at least I know the song. A look at Linus's angry, frustrated face completes my decision. Having broken us apart so publicly, he really, really doesn't want us to get back together. Taking a deep breath, I slide out of my seat and walk to the stage, while my heart does a drum 'n' bass track all of its own.

When I get to the stage, Linus gives the audience a charming smile and grabs me by the elbow, pulling me to the side. Rose follows, looking angry. Linus switches off his mic.

'What d'you think you're doing?' Linus asks her. He looks apoplectic. 'Come on, Rose, think about it. First you split up. Then you get back together. You're a soloist one minute, making secret band videos the next. Make your mind up.'

'I have made my mind up,' she says calmly. 'Sometimes I'm a soloist, sometimes I sing with my friends. That's music.'

'What are your fans going to think?'

'Finally, they're going to think that I'm lucky to have some good friends who stood by me.'

'*Who stood by you?*'

'Yes.'

She glares at Linus as forcefully as he's glaring at her.

'Sasha's been through hell because of what you told her to do, and she's never said a bad word in public about you, or me, or anyone. Think about that. If it wasn't for Sasha I'd still be a fat girl sitting on my own in my bedroom, hating the world and not believing I could do anything. And by the way, she has *never,*' Rose adds in a low voice, 'told me I was too big to sing love songs.'

'I never said that!'

'You implied it.'

Linus stops trying to argue and gapes at her. Rose smiles at him serenely.

'Fine,' he huffs. 'Fine. Fine. Fine. Fine. Fine. I'm glad you're happy. I just hope this is going to be good.'

I don't say a word. I'm just the guest artist. Someone gives me a stool and hands me the guitar. The audience claps and cheers. Rose gives me a satisfied smile. I have no idea how we're going to do this, because we've never played it just the two of us, but I suppose I'll follow her lead and we'll make it up somehow.

'You do the introduction,' she whispers. 'I'll join in.'

Oh. Fabulous. We'll do it like that, then.

I'm too high on adrenaline to argue. I strum the guitar a few times to get the feel of it, and practise a few notes. Even though I've practically lost the feeling in my fingers through nerves, the notes do at least sound like music, which is a start. I glance up, out at the audience and above, to the technical box, where I can just about make out the angular silhouette of Ivan Jenks against the light. He's watching. I don't want him to see me fail.

And so I start to play. And from the opening bars, it feels OK. Nell was right – I know the song. I kept the chords simple, so I don't have to do any virtuoso stuff. It's beautiful to hear the sound the guitar makes, and magical when Rose joins in on the piano. It's like we're going on an adventure together, down a path we don't quite know, through a bright, enchanted forest, holding hands.

We sing the first verse and our voices easily mingle. They always did, of course: we've sung together for so long. Her smoky, warm tones blend gently with my 'truckful of gravel'. I find myself looking out at the audience and not being scared to see their faces in the semi-darkness. It's the same soaring feeling I got at George's party and started to feel at the audition, before it went so wrong. I thought I'd lost it for ever but no: I can do this. In fact, I love to do this.

Rose grins at me and gets carried away, getting louder and changing key so I have to think really hard which chords to use to follow her. It sounds amazing, though. By the time we get to the final 'Get to know me', I can feel my whole body buzzing with exhilaration. We play the last chord together and move in so we can hug each other. The audience whoops and cheers. It's the best feeling in the world.

319

Afterwards, I long to talk to Rose about it, but Linus whisks her off to a special VIP area somewhere. Meanwhile, Ivan Jenks sends a couple of minions to find the rest of us so he can interrogate us about the new video, and what we knew about it, and whether we had anything to do with 'this whole fiasco'.

He calls us up to the technical box at the back of the hall and glowers over us, stroking his beard menacingly. We are, to be honest, brilliant. I'm still high from my performance, and Jodie and Nell understand instantly what we need to do. I've told them about Elliot, under my breath, but you'd honestly think they'd never heard of a computer, never mind a friend who could hack them. Nell is all wide-eyed sympathy for Ivan, I'm pure innocence and Jodie is flattering encouragement.

'Why, that's *terrible*, Mr Jenks.'

'It must be *awful* for you. What could have happened, do you think?'

'The video was on our band page – look – but how could it *possibly* have got into your system? I mean, you must have the most amazing security, right? Otherwise, nobody would ever use Interface, would they? They'd never put all their personal stuff up there.'

'Well, that's true,' Ivan acknowledges to Jodie, gruffly. 'We weren't *hacked*, obviously. It must have been some mistake with the engineers. A glitch. We'll be looking into it.'

'Oh, good luck,' Jodie tells him, with her TOTALLY SINCERE face on.

Sunglasses

Next day, at Jodie's, Elliot explains why he hacked the
song.

'It was kind of Sam's idea,' he admits. 'He said
Rose told you she hated the official one. And he told me
about this great song you did together in the studio. I
watched it on your band page. Then Interface did that
whole thing about moving schools. I thought they needed
a lesson.'

'So you just casually hacked into their system and
swapped the videos?'

He tuts at me. 'Not casually, Sasha. It took days of
work. And a friend at their HQ who's not too happy
about some of the stuff they do. But it was beautiful,

wasn't it? I like to think of it as art.'

'Beautiful,' I agree. 'But just . . . don't do it again, Elliot, please? You'll get arrested.'

'Yeah,' he sighs. 'Maybe. I think that might have been my finest hour. A billion devices!' He grins.

It was only available for two and a half minutes, but suddenly everyone's talking about it. Funnily enough, it was the fact that the song disappeared so fast that makes it so popular. People keep saying 'Oh, you should have heard it, it was amazing.' Then they try and find the link to it on our band page – until the page crashes under the pressure, after half a million views.

Dad calls from Vegas to tell me it's just like when they first played Elvis on the radio and people rang in to beg for more. Dad calls quite a lot, actually, to tell me how many hits 'You Don't Know Me' is getting (as if I don't already know), and to sing me his Elvis version of it down the line. It's surprisingly good.

It's Elliot who tells me I should put the song on iTunes, and shows me how to do it. It's easier than I thought, and once it's up there it sells ten thousand copies.

A *day*.

Every day. For three weeks. Which is not quite enough to take it to number one, but it's still five times more than 'Living the Dream: the Official Download', as Elliot often reminds me with delight.

It's enough to make a lot of money. Enough to get me noticed by two record labels. Enough to make me certain that songwriting is what I want to do.

Rose ignores everything the management team told her, and uses her page to tell the world how much our friendship means to her. At first, some of her fans try to talk her out of it, but eventually, watching the video and reading her comments online, they start to understand.

Slowly at first, but in increasing numbers, we start to get more fans of our own. Not people who just like our page, but people who want to share something with us. This is different from 'the one in the kilt has great legs'. It's sharing something precious, something important.

> *You know what it's like to go through all the hate and you stayed strong. 'You Don't Know Me' is what keeps me going in the dark times, when the haters try to get me.*

> *I've played your song a million times! It's beautiful. You made friends again with Rose and your friendship is more powerful than all the hate.*

> *I love your video – it's so gentle and inspiring. I want to learn to make music like all of you.*

Jodie's busy with the school play and Nell's smothered with science revision. Rose is on tour, but I take the time to answer as many of them as I can.

The strangest effect of all is that lots of the people visiting our page to find out about 'You Don't Know Me' end up seeing 'Sunglasses' too. Our silly, funny song about a messed-up relationship is viewed so often we release that on iTunes as well. It seems there are thousands of girls who love to dress up and be crazy. Who aren't necessarily cool, and don't necessarily care. They send us pictures of themselves in comedy glasses, boas and silly outfits. They do take-off videos of their own, which are fabulous. They proudly call themselves freaks and losers, and they don't care. Just like we don't, any more. I use one of the pictures they send as the new screensaver on my phone: four girls in sequins and spangles, laughing.

One day in June, on my way out of a Maths exam I spot Michelle Lee waiting by the school gates, looking out for someone. As usual whenever I see her, I put my head down, but it turns out it's me she's looking for.

She is super, hyper embarrassed about having to do it, though, and having caught my attention, she addresses all conversation to my toes.

'Er, look, Sasha. My uncle's the guy who runs the Bigelow Music Festival. You probably knew that.'

'No, I didn't.'

'Well, he is. And anyway, he was wondering . . . He wanted me to ask you . . . 'Cause you don't seem to have a manager he can call . . . Would you be interested in doing it?'

'Doing what?'

'The festival. The programme's sorted, but he can make space for you, because of the, er . . . you know . . . hit. I know you haven't got a band, but,' she rolls her eyes and swallows, 'Jim Fisher's a friend of my uncle's, and he's getting some guys together for a set, and they've offered to let you guys guest if you wanted. He asked Rose, of course, but she's busy.'

'Of course. Well, sure, we could think about it.'

Rose is always busy. I think she's playing at the White House around then. I suppose I could be insulted that we're second choice after her, but, hello? The Bigelow Music Festival? Of course we'll do it. However, it's nice to make Michelle sweat a little first. She did threaten to kill me, after all.

'So anyway,' Michelle mutters in the direction of my ankles, 'you could do that "Sunglasses" thing of yours, and the new song, and anything else you've got that's, er, good. Once you've done the Bigelow Festival it's, er . . . useful. For your CV.'

She grinds to a halt, wincing with the strain of asking. In fact, she looks as if she'd rather die. I hope her uncle doesn't get her to do all his bookings for him.

'I'll have to check with Nell and Jodie,' I tell her.

'OK. Whatever.'

But I don't really. I know already what they'll say.

For four weeks, we practise. Once exams are over, we spend our free time at Jim's place, working in the studio with Jim and whoever's available from his eclectic list of bandmates. They're all old hands, who've been playing for decades, so they're instantly brilliant at picking up the songs. It's more about us getting good enough to keep up with them. We do 'Sunglasses' and 'You Don't Know Me', and two of Jim's old songs from the Eighties that we already know by heart.

Now I understand completely why Rose put up with the stupid diet, and being made to talk about her parents, and Elsa, and everything else that Linus threw at her. If you can get to do this, even a little bit, you'd put up with anything. I can't quite believe I have Michelle Lee to thank for this chance.

Breathless Boy

On the Friday of the festival, it chucks it down with rain all day, forcing everyone to wander round in shorts and wellies. Typical Somerset July weather, in fact. But the Saturday dawns cloudless and beautiful. The site is set into the bowl of hills beyond the town, with pink and blue flags fluttering above a series of big music marquees, while little festival-goer tents cluster around the edges, dotting the hills with colour. We've been going for years, but never on a day quite as perfect as this.

Nell's dad arrives to pick me up in the 'band taxi', with Nell and Jodie already in the back. Mum will meet us there. The festival is always a busy time for her. There's a cake stall in the 'Sweet Treats' area that sells as many cupcakes as she can physically make.

We drive down the familiar lanes, skimming over-hanging hedgerows, past the station and round the edge of Castle Bigelow, towards the main festival entrance and then, beyond it, down a track we've never used before. We're following signs marked 'Artists'. Every time I see one, it makes me smile.

Our set is not until the evening, timed to coincide with sunset. Jim and his bandmates won't be here until later, but we wanted to make the most of the day. When we arrive, instead of having to queue for ages as usual, we're whisked to a smart, carpet-lined Portakabin, where a keen volunteer (who I recognise as last year's head boy from St Christopher's) gives our special, gold-rimmed backstage passes.

'I am so getting this framed,' Jodie mutters on the way out, marvelling at hers.

I agree. I'm already wondering where in my bedroom to put mine. Or maybe I'll just wear it all the time.

The backstage area has its own tents for artists to get changed and eat, plug in computers and generally hang out. Wherever I look there are people I recognise from gigs and previous festivals, favourite records and even the charts. The Bigelow Festival isn't big, but it's friendly and bands like to play here.

I can't believe we're really doing this.

'Something's going to go wrong,' Jodie says, still mes-merised by her golden pass. 'I mean, it's got to, right?'

I suppose it has, but I can't think what, apart from sun-stroke. There is still not a single cloud in the sky. The sun's getting hotter by the minute.

We head down the passageway to the main part of the

festival, and out into the riot of colour that Bigelow festival-goers always create – by what they wear, and sell, and the huge festival flags they carry.

'Can't we just enjoy it?' Nell begs. 'Our last proper time together.'

In September, Jodie's going to the sixth form college, where they do much better drama courses than at St Christopher's. Nell's parents have announced they're moving to Bristol, where there are plenty of schools offering great science A-levels. I'm trying to get a place somewhere I can study music and songwriting. The Manic Pixie Dream Girls are finally splitting up.

We wander over to the 'alternative' tent where a folk band are playing wild ceilidh music, all bright strings and fast, rhythmic drumming. Nell spots her dad in the crowd and goes off to join him. I realise I'd better find Mum and say hello.

I'm walking outside near the main stage when I could swear I hear someone calling my name. It's hard to be certain, because a large blues band is playing very loudly, through a speaker right behind my head. Still, I look around, wondering if someone from my class is here.

Instead I spot a different face looking straight at me. A beautiful face, with storm-cloud eyes under a mop of dark hair. He looks embarrassed to be waving at me, and many boys in his position would probably have pretended not to notice me at all. But he's too kind for that.

Gentleman Dan.

We meet up and walk as far away from the speaker as we can.

'So, how are you?' he asks.

The last time I saw him, he was staring at his shoes

while Rose sang about him reaching for the stars. Maybe that's why my first answer comes out 'Fhhhhggghh.' But once I've cleared my throat, my second answer is 'Fine'.

We make polite conversation for a couple of minutes. His family's fine. So's mine. Call of Duty are OK. They have a new bassist, but apart from that . . .

'And Rose?' I ask. I can't bear it any longer. I know she got in touch and apologised, and he went to visit her in London, but after that she stopped talking about him to me. I assume they've started dating again, secretly, like before, and she wanted to spare my feelings, which was kind of her.

'Rose?' he echoes.

'Is she . . . OK?'

He looks slightly confused. 'I assume so.' Then he looks embarrassed, as he works out what I really mean.

'Oh. I saw her a while ago,' he begins. 'It was good. We'd both assumed a lot of . . . stupid stuff. She said you helped fix it. Did you?'

I half nod and stare at the floor.

'Well, thanks,' he says awkwardly. And, realising that I'm waiting for more, he adds, 'We're not going out, though. I thought she'd have told you. We couldn't make it work again. It was too . . . intense the first time.'

Thanks for that, Dan. Way to put an image in my head I don't really want.

'Oh. Right.'

'It felt too strange being back together,' he goes on, even though I don't need him to. Really. Fine with not knowing the details.

'Uh huh.'

He still seems to think he owes me an explanation. 'It

was weird, you know, after those songs. Her life is so public now. If we'd gone back out, everyone would have known about us. I mean, I'm so proud of her, but I don't want to be the Breathless boy for the rest of my life.'

He laughs, embarrassed, and I laugh too, to be polite. He already *is* Breathless Boy, without the 'the'. To me, anyway.

He's still looking at me, and I know he's remembering when that song played in the Land Rover, and the kiss that didn't happen between us.

'I'm sorry,' he says, softly. 'About . . . everything.'

'I know. You told me.'

He laughs. 'I seem to apologise to you a lot.'

I smile too. 'You mess up a lot, Dan Matthews.'

'Yeah. I suppose I do.'

For a moment we look at each other and we wonder. There is nothing officially keeping us apart now. But we look and look and nothing happens. As always with Dan, the moment passes. There is too much history. Right boy, wrong time. I want to be the girl things got 'too intense' with, not the one who came next. His story was always Rose's, not mine.

Above us, a plane is flying quite low, coming in from the direction of the town and starting to form a lazy circle in the sky above us. We look up to watch it. It's an old-fashioned red biplane, towing a banner, but it's too far away for us to read the words.

'So you're singing later?' Dan asks, changing the subject, keen to move on.

'Yes. It's the strangest thing. We really are.'

'I bought the song. "You Don't Know Me", I mean.'

'Wow! Thanks. You helped *write* the song, by showing

330

me D minor. I probably owe you royalties.'

'No, you don't.'

He reaches out and gently moves a stray strand of hair from my eyes. In the sky, the plane rumbles on, getting closer. Another festival tradition. Someone proposing to his girlfriend, no doubt, with 'MARRY ME' in big letters in the sky.

'I'll be there tonight,' Dan says. 'In the audience somewhere.'

He dips his head to give me a fleeting kiss. The sweetest, softest, saddest goodbye. And then the tousle of his unruly hair disappears back into the crowd. For a while, I watch the space where he used to be.

Two minutes later, I'm still standing there, staring into space, when Jodie comes up to me.

'*There* you are. I've been trying to find you. Look.'

She points over towards an old-fashioned Womble on a stick. Somebody's holding it up, presumably so their friends can find them. It's a festival tradition. There are lots of fluffy animals like this, bobbing around above the heads of the crowd.

I can't see what's so special about the Womble, but my mind's elsewhere. I don't tell Jodie what happened with Dan. It's becoming *my* Bigelow Festival tradition: kiss a boy and keep it a secret.

'There! Can you see it?' Jodie insists.

'Uh huh.'

'Well? What do you think? Come on. We've got to find Nell.'

She seems bizarrely excited about this creature. I know Nell loves animals, but . . .

'Wombles aren't real, Jodie,' I point out. 'They're from an old TV show.'

I wonder if the sun is getting to her. Or maybe *I've* gone a bit crazy. I'm kind of devastated about losing Dan, but kind of OK. It's only now that I'm starting to realise just how difficult it was, imagining him and Rose back together. Now I know they aren't, the world is coming into a new sort of focus, and I'm still adjusting.

'I don't mean the stupid *Womble*,' Jodie snorts. 'I mean the plane. Look up in the sky. Big red thing. Noisy. OK, it's turning now. Watch.'

She puts her arm round me and holds me still while the biplane circles around and its banner comes into view. It's two words. I have to peer closely to make them out.

'Oh my God. Quick! Nell! Let's find her.'

We set off at a run, but with no real idea where we're going. Nell could be anywhere by now. Around us, various people are gazing skywards, looking confused.

'It's for us!' Jodie shouts joyfully at whoever will listen.

A plane. Rose hired a *plane*. And now Dan's not hovering beside her in my imagination, she's free. I'm free.

She hired a *plane*.

'Look! There!' Jodie says.

In the middle of a busy pathway, Nell and her dad are standing side by side, stock still, staring upwards. It's their stillness that makes them stand out. We rush over to them and all stand together.

'What does it mean?' Nell's dad asks.

'It means good luck,' I explain.

SEMINAL LEOTARDS, in big, black letters, flying above the festival, for everyone to see.

332

Flying

I text Rose, to say thank you. As usual, there's no reply. She's at an awards ceremony tonight, with Jessie J, and Adele, and quite possibly Paul McCartney. She's probably at a spa now or something, getting ready. Like you do.

But I wouldn't want to be anywhere except here right now. The three of us spend a couple of hours listening to bands and eating junk food, ignoring the butterflies in our stomachs, mentally rehearsing our own numbers.

I try to ignore the lyrics building up in my head about 'right boy, wrong time', and 'the only kiss you gave me was goodbye'. That's something Rose and I have in common about Dan Matthews: he's world-class for inspiring breakup songs. Later, I'll write mine, and I'll feel better when the feelings become notes on the guitar and words on the page. For now, I just want to enjoy this special day.

Gradually, the hill in front of the main stage starts to fill up. Lots of die-hard Jim Fisher fans are already getting into position, making sure they have a good view of the stage. Normally, we'd be among the crowd. So strange that this year we're heading backstage instead, to meet up with the band, stopping to sign the odd autograph and pose for pictures along the way.

We retrace our steps to the artists' area, flashing our gold passes at the security team. The band are waiting for us, chatting happily to the backstage crew. They've spent the day quaffing champagne around Jim's swimming pool, and playing with his children. They're all in a very good mood.

Mum arrives backstage, bearing spare cupcakes from her stall, so that she can help us out. Our changing room is another Portakabin, smelling faintly of antiseptic handwash, where we spend a happy hour transforming ourselves into the Dream Girls, using the hair and makeup techniques we've perfected over years of practice.

One of the crew knocks on the door.

'Line check!' he calls.

Still in our day clothes, we follow all the band except Jim to the main stage, to check that the sound levels are right for our mics and the instruments. Jim's staying behind so he can make a big entrance later. 'Preserving the drama', in fact. The rest of us spend five minutes onstage. I wish I could be wearing Nell's glasses, but instead I half-close my eyes, so the crowd is one big blur. Then we head quickly back. Our set starts in twenty minutes. Now the equipment is ready, we just have time to change.

'You have to admit, though,' Jodie says, wriggling into her leggings and checking her top hat for damage, 'it was kind of show-offy.'

'Are we still talking about the banner?' Nell asks.

'What else?'

'Well, I liked it,' Nell says, pouting into the mirror to check her lipstick.

'I'm not saying I didn't *like* it. I'm just saying it was grand.'

'You loved it!' I tease her, jostling Nell for space at the mirror. 'You were like a little kid.'

'I am never,' Jodie huffs, slipping her feet into her glitter shoes, 'like a little kid.'

'Oh dear,' Rose says, pushing open the Portakabin door, 'was it too much? I just got the idea and I couldn't resist.'

WAIT.

ROSE?

We all look round. Nell drops her lipstick. I nearly strangle myself with a boa. Jodie practically falls off her shoes.

'Rose?' Long pause. 'Aren't you in America?'

'I was,' she smiles from under her large, floppy hat. 'I landed this morning. Sorry I'm late.'

'But the awards . . .' I stutter. I think I know every day of her schedule. 'In London tonight. Jessie J. Adele. Your heroes. It says on the website you'll be there.'

Rose's smile turns to a grin. 'Don't believe everything you read on the web. I told them I couldn't make it.'

We cluster round her, eager for news. How was the

tour? How did she get here? Is she in trouble? Is she going to watch us? *Why* couldn't she make the awards? Even Kylie is going to be there. The actual Kylie.

She just stands there, smiling, letting us ask questions until we're all asked out.

'The tour was good, but this is better.'

'What? Better than the White House?' Jodie scoffs.

'Actually, yes. That was amazing, but this is . . . the best. I couldn't miss this gig. I came to wish you luck.'

'Like the banner wasn't enough?' Jodie asks, cocking an eyebrow at her.

'Actually, no. When I thought about it, actually, no.'

'And Linus said you could come?' I check, astonished.

Rose bites her lip. 'No. He said I couldn't come. He wanted a picture of me next to Kylie.' There's a flash of defiance on her face, but a frown of worry, too.

'You look exhausted,' Nell says, ignoring the fact that we only have five minutes left to get ready. 'Come and sit down.'

She opens the door to the only seating area we have, which is a white plastic Portaloo. Nell closes the seat for Rose and props the cubicle door open with a shoe. Rose giggles and thankfully sits.

'The thing is, I was in the limo this morning,' she says, 'coming back to London from the airport, and I was thinking about the biplane. I was checking it was set to go, and thinking what fun it would be, flying over the fields with all the tents and banners, and I realised I was jealous. Of a plane. It was crazy. It was here, and I wasn't.'

Nell laughs. 'So?'

'I suddenly thought, what's the point of it all if you can't do what really matters? So I got the car to turn round and take me to Reading station. It felt like the most rebellious thing I ever did.'

'Oh lord,' Jodie sighs, 'you haven't lived.'

'I think I have,' Rose corrects her, cocking an eyebrow in her direction.

She looks around and grins. She's here, tired and jet-lagged, hair all over the place, sitting on a Portaloo at a festival, chatting to three girls in glitter, sequins and feathers, who are about to sing a couple of hit songs with a band of top musicians. Yeah, this is probably living. Although the 'and then I took a car to Reading station' probably won't go down as major misbehaviour in the annals of rock history.

'So are you going to sing with us?' Nell asks.

Rose's smile fades slightly. She looks hesitant.

'It's OK if you're too tired,' Nell says quickly.

'No, it's not that. I mean, do you want me to? This is your gig.'

The three of us stare at her.

'Yes,' I say, speaking for all of us. 'We want you.'

'What about the band? I haven't rehearsed . . .'

'They'll be fine. We'll improvise. It's what we do.'

We rush around madly, rescuing a dress from Rose's suitcase (the one she wore at the White House, only slightly crushed), trying to sort her hair out, failing, deciding to hide it under the floppy hat. We talk to the band, who are perfectly happy – unsurprisingly – for us to be joined by a famous recording artist with a number one hit, who's good at improvising, and who Jim Fisher is very fond of anyway.

We're running late now, but we're the four of us, one

last time. And yes, it was worth it. Back in London, Kylie will probably cope.

While Jodie's busy doing her vocal exercises and Nell is calling her mum to tell her what's happening, I help Rose with her dress. In her bag, her phone goes off about once a minute.

'It'll be Elsa,' she says, rolling her eyes Jodie-style and ignoring it.

'Are you OK now?' I ask. 'Really?'

It seems a bit crazy to be asking someone this when you're zipping them into a custom-made black velvet evening dress, encrusted with silver musical notes, but I mean it. A life run by Elsa doesn't seem perfect to me.

'Yes,' she says, seriously. 'I think so. It's kind of unreal, but the music's real. That makes it worth it. Plus, Elsa's working for Roxanne Wills soon, so I'm getting this sweet girl called Gitte to help me. She's a jazz freak too. I miss you, though. So much.'

'I miss you too. I bumped into Dan today by the way. He said you weren't . . .'

'No. And you didn't . . . ?'

'No.'

She looks at me and laughs. 'I assumed . . .'

'So did I.'

There's a pause while I zip.

'Listen,' Rose says. 'There's a producer in Malibu.'

'What? *The* Malibu?'

'Yes. I'm working with him on some songs for the album. He's a genius. You'd love him. Do you want to come out, just for a few weeks? Maybe your mum could come and cook for us. You'd meet loads of musicians. We all hang out on the beach together and . . .'

'Yes. Just yes.'

'Oh, Sash! Thank you.'

She squeezes me close. The White House dress is very prickly. I make a mental note not to hug her too often when she's in her stage clothes.

The summer stretches out ahead. Me. Rose. America. Music. The beach. And songs. A whole summer of writing songs.

By now, the backstage crew are getting nervous, and the crowd are chanting for Jim. Mum hugs us goodbye and the organisers shepherd us through a secret backstage route towards the stage. Nell's the one who points out that this is totally like being in a Taylor Swift video. She's right. Maybe Rose Ireland videos will be like this one day.

I keep my eyes open properly this time. As we peer out from the back of the stage, Crakey Hill is stretched out before us, bathed in summer sun. Almost every bit of it is covered with people by now. Hundreds of them, hundreds and hundreds. With every moment that goes by, the gaps fill up and the sea of faces gets deeper. When the first band members take the stage, the crowd gives a roar.

It's like a living creature! A big, relaxed, cuddly animal, having a good time. Soon that crowd will be singing along to 'Sunglasses', then swaying to 'You Don't Know Me'. A billion devices all over the world are all very well, I think, but a thousand people who can sing your song back to you – well, that's something else. The butterflies in my stomach, which have been fluttering gently all day, now start doing a full-on gymnastics routine.

We walk to the front in our finery and hundreds of people start cheering. When Rose walks on behind us, unannounced, they all go mad. You can hardly hear yourself think for the noise.

Jim Fisher comes on last, in a gold lamé jacket and one of his old silk shirts, slit to the waist, looking slightly ridiculous and very cool. The crowd goes insane.

'It's good to be here tonight,' he says, filling the hills with his sexy voice. More cheering and waving. 'We've got a lot of great numbers to play for you, but first I'd like to introduce some friends of mine. I think you know who they are. Here, reunited for one night only, I give you . . . the Manic Pixie Dream Girls!'

I have never heard so much happy screaming. And then I spot something that makes me want to scream too. Almost everyone in the front few rows is wearing sunglasses. Silly, plastic ones, like the ones Rose bought here last year, that we used in our video. Some are dressed up as chambermaids. Others are waving feather boas and rocking sequin shorts. They're here for us! Not just for Jim, but us too. I want to cry all over again. I love these people, each and every one.

We hold hands and face the crowd together. I squeeze Rose's hand, and she squeezes back. Jim shouts 'One, two, three,' and launches into the opening bars of 'Sunglasses'. Ahead of us, the hill is alive with happy faces. I already have that flying feeling again.

One last time, we step up to the mics to sing.

ACKNOWLEDGMENTS

I'd like to say a big thank you to:

All the students at schools I visited in 2012, who gave me the courage and inspiration to keep writing this story.

Gaby Munyard and Sophie Elliot, who read the manuscript for me and gave me lots of useful advice.

Keith Richards (the autobiography) and Adam Norsworthy for insights into the music side.

My Facebook friends, for some of the shares I shamelessly stole for this story.

Wayward Daughter, whose YouTube video for 'You Lost Your Place' was part of my playlist for this book. ('She's wearing your clothes' is one of my favourite lines.)

My writer friends at the Sisterhood: I couldn't do it without you.

My husband Alex, for everything, from D minor chords to iPhones. And for my sanity.

Emily, Sophie, Freddie and Tom, who are living, breathing members of the wired generation, and who this time had to share me with Sasha, Rose, Jodie and Nell.

And last, but never least, my wonderful editor Imogen Cooper, Barry Cunningham, Rachel Hickman and the rest of the team at Chicken House. You really do know me!

WHAT YOU CAN DO

If you are worried about being bullied online, make sure you talk to someone. You can block it or report it, and there are other things you can do. To get or offer support, check out www.childline.org.uk, and www.thinkuknow.co.uk.

And if you are having a joke online at someone else's expense . . . don't. Just don't. This is why.

Feeling inspired?
Share the fun!

Do you have a passion for singing, a talent for writing lyrics, or do you simply like to have fun with your friends in front of the camera?

Then I need you!

I'd love to see your *You Don't Know Me* inspired videos, pics and lyrics. I will be sharing a selection on my website, with prizes to be won for the best and most fun uploads.

For details of what I am looking for and how to upload your stuff visit:

www.SophiaBennett.com

Let's show off the best of what girls can do, and have fun doing it!

Love,

Sophia

Competition open to UK residents only. Closing date: 6th September 2013.